FABLED LANDS

THE PLAINS OF HOWLING DARKNESS

Dave Morris and Jamie Thomson

Illustrated by Russ Nicholson
Cover painting by Kevin Jenkins

Fabled Lands Publishing

CRAGDRIFT SEA
THE ARCHES of JARM
The Peaks at the Edge of
Pyramid of Xinoc
Ruby Citadel
HORDE OF THE THUNDERING SKIES
HORDE OF TH THOUSAND WIND
RIVER of LIFE
R. of DESTINY
OLD EAGLE RIVER
Tigre Bay
Great Steppes
The Rimewater
City of Ruins
Sky mtn
Icemine
Krateros
Icicle Woods
The Spine of Harkun
Lake of Demons
OLD HARKUNA
Haunted Hills
Onaros
Marmorek
Forest
Lake of Seven Needles
The HIGH KINGS Seat
Endless Plains
Carapace
of Woes
Wheatfields
RUNEL RIVER
The Singing Forest
GOLNIR
Pass of Sighs
The GREAT TURTLE
R. of RUBY
Castle Ravayne
Kunrir
The Grumm
Ringhorn
Thanatos Caverns
Metriciens
ATTICALA
Iskandar River
Skios
UTTAKU
Grindel's Hall
Ignus Light
Dweomar
Sea of Weeds
The Oracle
Limbart's Vortex
Aku
SORCERERS ISLE
R. Wyrd
Teleos
THE VIOLET
The Innis Shoals
Forest of Remorse
SEA OF STILTS
Sleeping Isle
Ruined Tarshesh
The Walking City
The Straits of Almir
Hoplas
City of STARGAZERS
Borotek
FOREST of the Rakshasas
THE GREAT RIVER
The Crimson Fort
Vulture Peak
The Blue Grassland
The Hole in the World
Kurani
ANKON
Forest of the Apsaras
The Temple of the Eye
R. Aljantar
Mithdrak
Noral
Pethumar
Country of the Chandor
CHRYSOPRAIS
Auricilum
Desert of Bones
Ark Ships of the Golden Men
Hidden Ones
Pevek
Korevar

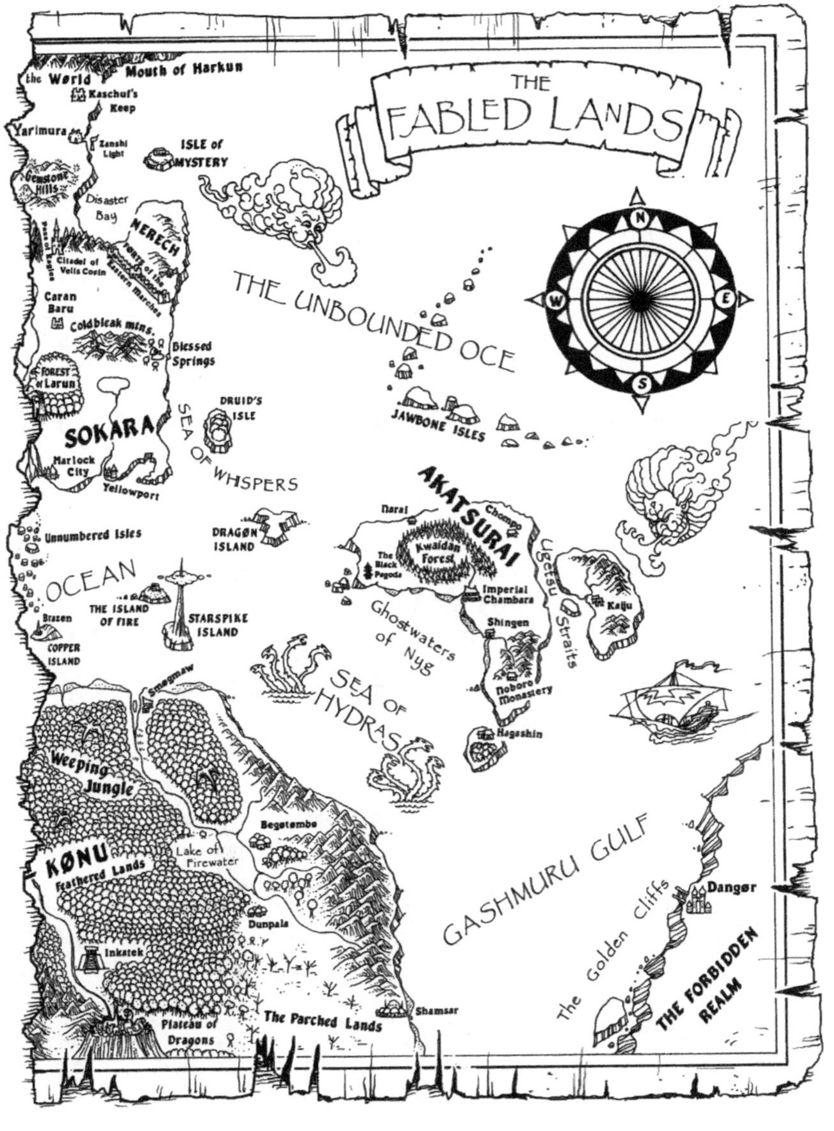

THE FABLED LANDS
the World
Mouth of Harkun
Kaschul's Keep
Yarimura
Zanshi Light
ISLE of MYSTERY
Gemstone Hills
Disaster Bay
NERECH
County of the Eastern Marches
Citadel of Velis Corin
Caran Baru
Coldbleak mtns.
Blessed Springs
FOREST of Larun
DRUID'S ISLE
SEA OF WHISPERS
SOKARA
Marlock City
Yellowport
THE UNBOUNDED OCE
N
W
E
S
JAWBONE ISLES
Unnumbered Isles
DRAGON ISLAND
OCEAN
THE ISLAND OF FIRE
STARSPIKE ISLAND
Brazen
COPPER ISLAND
AKATSURAI
Narai
Chomp
Kwaidan Forest
The Black Pagoda
Imperial Chambara
Shingen
Ugetsu Straits
Kaiju
Noboro Monastery
Hagashin
Ghostwaters of Nyg
Smugmaw
SEA OF HYDRAS
Weeping Jungle
Begotombo
KONU
Lake of Firewater
Feathered Lands
Dunpala
Inkstek
GASHMURU GULF
The Golden Cliffs
Danger
THE FORBIDDEN REALM
Plateau of Dragons
The Parched Lands
Shamsar

First published 1996 by Macmillan Publishers Ltd

This edition published 2010 by Fabled Lands Publishing,
an imprint of Fabled Lands LLP

ISBN 978-0-9567372-3-6

Adventuring in the
Fabled Lands

Fabled Lands is unlike any other solo role-playing games. The reason is that you can play the books in any order, coming back to earlier books whenever you wish. You need only one book to start, but by collecting other books in the series you can explore more of this rich fantasy world. Instead of just one single storyline, there are virtually unlimited adventures to be had in the Fabled Lands. All you need is two dice, an eraser and a pencil.

If you have already adventured using other books in the series, you will know your entry point into this book. Turn to that section now.

If this is your first Fabled Lands book, read the rest of the rules before starting at section 1. You will keep the same adventuring persona throughout the books – starting out as 4th Rank in *The Plains of Howling Darkness*, and gradually gaining in power, wealth and experience throughout the series.

ABILITIES

You have six abilities. Your initial score in each ability ranges from 1 (low ability) to 7 (a high level of ability). Ability scores will change during your adventure but can never be lower than 1 or higher than 12.

CHARISMA	the knack of befriending people
COMBAT	the skill of fighting
MAGIC	the art of casting spells
SANCTITY	the gift of divine power and wisdom
SCOUTING	the techniques of tracking and wilderness lore
THIEVERY	the talent for stealth and lock picking

PROFESSIONS

Not all adventurers are good at everything. Everyone has some strengths and some weaknesses. Your choice of profession determines your initial scores in the six abilities.

- **Priest:**
  Charisma 5, Combat 3, Magic 4,
  Sanctity 7, Scouting 5, Thievery 2
- **Mage:**
  Charisma 3, Combat 3, Magic 7,
  Sanctity 1, Scouting 6, Thievery 4
- **Rogue:**
  Charisma 6, Combat 5, Magic 5,
  Sanctity 2, Scouting 3, Thievery 7
- **Troubadour:**
  Charisma 7, Combat 4, Magic 5,
  Sanctity 4, Scouting 3, Thievery 5
- **Warrior:**
  Charisma 4, Combat 7, Magic 2,
  Sanctity 5, Scouting 4, Thievery 3
- **Wayfarer:**
  Charisma 3, Combat 6, Magic 3,
  Sanctity 4, Scouting 7, Thievery 5

Fill in the Adventure Sheet at the back of the book with your choice of profession and the ability scores given for that profession.

STAMINA

Stamina is lost when you get hurt. Keep track of your Stamina score throughout your travels and adventures. You must guard against your Stamina score dropping to zero, because if it does you are dead.

Lost Stamina can be recovered by various means, but your Stamina cannot go above its initial score until you advance in Rank.

You start with 20 Stamina points. Record your Stamina in pencil on the Adventure Sheet.

RANK

You start at 4th Rank, so note this on the Adventure Sheet now. By completing quests and overcoming enemies, you will have the chance to go up in Rank.

You will be told during the course of your adventures when you are entitled to advance in Rank. Characters of higher Rank are tougher, luckier and generally better able to deal with trouble.

Rank	Title
1st	Outcast
2nd	Commoner
3rd	Guildmember
4th	Master/Mistress
5th	Gentleman/Lady
6th	Baron/Baroness
7th	Count/Countess
8th	Earl/Viscountess
9th	Marquis/Marchioness
10th	Duke/Duchess

POSSESSIONS

You can carry up to 12 possessions on your person. All characters begin with 16 Shards in cash and the following possessions, which you can record on your Adventure Sheet: **sword**, **chain mail (Defence +3)**, **map**.

Possessions are always marked in bold text, like this: **gold compass**. Anything marked in this way is an item which can be picked up and added to your list of possessions.

Remember that you are limited to carrying a total of 12 items, so if you get more than this you'll have to cross something off your Adventure Sheet or find somewhere to store extra items. You can carry unlimited sums of money.

DEFENCE

Your Defence score is equal to:
  your COMBAT score
  plus your Rank
  plus the bonus for the armour you're wearing (if any).

Every suit of armour you find will have a Defence bonus listed for it. The higher the bonus, the better the armour. You can carry several suits of armour if you wish – but because you can wear only one at a time, you only get the Defence bonus of the best armour you are carrying.

Write your Defence score on the Adventure Sheet now. To start with it is just your COMBAT score plus 7 (because you are 4th Rank and have +3 armour). Remember to update it if you get better armour or increase in Rank or COMBAT ability.

FIGHTING

When fighting an enemy, roll two dice and add your COMBAT score. You need to roll higher than the enemy's Defence. The amount you roll above the enemy's Defence is the number of Stamina he loses.

If the enemy is now down to zero Stamina then he is defeated. Otherwise he will strike back at you, using the same procedure. If you survive, you then get a chance to attack again, and the battle goes on until one of you is victorious.

Example:

You are a 3rd Rank character with a COMBAT score of 4, and you have to fight a goblin (COMBAT 5, Defence 7, Stamina 6). The fight begins with your attack (you always get first blow unless told otherwise). Suppose you roll 8 on two dice. Adding your COMBAT score gives a total of 12. This is 5 more than the goblin's Defence, so it loses 5 Stamina.

The goblin still has 1 Stamina point left, so it gets to strike back. It rolls 6 on the dice which, added to its COMBAT of 5, gives a total attack score of 11. Suppose you have a chain mail tabard (Defence +2). Your Defence is therefore 9 (=4+3+2), so you lose 2 Stamina and can then attack again.

USING ABILITIES

Fighting is often not the easiest or safest way to tackle a situation. When you get a chance to use one of your other abilities, you will be told the Difficulty of the task. You roll two dice and add your score in the ability, and to succeed in the task you must get higher than the Difficulty.

Example:

You are at the bottom of a cliff. You can use THIEVERY to climb it, and the climb is Difficulty 9. Suppose your THIEVERY score is 4. This means you must roll at least 6 on the dice to make the climb.

CODEWORDS

There is a list of codewords included in the back of the book. Sometimes you will be told you have acquired a codeword. When this happens, put a tick in the box next to that codeword. If you later lose the codeword, erase the tick.

The codewords are arranged alphabetically for each book in the series. In this book, for example, all codewords begin with D. This makes it easy to check if you picked up a codeword from a book you played previously. For instance, you might be asked if you have picked up a codeword in a book you have already adventured in. The letter of that codeword will tell you which book to check (i.e. if it begins with C, it is from Book 3: *Over the Blood-Dark Sea*).

SOME QUESTIONS ANSWERED

How long will my adventures last?
As long as you like! There are many plot strands to follow in the Fabled Lands. Explore wherever you want. Gain wealth, power and prestige. Make friends and foes. Just think of it as real life in a fantasy world. When you need to stop playing, make a note of the entry you are at and later you can just resume at that point.

What happens if I'm killed?
If you had the foresight to arrange a resurrection deal (you'll learn about them later), death might not be the end of your career. Otherwise, you can always start adventuring again with a new persona. If you do, you'll first have to erase all codewords, ticks and money recorded in the book.

What do the maps show?
The map at the back of the book shows the Great Steppes, which is covered by this adventure: *The Plains of Howling Darkness*. The map at the front shows the whole extent of the known Fabled Lands.

Are some regions of the world more dangerous than others?
Yes. Generally, the closer you are to civilization (the area of Sokara and Golnir covered in the first two books) the easier your adventures will be.

Where can I travel in the Fabled Lands?
Anywhere. If you journey to the edge of the map in this book, you will be guided to another book in the series. (*The War-Torn Kingdom* deals with Sokara, *Cities of Gold and Glory* deals with Golnir, *Over the Blood-Dark Sea* deals with the southern seas and so on.) For example, if you are enslaved by the Uttakin, you will be guided to *The Court of Hidden Faces* **321**, which refers to entry **321** in Book Five.

What if I don't have the next book?
Just turn back. When you do get that book, you can always return and venture onwards.

What should I do when travelling on from one book to the next?
It's very simple. Make a note of the entry you'll be turning to in the new book. Then copy all the information from your Adventure Sheet and Ship's Manifest into the new book. Lastly, erase the Adventure Sheet and Ship's Manifest data in the old book so they will be blank when you return there.

What about codewords?
Codewords report important events in your adventuring life. They

'remember' the places you've been and the people you've met. Do NOT erase codewords when you are passing from one book to another.

Are there any limits on abilities?
Your abilities (COMBAT, etc) can increase up to a maximum of 12. They can never go lower than 1. If you are told to lose a point off an ability which is already at 1, it stays as it is.

Are there any limits on Stamina?
There is no upper limit. Stamina increases each time you go up in Rank. Wounds will reduce your current Stamina, but not your potential (unwounded) score. If Stamina ever goes to zero, you are killed.

Does it matter what type of weapon I have?
When you buy a weapon in a market, you can choose what type of weapon it is (i.e. a sword, spear, etc). The type of weapon is up to you. Price is not affected by the weapon's type, but only by whether it has a COMBAT bonus or not.

Some items give ability bonuses. Are these cumulative?
No. If you already have a set of **lockpicks (THIEVERY +1)** and then acquire **magic lockpicks (THIEVERY +2)**, you don't get a +3 bonus, only +2. Count only the bonus given by your best item for each ability.

Why do I keep going back to entries I've been to?
Many entries describe locations such as a city or castle, so whenever you go back there, you go to the paragraph that corresponds to that place.

How many blessings can I have?
As many as you can get, but never more than one of the same type. You can't have several COMBAT blessings, for instance, but you could have one COMBAT, one THIEVERY and one CHARISMA blessing.

QUICK RULES

To use an ability (COMBAT, THIEVERY, etc), roll two dice and add your score in the ability. To succeed you must roll higher than the Difficulty of the task.

Example: You want to calm down an angry innkeeper. This requires a CHARISMA roll at a Difficulty of 10. Say you have a CHARISMA score of 6. This means that you would have to roll 5 or more on two dice to succeed.

Fighting involves a series of COMBAT rolls. The Difficulty of the roll is equal to the opponent's Defence score. (Your Defence score is equal to your **Rank** + your **armour bonus** + your **COMBAT score**.) The amount you beat the Difficulty by is the number of Stamina points that your opponent loses.

That's pretty much all you need to know. If you have any detailed queries, consult the detailed rules in the preceding pages.

A selection of pre-generated characters, colour maps of the Fabled Lands world and other bonus material are available on the website:

www.fabledlands.com

1

You are alone in an open boat waiting for death. How your life has changed since that day when you set out from your homeland across the Unbounded Ocean! You had signed on board a ship with the hope of visiting a dozen ports and seeing a thousand wonders. But calamity overtook your voyage in the first week, when pirates swooped down upon the vessel. You and a handful of shipmates managed to get the cutter down into the water and were making off, but some of the pirates leapt down from the rail right in your midst. The fighting was hard. You remember little of it now, but when it was over the boat was awash with blood and you were the only one left alive. Of your own ship and the pirates' craft there was no sign – the current had carried you out of sight of any living thing.

Best not to think how you've survived since then. At the mercy of the wind and sea currents, you have been swept steadily westwards into regions completely unknown to you. Drinking water has been your biggest problem – you've had to rely on rain, and there has been none for days. Your body is weak, your spirits low. Then, just as death seems ready to draw his boat alongside, you see something that kindles new hope: white clouds; birds turning high above; the grey hump of land on the horizon!

Steering towards the shore, you feel the cutter lurch as it enters rough water. The wind whips up plumes of spindrift and breakers pound the cliffs. The tiller is yanked out of your hands. The little boat is spun around, out of control, and goes plunging towards the coast.

You leap clear at the last second. There is the snap of timber, the roaring crescendo of the waves – and then silence as you go under. Striking out wildly, you try to swim clear, then suddenly a wave catches you and flings you contemptuously up on to the beach.

You are battered, bedraggled, but alive.

Nearby, a great city dominates the skyline. Turn to **280**.

2

Which of these codewords do you have?

Defend	turn to **57**
Deliver	turn to **134**
Assist or *Dread*	turn to **242**
None of them	turn to **97**

3

Once you have boarded the barge, it judders into life with a low groaning sound, and floats off westward. You find some food on board – restore 3 Stamina points.

Eventually, the barge pulls up at a quay, jutting out from the cliff-face into the star-filled blackness beyond the edge of the world. You step on to it. Turn to **195**.

4

A great curtain of flames rises in front of you, and roars away, rushing toward the druidess. She has unleashed a huge hedge of thorns, which hurtles toward you and threatens to rip you to shreds. Your fiery spell, however, crisps the deadly brambles to cinders, and rolls on. Dialla manages to throw herself aside, and escapes with a few minor burns. You are declared the winner.

Turn to **24**.

5

If you have the codeword *Dotage*, turn to **640**. If not, but you have the codeword *Alissia*, turn to **251**. If you have neither codeword, read on.

As you draw nearer to the hill, dozens of figures rise up from behind the crest of a low mound. They wear massive helmets, sculpted to resemble beast faces – boars, dragons, pigs and the like. Their bodies are human but gnarled and deformed, and covered in mottled, silvery-grey fur. At the sight of you they give a roar of blood-lust and charge! There are so many of them, that you have no choice but to flee for your life.

Roll a die and add one. If the result is less than or equal to your Rank, turn to **460**. If it is higher than your Rank, turn to **180**.

6

The interior of the cave is jet black and has the pungent smell of ammonia. 'Bat guano...' breathes the bosun with a shudder. 'I hate bats.'

Without a source of light, such as a **candle** or **lantern**, you are unable to proceed.

Proceed with a source of light	turn to **115**
Return to the ship	turn to **191**
Push further inland	turn to **41**

7

You are dead. Cross off the possessions and money listed on your Adventure Sheet.

If you have a resurrection arranged, you can now turn to the entry marked for it. If not, it really is the end; you should delete all ticks and codewords in all your Fabled Lands books and start again (at 1 in any book in the series) with a new character.

8

It looks slightly askew to you, as if the beacon is in the wrong place. 'You might be right, cap'n,' says the first mate, 'but then again, it is said the reefs and rocks of the bay can change position – perhaps the beacon's been moved to take that into account.'

'Bah,' says the helmsman. 'You're the most superstitious mate I ever served under! Who ever heard of rocks and reefs moving?'

Sail straight for the beacon	turn to **79**
Follow your own route	turn to **208**

9

You remember the love ballad that was sung at the court of the High King, for him and his consort, Princess Leonora. Perhaps that might soften the frozen heart of the spectral Ice Queen, the ghost of Leonora, condemned by sorcery to haunt this place.

Make a CHARISMA roll at Difficulty 16. Add one to this roll if you are a Troubadour.

Successful CHARISMA roll	turn to **130**
Failed CHARISMA roll	turn to **235**

Yarimura is a young city. Its buildings are finely constructed houses of wood and stone with pagoda-style roofs.

The Clan of the White Spear, exiles from the east, rules the city. A hundred years ago, civil war raged in Akatsurai. The clan was forced to flee in its ships to the west. Unable to find refuge in Sokara, the clan founded Yarimura – the clan's fiercely loyal samurai warriors easily suppressing the local nomad tribes.

The current daimyo – the chief of the clan – is Lord Kumonosu. He dreams of the day he will return to Akatsurai as Shogun of the empire.

Yarimura's streets and plazas are cosmopolitan indeed. Finely dressed samurai swagger and strut alongside nomad traders from the plains and merchants and mercenaries from Sokara and Golnir. This is a city where east meets west. The Clan of the White Spear, however, governs it with a rod of iron. Yarimura is in a perpetual state of readiness for war as the armies and fleets of Akatsurai constantly seek to seize the city for the empire.

You can buy a town house in Yarimura for 150 Shards. Owning a town house gives you a place to rest, and to store equipment. If you buy one, tick the box by the town house option, and cross off 150 Shards.

To leave Yarimura by sea, or to buy and sell ships, visit the harbourmaster at the Sea Barrier. To buy or sell cargo, visit the Silk Market.

Tambu, the great spirit of the plains people, has a temple here. The invaders, however, have brought the religion of Akatsurai with them: their temples can be found in the Plaza of the New Gods.

Visit your town house ☐ (if box ticked)	turn to **160**
Go to the temple of Tambu	turn to **33**
Go to the Plaza of the New Gods	turn to **58**
Explore the south sector	turn to **77**
Go to the daimyo's palace	turn to **101**
Go to Thieves' Kitchen	turn to **182**
Go to the Tower of Bakhan	turn to **199**
Go to the merchant's guild	turn to **220**
Go to the Silk Market	turn to **252**

Visit the harbourmaster   turn to **141**
Go to the Horse Market   turn to **231**
Leave the city   turn to **280**

11

A darkening of the heavens heralds the gathering storm. A ferocious wind sweeps the rain in sheets over your ship, and the waves rise and fall inexorably, lifting you up, and then dashing you down.

If you have the blessing of Alvir and Valmir, which confers Safety from Storms, you can ignore the storm. Cross off your blessing and turn to **236**.

Otherwise the storm hits with full fury. Roll one die if your ship is a barque, two dice if it is a brigantine, or three dice if it is a galleon. Add 1 to the roll if you have a good crew; add 2 if you have an excellent crew.

Score 1-3   Ship sinks   turn to **135**
Score 4-5   The mast splits   turn to **106**
Score 6-20   You weather the storm   turn to **236**

12

It is an easy matter to sell the gold-scribed scroll that carries the curse of Tambu to an unsuspecting merchant.

As you part company, you see he is quickly stricken by the ague when he reads the scroll. You, however, feel much better now that the curse is lifted. Restore one point to your CHARISMA, COMBAT and SCOUTING ratings. Turn back to the paragraph you noted.

13

There are no more bouts, as no contestants have enrolled for battle.

'Perhaps in a few weeks, someone will turn up,' comments a passing mage.

It is quite common for the arena to be dormant for days on end, yet sometimes there are bouts every day for weeks. The coveted title of Arena Champion, and the rewards that go with it always draw someone. Only those that are Mages by profession may enter the contest.

Fight in the arena (Mages only)	turn to **214**
Visit the market	turn to **111**
Go to the temple of Molhern	turn to **637**
Go to the White Warlock Tavern	turn to **455**
Visit the chief mage	turn to **403**
Leave the City of Mystery	turn to **90**

14

You can only imagine that the stairs were built by a race of giants. You clamber up and up, into the thin, icy air. The Great Steppes are spread out below you, and the pyramid looks like a toy from here. Above you, the stairs climb up to the top of the volcano. Soon the cold becomes unbearable, and it becomes difficult to breathe the rarefied air.

Continue up	turn to **684**
Go down	turn to **271**

15

Ice and snow cover the northern steppes, which stretch away to the south and west as far as the eye can see. To the north, the snow-covered peaks mark the edge of the known world. You can see a sheer cliff-face, with something indistinct at its base.

Investigate the cliff	turn to **706**
East	turn to **398**

West   turn to **535**
South   turn to **442**

16

You are trampled by many of the herd – as if deliberately. Roll three dice, and lose that many Stamina points. If that kills you, turn to **7**. If you are still alive, the horses ride on into the darkening night. You pick yourself up. Turn to **666**.

17

You are crossing the windswept northern steppes. It is bitterly cold. Roll two dice.

Score 2-5	A voice on the wind	turn to **525**
Score 6-7	No event	turn to **65**
Score 8-12	A band of nomads	turn to **647**

18

The golem squashes you flat with a single blow of its huge stone fist.

If you have a resurrection deal, turn to the entry marked for it on your Adventure Sheet. Otherwise your only option is to start again with a new character after first deleting all ticks and code-words in your Fabled Lands books. (You can start again at **1** in any book in the series.)

19

You are nothing if not brave. The warriors are only too happy to oblige by drawing short, curved swords and leaping on to you from all sides.

Make a COMBAT roll at a Difficulty of 20.

Successful COMBAT roll	turn to **577**
Failed COMBAT roll	turn to **379**

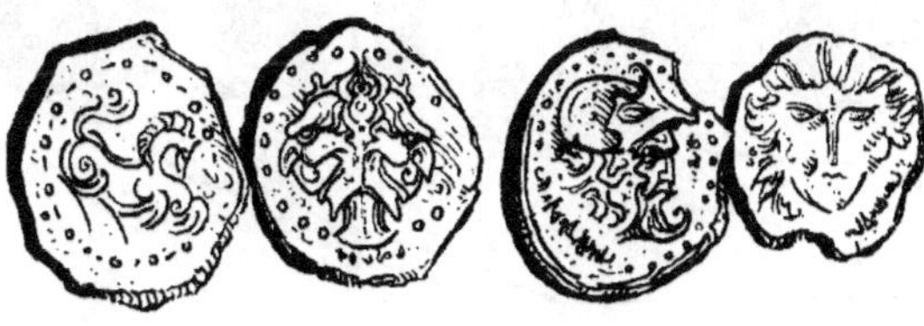

20

The guards at the fort think you are mad to enter the land of Nerech.

'Goodbye, then,' one of them says, 'for ever!' The others laugh cruelly, as they open the gates.

Turn back	*The War-Torn Kingdom* **299**
Venture forth	turn to **32**

21

The open gateway is flanked by two stone idols, man-like but with the heads of jackals. Their jewelled eyes gaze impassively at you. You are not sure, but you think their eyes are following your movements.

If you have the codeword *Cheops*, turn to **689**. If not, read on.

Leave	turn to **472**
Walk past the idols	turn to **49**

Cross off the 10 Shards. One of the men leads you through the mine. The walls are like frosted glass, and the ice radiates a bluish glow that fills the mine with an eerie wintry beauty. Miners work with axes and saws, cutting blocks of blue ice from the walls.

You come to a large chamber, where several tunnels meet. One tunnel looks black and abandoned. Not even the chill radiance of the ice lights its dark passages.

'What's down there,' you ask.

'Down there? Why, that's the old mine. It's abandoned now,' says the miner.

'Why hasn't it been flooded?'

'We tried, but the water wouldn't freeze. It is an evil place — haunted, that's for sure.'

'A ghost?'

The miner just looks at you and says nothing.

Leave the tunnels	turn to **320**
Go down the dark tunnel	turn to **663**

To renounce the worship of Juntoku, you must pay 40 Shards to the priesthood by way of compensation.

The high priest warns you that if you turn your back on Juntoku, your fellow man will turn his back on you. Do you want to change your mind?

If you are determined to renounce your faith, pay the 40 Shards and delete Juntoku from the God box on your Adventure Sheet. When you have finished here, turn to **58**.

Your next opponent is ushered into the arena. The referees announce him as Vulcis Embers from Metriciens, in Golnir. He is dressed in rich red and gold robes. The drum rattles once more, and the contest begins. Decide which spell to cast.

Wall of fire	turn to **203**
Wall of water	turn to **179**
Wall of thorns	turn to **151**

25

The fisherman drops you off on the coastline outside the city of Yarimura – he refuses to take you into the harbour.

'I'll not pay their damned harbour tax!' he growls.

Turn to **280**.

26

Get the codeword *Dread*.

'Excellent!' beams Commander Telana. 'The hopes and prayers of Sokara go with you. Well, the hopes and prayers of the army, at any rate! Still, good luck!'

If you have the codeword *Deep*, turn to **644**. If not, you leave. Turn to **152**.

27

The pirates kill all the crew, but spare the galley slaves – for now. You are hauled before the captain, a hugely fat barrel of a man with only one ear, for judgment. Those not good enough are chucked overboard; some are taken on as shipmates on the pirate ship to replace their losses.

If you have the codeword *Clutch*, turn to **287** immediately. Otherwise, make a CHARISMA roll at Difficulty 12.

Successful CHARISMA roll	turn to **176**
Failed CHARISMA roll	turn to **253**

28

Your experience with the harmonics of music has taught you much. Gain 1 Rank. Roll one die and add the result to your total, unwounded Stamina score permanently. Don't forget that going up in Rank will also increase your Defence by one. When you are ready, turn to **499**.

29

To the west, the endless monotony of the undulating steppes is broken by the River of Destiny, its half-frozen waters flowing sluggishly to the Rimewater. Roll two dice.

Score 2-5	A caravan	turn to **705**

| Score 6-7 | No event | turn to **676** |
| Score 8-12 | A black stallion | turn to **382** |

30

At the sight of you, the stallion snorts fearfully, and dives into the river, changing its shape in mid-flight, arrowing into the water like a beaver. It doesn't come out.

Turn to **676**.

31

Cross off the 5 Shards. You take the scroll and read it. It says: 'The Curse of Tambu, Khan of the Skies, upon the bearer of this scroll!' Instantly, you are struck by an enfeebling ague.

The pedlar leaps up, suddenly healthy. 'Free at last!' he yells, and runs off, leaping for joy.

You try to stop him, but the curse has left you reeling. Note you have the Curse of Tambu and lose 1 point from your CHARISMA, COMBAT and SCOUTING abilities until you can lift the curse. Judging by the pedlar's behaviour, if you can get someone to buy the scroll off you, the curse will go with it.

You struggle onward. Turn to **144**.

32

Nerech is a barren peninsula of wind-blasted rolling heathland. The sky is a dismal grey; a lone crow circles overhead, cawing mournfully. Wild cliffs overlook the sea. Inland, you see a tall hill in the distance.

Head for the hill	turn to **5**
Climb down to the shoreline	turn to **688**
Go west to Fort Mereth	*The War-torn Kingdom* **299**
Go west to Fort Estgard	*The War-torn Kingdom* **472**
Go west to Fort Brilon	*The War-torn Kingdom* **259**

33

The temple of Tambu is a wooden structure built to resemble one of the round tents of the nomads of the steppes. Tambu is the Great Spirit of the Steppes. When the Northern Lights flicker in the sky, it is said that the spirits of earth, sky and water are dancing for him. Tambu's blessing is said to aid those who travel across the steppes.

Become an initiate of Tambu	turn to **291**
Renounce his worship	turn to **143**
Seek a blessing	turn to **388**
Talk to the chief shaman	turn to **457**
Leave the temple	turn to **10**

34

You slip and fall almost immediately. You hit the ground, but the thick snow cushions you somewhat. Lose 1-6 Stamina points.

Try again	turn to **175**
Give up	turn to **668**

35

If you have the codeword *Deep* or *Dim*, turn to **289**. If not, read on.

You come to a network of underground tunnels that run under the mountains. It is pitch dark, and you must have a **lantern** or **candle** to proceed.

Explore the tunnels	turn to **174**
No source of light	turn to **558**

36

You convince him it will be safe, playing on his greed. The merchant agrees to go along with your plan. Cross off the 75 Shards. You hide in an empty wine barrel. The merchant's trading pass is good, and he is allowed into the citadel without a hitch. You sneak out of the barrel that night. Turn to **295**.

37

You summon a wall of water twenty feet high and send it gushing toward your opponent. The druidess unleashes a bristling hedge of thorns and brambles, dense and thick, that rushes headlong to meet your wall of water. To your horror, the thorns break the water into rivulets and streams that dissipate over the floor of the arena and then grind on toward you. You only have the barest moment to dive aside. Roll two dice, and lose that many Stamina points, as the thorns rip you in passing.

Down to zero Stamina	turn to **7**
Still alive	turn to **81**

38

You step back to the window. The concubine suddenly sits up; her pale white face, framed with long dark hair, looks like the moon shining in a black, night sky. You think it is all up, but she just smiles coyly at you, and turns over.

You make your way back down the tower, without a hitch.

The next day you pay a visit to Lochos Veshtu at the headquarters of the Brotherhood of the Night. Turn to **444**.

39

You come across a tall stone slab, set into the side of a hill. A rune has been carved on it, which you reckon to be the mark of the trau, creatures of the underworld.

Knock on the slab	turn to **573**
Leave	turn to **102**

40 ☐

If there is a tick in the box, Orin Telana refuses to talk to you until you have completed your mission — turn to **152** immediately. If not, put a tick there now, and read on.

Orin is surprised to see you. 'It is vital for us all that you kill Beladai,' he says. 'You must infiltrate his camp to the north, find his tent and kill him! If you are having trouble penetrating the camp, perhaps this will help.'

He gives you a **Potion of THIEVERY +1**. It can be used *once* only, just before you make a THIEVERY roll, to add one to your THIEVERY ability, for that roll only. Note it on your Adventure Sheet. If you have the codeword *Deep*, turn to **644**. If not, you leave; turn to **152**.

41

You come to a river. The water is icy green and fast-flowing. Just as you are steeling yourself to plunge in and swim to the other bank, the bosun points out a covered bridge not far off.

'Why get our feet wet, cap'n?' he asks.

Swim the river	turn to **257**
Cross using the bridge	turn to **328**

42

You climb a rocky, wind-blasted path up the hill. The icy gusts that howl around the hill chill your bones, and the grim, grey keep that looms over you chills your soul. Two massive iron-bound doors are set into its featureless walls. No guards stand beside the gate, and no one appears at the battlements.

Knock on the doors	turn to **486**
Leave Vodhya	turn to **398**

43

The storm demon shudders as you call upon Elnir to banish it. Unable to stand the power of the Sky God, the demon departs, shooting into the firmament like an arrow of green light. As it goes, the storm ceases.

You have won the favour of Elnir. Roll two dice. If the score is greater than your CHARISMA rating, you can add one to your CHARISMA, permanently.

Also, the storm demon has dropped the missile it was about to throw at you. Take the **selenium ore** and add it to your Adventure Sheet. When you are ready, turn to **65**.

44

You are trekking across the endless steppes. Your vision is filled with vast blue skies, and tall grasses that stretch away in all directions, dotted with clumps of scrubby, ground-hugging vegetation.

After a time, you come to an area of marshy ground, fed by a trickling stream. Gnarled trees have taken root around the marsh.

Roll two dice.

Score 2-5	A light in the marsh	turn to **707**
Score 6-7	No event	turn to **92**
Score 8-12	A hut on stilts	turn to **126**

45

You move with calm assurance across a dizzying rock-face that many brave men would go weak at the knees simply to behold. You know that the trick is to keep your body out from the cliff and test each handhold carefully before putting your full weight on it.

Roll two dice, and if you get more than your SCOUTING score you can increase it permanently by 1.

Climb to the top of the cliff	turn to **164**
Descend to the ground	turn to **706**

46

You are not sure if the beacon is in the right place or not.

Sail straight for the beacon	turn to **79**
Follow your own route	turn to **208**

47

Record the codeword *Defend*.

You are spotted outside Beladai's tent by a group of torch-wielding soldiers.

'Stinking assassin!' yells one of them, and they fall upon you in a rage.

You are hacked to pieces in moments. Turn to **7**.

48

To renounce the worship of Amanushi, you must pay 40 Shards to the priesthood by way of compensation.

The priest begs you to reconsider. 'Do not forget that Amanushi can protect you from the knife in the dark, and the depredations of those who would steal from you.'

Do you want to change your mind? If you are determined to renounce your faith, pay the 40 Shards and delete Amanushi from the God box on your Adventure Sheet.

When you have finished here, turn to **194**.

49

As soon as you step between the idols, their heads whip forward and bite at you with sharp, flinty teeth.

Make a COMBAT roll at Difficulty 14.

Successful COMBAT roll	turn to **617**
Failed COMBAT roll	turn to **675**

50

You are sailing along the southerly shores of Nerech, the Land of the Manbeasts. The coastline is one long stretch of cliff. The waters are shallow and rocky, making it impossible to land here. Misshapen figures cavort and yell on the clifftops, shaking their fists in impotent rage at your ship and crew.

Roll two dice.

Score 2-4	Storm	turn to **11**
Score 5-6	An uneventful voyage	turn to **236**
Score 7-10	A ship-wrecked mariner	turn to **173**
Score 11-12	A merchant ship	turn to **514**

51

Unfortunately for you, the captain of the vessel is Avar Hordeth: a powerful man, and one who you have crossed before.

'Wait a minute,' he bellows. 'I know you – you're that snot-nosed little bandit who robbed my villa in Yarimura! Well, well, how sweet that the Fates should bring us together again.'

You are too weak to put up much of a fight and his crew seize you, clap you in irons and throw you into the brig. You can hardly believe your misfortune – of all the people to be picked up by! Avar Hordeth takes all the money and items you were carrying.

Later, you are taken to Yarimura, where you are sold to the city's small navy and put to work as a galley slave, condemned to row under the lash.

Turn to **222**.

52

You camp for the night. If you have a **wolf pelt**, the fur helps to keep you warm. If you do not, lose 1 Stamina from the cold.

You need to hunt for food. Make a SCOUTING roll at Difficulty 11. If you succeed, you find some voles to eat. If you fail, you go hungry and must lose 1 Stamina point.

If you still live, the next day dawns.

Go north	turn to **15**
Go east toward Yarimura	turn to **280**
Go south	turn to **234**
Head west deeper into the steppes	turn to **17**

53

If you have the title Arena Champion, turn to **71**. If not, read on.

Starstone Arena is so called because it is built upon a flat bed of rock – a meteorite that fell to earth many centuries ago. The rock has strange properties. It enables those trained in the magical arts to cast powerful spells based on the elements of fire, water and wood. Magicians battle it out in the arena on a regular basis, each struggling for the coveted title of Arena Champion, and the rewards that go with it. To earn the title, you must win two bouts. Only Mages can enter the contest.

Fight in the arena (Mages only)	turn to **117**
Watch a contest	turn to **127**
Visit the market	turn to **111**
Go to the temple of Molhern	turn to **637**
Go to the White Warlock Tavern	turn to **455**
Visit the chief mage	turn to **403**
Leave the City of Mystery	turn to **90**

54

Its walls, though crumbling, are still so massive and sheer that they are unclimbable. The gates, however, hang from their hinges, their rotting timbers groaning in the wind. Runes, in the language of the long-lost Shadar empire, are carved above the gate. As you step past them, a gigantic head materializes in the air before you. It looks like a jackal, with burning eyes of fire.

If you have a **banner of the Shadar**, turn to **695**. If not, turn to **539**.

55

Cross off the 10 Shards. The woman lays out some oxhide cards, painted with primitive looking runes.

'Aha!' she cries, 'the Piper and the Snake.' She shoves her face
close to yours and barks, 'Be prepared to be the Piper, if you
travel there.'

'And that's all, is it?' you ask.

She grunts, and stares out the window.

You leave the wood. Turn to **325**.

56

One of the nomads, presumably the leader of the warband, tosses
his horse's reins to another and comes striding up to you. He pokes
you in the chest, seizes you by the back of the neck, presses his face
nose-to-nose with yours, and says: 'Fineitri.'

Wrestle him to the ground	turn to **229**
Say 'Fineitri' back at him	turn to **639**
Attack him and his men	turn to **19**
Break away and run	turn to **664**

57

You are recognized by the guards. They salute you and escort you
into the citadel. The commander, Duke Orin Telana, welcomes
you as the saviour of the citadel. You are free to stay here as long
as you like. Restore any lost Stamina points. The knights treat you
with respect, saluting constantly.

When you are ready, you can leave the citadel.

Head north into the plains	turn to **145**
Head south into Sokara	turn to **400**

58

The Plaza of the New Gods is a large oval, the floor of which is
covered in a mosaic of multi-coloured bricks that depicts a woman
whose face shines like the sun, the chief goddess of the pantheon
of the Akatsurai. Around the oval are several magnificent temples;
their mirrored spires and gabled pagodas sparkle in the sun.

Many people throng the plaza: priests and holy men, hawkers
and hucksters, samurai and nomads. You learn a little about the
gods of Akatsurai from them.

In the plaza there are temples to Nisoderu, Goddess of the

Rising Sun, and Queen of the Other Gods; Juntoku, Lord of War; Nai, Sender of Earthquakes; and Amanushi, Master of the Night.

You also hear a rumour that the temple of Nisoderu is looking for a courageous priest to help them with a task.

Visit the temple of Nisoderu	turn to **89**
Visit the temple of Juntoku	turn to **462**
Visit the temple of Nai	turn to **614**
Visit the temple of Amanushi	turn to **194**
Leave the plaza	turn to **10**

59

With regret, Bakhan tells you that she cannot make you another selenium wand.

'A wizard can make only one such wand in a single lifetime,' she explains.

All Bakhan can do for you is to lift a curse, if you are suffering from one. This she will do at no cost because you saved her from her own curse. Cross off any curses you have recorded and adjust any affected abilities to normal.

When you are finished, turn to **10**.

60

You conjure up a bristling wall of thorns, twenty feet high, and send it hurtling toward your opponent. At that instant, Dialla Earthdaughter does the same. The two walls meet in the middle of the arena with a thunderous crash. The thorns and brambles wrestle with each other, and you have to concentrate hard to maintain your wall of thorns, but Dialla's druidic background gives her the edge. Your spell is broken, and her wall of thorns smashes through the remnants of your own wall, to bear down on you with frightening speed.

You have only the barest moment to dive aside. Roll two dice, and lose that many Stamina points, as the thorns rip you in passing.

Down to zero Stamina   turn to **7**

Still alive   turn to **81**

61

After the battle, you are taken to see General Beladai. His beaming smile looks out of place on his dour, grizzled, veteran's face. He embraces you and says in his booming voice, 'The Northern Alliance and King Nergan will honour you above all others, my friend.'

Beladai gives you personal training in the art of war. Add 1 to your COMBAT ability permanently.

After a few days, King Nergan and his court arrive to set up base at the citadel. The King rewards you with a title, in this case, the title of your next Rank. You gain a Rank. Also, roll one die and add the result to your unwounded Stamina total. The King also gives you 500 Shards. After a victory banquet at which you are the guest of honour, you leave the citadel. Turn to **152**.

62

The faery hound snaps at you with its vicious-looking teeth. You find it hard to make out where to strike the shadowy beast in this gloom.

Faery Hound, COMBAT 7, Defence 10, Stamina 12

If you win, you can step through the basalt door it guards by turning to **108**. If you lose, turn to **7**.

63 □

If there is a tick in the box, turn to **279** immediately. If not, put a tick there now, and read on.

At a table in a shadowed corner, two people are talking. One is a short, disreputable-looking fellow, a nomad of the plains judging by his looks. The other is a large, fat, red-faced woman. You walk over, and introduce yourself. They react with astonishment at your temerity, and the man reaches for the long dagger at his belt.

Make a CHARISMA roll at Difficulty 14. Add one to the roll if you are a Rogue by profession, and add an additional one if you have the title Nightstalker.

Successful CHARISMA roll	turn to **146**
Failed CHARISMA roll	turn to **109**

64

Your boasts are unconvincing, and your insults fail to rouse the laughter of the onlookers. Yagotai walks away the victor, by popular demand. You are seized by many hands and bound, hand and foot. Yagotai ties one end of the rope to his horse's saddle and rides around the camp three times, whooping and yelling, dragging you behind him. The nomads look on, laughing cruelly. Lose 2-12 Stamina points (the roll of two dice).

If you still live, they cut your bonds, and dump you out on the steppes. Impressed by your hardiness, they decide not to rob you. Turn to **52**.

65

Another day dawns on the freezing steppes. If you have a **wolf pelt**, the fur helps to keep you warm. If you do not, lose 1 Stamina from the cold.

According to your map, you are somewhere south of the Ruby Citadel.

North	turn to **535**
West	turn to **383**
South	turn to **44**
East	turn to **442**

66

You make it safely on to the roof. Luroc nods, slapping you on the back. Silently, you both steal into the inner courtyard below, where a fountain bubbles merrily.

Lurking in the shadowed cloisters, you and Luroc descend a stairway that leads below the villa. At the bottom, you find a set of heavy bronze doors, and a guard. Fortunately, he is snoring loudly. Luroc explains that the guard has been drugged by Floril. Luroc tries the door, and it swings open – again, Floril's work. You step into the treasure chamber of Avar Hordeth.

Turn to **88**.

67

You are washed up on to a pebble beach, gasping for breath, and only half-conscious. You are barely aware of grasping hands rifling through your things. You have been found by wreckers. You lose all your possessions and money – cross them off your Adventure Sheet. When you come to, you have been dragged up the beach, beneath towering cliffs. You have probably been washed up on the shores of Nerech, the Land of the Manbeasts. Turn to **688**.

68

The bells toll a deep sonorous note. But then the other bells begin pealing, set off somehow by the first. The ringing becomes so loud that it sends you running for the exit, hands clapped over your ears, shrieking in agony. Blood runs from your ears. Lose 1-6 Stamina points. You run out into the ruin, away from the Cave of Bells.

Visit the Vault of the Shadar	turn to **107**
Visit the Crypt of Kings	turn to **298**
Leave the City of Ruins	turn to **266**

70

You are clinging to glassy-smooth cliffs above an abyss that goes down to the sunless depths of the night sky. If only you could wake up and discover this isn't real.

Ascend	turn to **423**
Descend	turn to **204**

71

You are welcomed at the arena as a champion. You cannot compete again but you do have the right to stay in the champion's suite, a luxurious apartment built in the arena. Here you can rest for as long as you like free of charge, and regain any lost Stamina points. The mages can also cure poison, disease and lift a curse (such as the Curse of the Shadar or the Blight of Nagil). When you are ready, turn to **274**.

72

If you have the codeword *Dread* turn to **40**. If not, read on.

Orin Telana is a slim, handsome man. He greets you warmly but his eyes are grim and determined. He explains that the army to the north is fighting not just for the peoples of the steppes but for the Sokaran rebels who still support the old king. The Northern Alliance is held together by the charismatic Beladai.

'Cut off the head, and the body will die,' he says. 'If Beladai is killed his army, and the alliance, will fall apart, and the new order will be safe.'

Orin Telana wants you to find a way into the enemy camp and assassinate General Beladai.

If you agree to take up the mission, turn to **26**. If not, you are shown out, turn to **152**.

73

Despite your best efforts, you get completely lost in the maze of underground tunnels. Roll two dice. If you score less than your Rank, you manage to find a way out – turn to **558**. If you score greater than your rank, you get lost for ever, and starve to death. Turn to **7**.

74

The man is hauled aboard. You find a waterproof pouch on his belt. Inside is one half of what is clearly a treasure map. The directions, however, have been written in some code you cannot understand.

When the ship-wrecked mariner has been revived, you have him brought to your cabin and he tells you his story. His name is Etla,

once first mate to a blackhearted pirate captain called Nyelm
Starhand. Nyelm betrayed his crew, taking the map that showed
the location of the pirate's treasure, but Etla managed to steal half
the map, and escape, throwing himself on the mercy of the sea. He
believes that Nyelm is in Yarimura.

'If we can get Nyelm's half, we'll know the location of the
treasure – you an' me, we'll be rich.'

Etla gives you his half, and says that'll he'll meet you in Yarimura,
when you're ready. He points out that you still need him – only
Etla and Nyelm know the code to translate what the map says.

Record the codeword *Dirk*. Afterwards, Etla hitches a lift on a
passing merchant ship.

'See you in Yarimura!' he says with a toothless grin.

You sail on. Turn to **236**.

75

At the far end of the chamber, a stone plinth is raised above the rest.
On it sleeps a man dressed in purple-hemmed cloth of gold. On his
bearded and patriarchal head rests a golden crown, which glints in
the quivering light you have brought with you. His hands are
crossed over his chest. In one he holds a steel mace, the head of
which is fashioned in gold to resemble a flaming sun. In the other,
he holds a silver scythe, its blade fashioned into a crescent moon.
It is the High King, sleeping through the lost centuries, awaiting
the day of his awakening.

Suddenly the temperature drops even lower – a sudden cold that
threatens to stop your heart. If you have a **wolf pelt**, it protects
you from the cold. If you haven't, lose 2-12 Stamina points (the
roll of two dice).

If you still live, a smoky, phantasmal shape appears in the centre
of the chamber. Her spectral white face is as blank and smooth as
snow, and her ghostly robes, pale as moonlight, billow out behind
her like a trail of stars. Taloned hands, like the wind-blasted
branches of a winterbound tree, clutch at you.

If you have the codeword *Evergreen*, turn to **9**.

If not, turn to **110**.

76

You hurry forward with your men, but instead of gold you find only a heap of old polished brass.

'Nice of you to drop in,' says a voice.

You whirl round. Hanging head-down from the ceiling of the tunnel is a long lean vampire wrapped in a black shroud. He reaches out with thin arms to clutch his victims: you and your shipmates!

Vampire, COMBAT 8, Defence 12, Stamina 18

Only if you defeat the vampire can you get past its dangling carcass and leave – turn to **157**.

The south sector is a part of the city given over to visitors to the city. It is known as the Foreigners' Quarter.

If you have the codeword *Dirk*, turn to **686**. If not, read on.

You find an inn, called the Nomad's Rest.

Visit the inn	turn to **542**
Leave south sector	turn to **10**

78

The undead warriors fall to your martial skill. If you were wounded in the fight, you have been infected with a horrible disease, the Blight of Nagil, which causes boils and gangrene. Note you have the Blight of Nagil, and reduce your CHARISMA and COMBAT by one until you can find a cure.

You step into the main hall. Turn to **372**.

79

You sail for the beacon, a dim orange glow on the dark, stormy horizon of Disaster Bay. You are quite close, passing through a patch of mist, when a horrible rending sound alerts you to an awful danger. The ship has struck a submerged rock, and already it is breaking up.

The mist clears suddenly, and you see that your ship has been dashed against a small island of jagged rock. Armed men are standing on it.

'Wreckers!' cries the first mate, 'They must have lit the fire to lure us on to the rocks!'

Already, some of your crew have been washed overboard. They swim for the island, where the wreckers are waiting for them. Cruelly, they spear your defenceless men and loot the dead bodies. Barrels and bales of your ship's stores are washed up, to be seized by the wreckers' eager hands.

Turn to **411**.

80

You stun your opponent with a forearm smash across the bridge of the nose and follow it up with an arm lock that leaves him howling for quarter. You release him, now that you have shown your strength. The nomads respect your noble action and welcome you to their camp. Turn to **246**.

81

Your opponent is pronounced the winner. You are escorted from the arena.
  Turn to **274**.

82

You clear away the pile of stones and squirm through into a low-roofed chamber where there are many silver and blue jade funerary trinkets strewn around a stone casket.
  You stuff your jerkin full of loot; add 3000 Shards to the cash recorded on your Adventure Sheet. Then you turn your attention to the stone sarcophagus.

Open the sarcophagus	turn to **527**
Leave the mound	turn to **226**

83

The manbeast closes in. You must fight it.
  Manbeast, COMBAT 8, Defence 5, Stamina 10
  If you lose, turn to **7**. If you win, turn to **124**.

84

You come across a circle of ancient, wind-pitted standing stones. In the centre stands a weathered stelae, carved with Shadar runes and symbols.

Enter the circle	turn to **696**
Leave	turn to **224**

85

There is a blinding flash of light, and you feel a momentary sense of oblivion before you appear in mid-air. You crash into a heap on the ground. Picking yourself up, you look around, shivering because of the sudden cold. You have come to the Great Steppes. Turn to **668**.

86

You are right in their path but the horses surge around you, and then they come to a halt, stamping and snorting, their breath like clouds in the cold air. The black stallion trots up to you and regards you with eyes filled with an unnatural intelligence. You realize it is the Steed of Tambu, the Great Spirit of the Steppes. The steed can be ridden only by the worthy; it has deemed you of sufficient piety to receive that honour.

Mount the Steed of Tambu	turn to **239**
Leave the herd of horses	turn to **666**

87

If you have the codeword *Citrus*, turn to **367** immediately. If not, read on. You must fight.

Kaschuf, COMBAT 8, Defence 8, Stamina 20

If you win, turn to **304**. Otherwise, turn to **7**.

88

You have entered a long, low hall of a dark grey stone. Riches abound. Crates filled with objets d'art, bolts of silk from Akatsurai, jars of oleum oil from the Feathered Lands, ingots of gold and silver, chests of gems and coins – the treasure house of one of the richest merchants in the world.

'Well,' says Luroc, 'it's just a question of how much we can carry, and get away with, isn't it?'

But then you notice him eyeing you oddly, distrustfully, as if unsure of your intent. Come to think of it, you don't trust him an inch. It might be better to kill him and take everything for yourself – after all, it's only what he's bound to try to do to you. Every passing second seems to make you more uneasy, more certain that you'll have to kill Luroc.

Make a MAGIC roll at Difficulty 13.

Successful MAGIC roll	turn to **137**
Failed MAGIC roll	turn to **113**

89

The temple to Nisoderu, Goddess of the Rising Sun, is built around an open courtyard with a great shrine in the middle, covered in lit candles. Inside, a hundred nuns, dressed in flowing white robes, and wearing elaborate, wide-brimmed hats, sing a continuous chant in praise of her. The goddess is depicted everywhere as a beautiful woman with a face that shines like the sun. She represents not only the sun, but piety, faith and purity.

The nuns of Nisoderu are skilled in the ways of petitioning the goddess to bring the dead back to life.

If you are a Priest by profession, the high priestess will give you an audience.

Speak to the high priestess (Priests only)	turn to **618**
Become an initiate of Nisoderu	turn to **125**
Renounce her worship	turn to **165**
Seek a blessing	turn to **223**
Arrange a resurrection deal	turn to **268**
Leave the temple	turn to **58**

90

A young mage accosts you on the way out. 'Wait, sir!' he wheedles. 'Why slog your way home by the mundane means used by the common mass of men? I, Firgol the Accomplished, can cast a spell that will take you to the city of Yarimura in an instant! And for only a paltry 100 Shards.'

Pay 100 Shards for the teleport	turn to **280**
Leave the city on foot	turn to **407**

91

If you have the codeword *Diamond*, turn to **346**. Otherwise, read on.

You arrive at the river plain, where three rivers wend their sluggish, half-frozen course to the Rimewater. A freezing fog spills off the river, filling this whole area with an impenetrable grey haze.

Finding your way through this mist will not be easy.

Make a SCOUTING roll at Difficulty 14.

Successful SCOUTING roll	turn to **599**
Failed SCOUTING roll	turn to **697**

92

The sun is swallowed up by the horizon as night falls. You make camp. You are not far enough north for the cold to be a serious problem, but you still need to hunt for food.

Make a SCOUTING roll at Difficulty 11. If you succeed, you find a wild hare to eat. If you fail, you go hungry and must lose 1 Stamina point.

If you still live, in the morning you reckon that you are north of Sky Mountain and south of the Ruby Citadel.

North	turn to **17**
West	turn to **118**
East	turn to **234**
South	turn to **668**

93

You order the crew to sail into the fog.

The first mate says, 'They'll not follow you there, cap'n. It'll be mutiny if you go on.'

The men stand around shuffling their feet nervously, looking at the fog with fearful glances.

If you decide against taking the ship into the fog, turn to 296 and choose again.

If you want to try to persuade the crew to follow you to the isle, make a CHARISMA roll at Difficulty 13. For every Rank you are above one, you can add one to the die roll (i.e. if you are 5th Rank, add four to the roll; if you are 3rd Rank, add two to the roll), and for every 50 Shards you cross off and give to the crew, you can add one. You can also add one if the crew is of good or excellent quality.

If you succeed, turn to **138**. If you fail, they refuse and you'll have to turn to **296** and choose again.

94

As soon as you step into the hole, you feel strangely light-headed, as if you were in a dream. Nothing seems quite real. It is lit by a dull, reddish glow, although where the light is coming from you cannot tell. It is as if the very air were aglow. It smells damp, musty and spicy, all at once.

You proceed down a tunnel that slopes steeply downward, into the bowels of the earth. It soon branches into a veritable maze of tunnels.

Make a SCOUTING roll at Difficulty 14.

Successful SCOUTING roll   turn to **360**

Failed SCOUTING roll   turn to **510**

95

The stallion smells you and snorts. It trots up, and stands beside you, as if waiting for you to mount it.

Leave   turn to **676**

Mount the horse   turn to **116**

96

Becoming an initiate of Juntoku gives you the benefit of paying less for blessings and other services the temple can offer. It costs 50 Shards to become an initiate. You cannot do this if you are already an initiate of another temple. If you choose to become an initiate, write Juntoku in the God box on your Adventure Sheet – and remember to cross off the 50 Shards. Once you have finished here, turn to **462**.

97

The main gate is guarded by the Knights of the Northern Shield, the permanent garrison of the citadel. If you have the title Protector of Sokara or an **officer's pass**, the guards wave you through – turn to **295**. If not, you are denied entry. Turn to **596**.

98

Fortunately for you, a passing merchant ship picks you up. The captain, a merchant from Yellowport, is taking a cargo of textiles to Yarimura. He is happy to take you along for the ride.

'Always pick up the shipwrecked,' he says. 'You never know when you'll end up the same way.' After an uneventful journey you disembark at Yarimura. Turn to **10**.

99

Szgano finishes untying the woman as the last of your opponents falls beneath your blade. The old shaman, however, is still alive; the woman grabs his head, and looks deep into his eyes. He screams horribly as his soul, a grey gibbous thing, is sucked out of him into the woman's mouth. All that is left of the shaman is a dry husk, withered like a thousand-year-old mummy.

Lose 1 point of SANCTITY permanently, for saving the witch.

The Ruzbahn's skin becomes fresh and rosy, and she laughs a rich vibrant laugh. Szgano falls to his knees and kisses her feet devotedly.

'Thank you, my pet,' she says in a creamy voice, absently patting Szgano's head.

'They were right, of course,' she says, fixing you with her emerald eyes. 'I am the vampire witch. But you did save me, so I will let you live. Indeed, I have certain other powers. Give me some of your blood, and I will transmute it into gold.'

Give her some blood	turn to **227**
Run off	turn to **472**

100

You are travelling through the mountains.

Go south	*Cities of Gold and Glory* **282**
Go north to the steppes	turn to **643**

101

The daimyo's palace rises up from the centre of Yarimura, straddling it like a colossus, lord of its domain. It is built in the Akatsuran style, with massive walls and towers — more a fort than a palace.

If you have the codeword *Dare* and do *not* have the title Nightstalker, turn to **354**. Otherwise, turn to **665**.

102

The Gemstone Hills seem deserted. You spot neither hide nor hair of anything.

North to Yarimura	turn to **280**
West into the plains	turn to **234**
South	turn to **145**

103

You are brought into the presence of the god himself. He wears the war-gear of a mighty overlord, his face hidden in the gloom of a great iron visor.

'You have striven long and hard in my service,' he says. 'Now is the time for your reward.'

A seneschal, bony and lavender of skin, comes forward bearing a magnificent sword of white metal. This is bestowed on you amid much ceremony. The assembled dead give a cheer — though it sounds like the death-groan of a multitude — as you buckle the sword to your belt.

Add the **white sword (COMBAT +8)** to your list of possessions. You can never lose this sword; it cannot be stolen from you or lost. Even if you die and are resurrected elsewhere, the sword will still be with you.

If you are an initiate of Nagil, turn to **551**. If not, turn to **387**.

104

You slip on a loose tile; you and it crash to the ground with a shattering clatter.

'Idiot!' hisses Luroc, as he scrambles back down.

The noise has brought some guards, and at the sight of you, they raise a hue and cry.

'Run!' he screams and races off into the shadows, leaving you pursued by half a dozen armed men. You will have to try to lose them in the night.

Make a SCOUTING roll at Difficulty 14.

Successful SCOUTING roll	turn to **133**
Failed SCOUTING roll	turn to **168**

105

If you have the **mirror of the Sun Goddess**, turn to **710**.

If you haven't found it yet, turn to **435**.

If you found it, but have since lost it (through being robbed, killed, cursed, or worse!), turn to **361**.

106

Your ship is thrown about like flotsam and jetsam. When the storm subsides, you take stock. Much has been swept overboard — you lose 1 Cargo Unit, if you had any, of your choice. Also, the ship has been swept way off course and the mate has no idea where you are.

'We're lost at sea, cap'n!' he moans.

Turn to **390**.

107

The Vault of the Shadar is a large, square building of solid granite, unadorned and bare. There is no door, and there are no windows. You cannot find a way in.

Visit the Cave of Bells	turn to **657**
Go to the Crypt of Kings	turn to **298**
Leave the City of Ruins	turn to **266**

108

You enter a small chamber. It is stacked with glass chests, and inside you can see thousands of priceless gems. But no matter how hard you try, the chests will not move, nor will they break. Still, there are a few lying around that aren't in chests.

You find a large yellow gem. When you look through it, you notice some fine lines, like a kind of map. There is also a little arrow, which always points north. Note the **pathfinder's gem (SCOUTING +1)** on your Adventure Sheet.

The other gems that are lying around are worth 350 Shards. Note the cash on your Adventure Sheet.

There is nothing else here, so you continue on your way through the tunnels.

Turn to **123**.

109

You try some streetwise patter, but you succeed only in offending them.

'If it's trouble you want, then that's what you'll get!' yells the man. He tips up the table, and draws a long, barbed knife. The woman backs away. You must fight.

Nomad, COMBAT 7, Defence 6, Stamina 11

If you win	turn to **197**
If you lose	turn to **169**

You try to fight, but it has become so cold that you can hardly breathe. Your eyelids freeze together, and you cannot see. Suddenly, you are struck senseless.

You come round on the shore of the lake, but you have been drained of your vital energy by some vampiric force. Reduce your Rank by one, and roll a die. The result is the number of Stamina points you lose, permanently.

Turn to **320**.

The market of the City of Mystery consists of a single shop that specializes in magic. There is also a stall, where a scholar mage is looking to buy and sell ancient artifacts of the Shadar.

If you have the Curse of Tambu, note this paragraph down (**111**) and turn to **12**. If not, you can visit the market.

Magical equipment	To buy	To sell
Amber wand (MAGIC +1)	500 Shards	400 Shards
Ebony wand (MAGIC +2)	1000 Shards	800 Shards
Cobalt wand (MAGIC +3)	2000 Shards	1600 Shards
Selenium wand (MAGIC +4)	4000 Shards	3200 Shards
Celestium wand (MAGIC +5)	8000 Shards	6400 Shards

Potions	To buy	To sell
Strength (COMBAT +1)	100 Shards	90 Shards
Comeliness (CHARISMA +1)	100 Shards	90 Shards
Intellect (MAGIC +1)	100 Shards	90 Shards
Godliness (SANCTITY +1)	100 Shards	90 Shards
Stealth (THIEVERY +1)	100 Shards	90 Shards
Nature (SCOUTING +1)	100 Shards	90 Shards

Artifacts	To buy	To sell
Banner of the Shadar	800 Shards	400 Shards
Shadar scroll	—	150 Shards

Potions can be used just before a Difficulty roll or a fight to add +1 to the relevant ability and have *one* use only.

The shopkeeper tells you he can make you a special potion for 150 Shards, but he needs an **ink sac** as an ingredient. If you pay the money, and have an **ink sac** (cross it off your Adventure Sheet) he can make you a **potion of restoration** (one use only, heals all lost Stamina points).

Turn to **274**.

112

You succeed only in offending the merchant. He yells for the guards, and a dozen soldiers run out to arrest you. There are too many of them – you are seized and clapped in irons. Lose all your money and possessions on your Adventure Sheet. After a few weeks in a cell, you are sold to slavers from Caran Baru. Eventually, you are bought by the navy of Yarimura.

Turn to **222**.

113

You haven't much time to take what you can. Choose three things only from the following list:

1   500 Shards
2   **Dust of tranquillity**
3   **Battle-axe (COMBAT +2)**
4   **Casket of gems**
5   **Selenium ore**
6   **Silver holy symbol (SANCTITY +2)**

When you are ready, turn to **163**.

114

Avar Hordeth falls at last. Record the codeword *Dead*.

You can take Hordeth's ship if you like. To do so, fill in the details on the Ship's Manifest. It is a galleon, called the *Sea Centaur*; you can transfer the crew from your own ship to the *Sea Centaur*.

Decide which ship you want to travel on. The ship you don't want to use sails to Yarimura with a poor quality crew. Note that it is docked in Yarimura.

The *Sea Centaur* was carrying 1 Cargo Unit of spices, which is yours now. You also find 150 Shards in Avar's sea-chest, and a **mariner's ruttier**. Note it on your Adventure Sheet. Your first mate tells you that the ruttier will help in navigating certain dangerous waters.

When you are ready, you sail on. Turn to **236**.

115

Your light picks out the glint of gold at the end of a long tunnel.

Head along the tunnel	turn to **76**
Leave the cave	turn to **157**

116

You vault nimbly on to its back. Instantly, it neighs wildly and leaps into the river. As soon as it hits the water, it begins to change shape, sprouting fins, and webbed hands and feet. It dives deep into the river, and out of sight. You are left floundering in the water.

When you manage to pull yourself up on the bank, you discover you have lost some possessions. Cross three items (your choice) off your Adventure Sheet.

Turn to **676**.

117

You must be a Mage to enter the arena contest. If you are not, turn to **274**.

If you are a Mage, you must first pay an entrance fee of 50 Shards. If you cannot or will not pay, turn to **274**. Otherwise, cross off the money and turn to **214**.

118

The steppes are vast indeed. Here, in the middle of nowhere, you feel a keen sense of isolation, a lone traveller in an abandoned land. But you notice a welcome change in the endless monotony of the plains — a depression in the earth a little way off.

Investigate the gully	turn to **683**
Go north	turn to **383**
Go south	turn to **266**
Go west	turn to **29**
Go east	turn to **44**

119

You take them by surprise, and cut them down without a sound. You heave down on a massive lever, and the great gates begin to grind slowly open. Within seconds, the citadel is in uproar.

Outside, on the northern plain, a deafening shout, from a thousand voices, splits the quiet of the night, and an elite force of Beladai's army charges the gate. Inside, the garrison rushes to the defence.

In the confusion, you hope to make your escape. If you have the codeword *Dim*, turn to **655**. If not, roll two dice. If the score is less than or equal to your Rank, turn to **606**. If it is higher than your Rank, turn to **375**.

120

You are sailing around the tip of Nerech. Out to sea, a great cloud of roiling fog, tinged with an eerie greenish glow, surrounds a mountain that climbs out of the mist.

'That's the Isle of Mystery,' says the first mate. He spits and makes a sign against evil.

The men mutter among themselves; they are afraid of the misty isle.

Roll two dice.

Score 2-4	Storm	turn to **161**
Score 5-7	An uneventful voyage	turn to **296**
Score 8-12	Spectral pirates	turn to **443**

121

Your hair stands on end, and you feel a prickly sensation all over your body. Suddenly, you find yourself on an island beach. A thick, greenish fog-bank hangs out to sea, completely surrounding the isle. Inland, it is covered in a hot, steamy jungle from which rises a forested mountain. You have arrived on the Isle of Mystery.

Turn to **564**.

122

If you have the codeword *Dove* or the title Arena Champion, turn to **302** immediately. If not, but you have the title Illuminate of Molhern, turn to **478**. Otherwise, turn to **552**.

123

You come out into a large cavern. Radiating from it are four more tunnels. Above each tunnel, a plaque is set, engraved with trau runes. You try to decipher them.

Make a MAGIC roll at Difficulty 13.

Successful MAGIC roll	turn to **495**
Failed MAGIC roll	turn to **233**

124

The manbeast collapses. Its body begins to smoke and burn, and then suddenly vaporizes in a flash of incandescent flame. All that is left is its bird-helm.

Put the helmet on	turn to **219**
Leave it and press on	turn to **627**

125

Becoming an initiate of Nisoderu gives you the benefit of paying less for blessings and other services the temple can offer. It costs 50 Shards to become an initiate. You cannot do this if you are an initiate of another temple. If you choose to become an initiate, write Nisoderu in the God box on your Adventure Sheet – and remember to cross off the 50 Shards.

Once you have finished here, turn to **89**.

126

You see a strange, leathery-looking hut, resting on thin stilts that are sunk into the marsh like the legs of some giant insect.

Make a MAGIC roll at Difficulty 12.

Successful MAGIC roll   turn to **153**
Failed MAGIC roll   turn to **178**

127 ☐

If there is a tick in the box, turn to **13** immediately. If not, put a tick there now and read on.

The floor of the arena is solid rock, smooth as marble, but glowing slightly with an eerie greenish radiance.

The arena referees announce a bout between a shaman of the finmen, a race of aquatic humanoids, and a wizard dressed in orange robes who calls himself the Red Flame. They face each other across the arena.

You can bet on the outcome, if you wish, up to 50 Shards. Decide which contestant you will bet on (if you want to bet at all) and how much, then note it down. The odds are the same for both (evens) so if you bet 20 Shards and win, you'll get 20 Shards profit. When you are ready, turn to **263**.

128

You pass close by a windswept place where a grisly scene is being enacted. A band of nomad warriors have tethered a captive to a rock and are watching as he slowly dies of exposure. The nomads' attention is fixed solidly on their victim, so you have the opportunity to slip away unnoticed.

Continue on your way	turn to **52**
Announce your presence	turn to **56**
Sneak closer	turn to **480**

<h1 style="text-align:center">129</h1>

He gives a faint moan of relief as you loosen the tight bonds. You see at once that he is close to death, but his eyelids flutter open and he manages a weak smile.

'At least I die comfortable,' he says in a Sokaran accent. 'Those devils think that a man who dies in pain will suffer agony for eternity. Thanks to you they didn't get their way.'

He is fading fast. 'Don't speak,' you tell him.

'Why not?' he chuckles. 'I won't get much chance later. Listen, you've done me a kindness and I'll do you one in return. Go to the northern mountains — find a bronze gate. Bow to it three times with your hand on your heart...'

'What then?' you ask, but he is gone.

Get the codeword *Duress* and turn to **52**.

<h1 style="text-align:center">130</h1>

Your song is sweet. The spectre hesitates and draws back. She tilts her featureless head, and swirls away from you. Then she begins to dance to the music of the song, haltingly at first, and then more surely, the haunter itself haunted by a familiar melody.

'Leanora,' says a voice tinged with infinite sadness.

You turn to look in astonishment. The High King has sat up, awakened by the ancient ballad.

The spectre of Princess Leanora sinks to her phantasmal knees before the king. She reaches up, and pulls away the blank, white mask that hid her features: underneath there is only faceless emptiness, the emptiness of desolate snow-covered wastes and ice-bound seas.

'Ah, Leanora...' sighs the king.

Icy tears fall from her empty face to clatter like silver dewdrops on to the stony floor of the chamber. The High King touches her spectral form tenderly with his mace. A ghostly wind strikes up.

'Peace at last,' whispers the spectre and she is borne away by the wind. With a wail, she melts away.

The High King bows his head sorrowfully.

After a while, he looks up at you. Turn to **198**.

131

You are clubbed into unconsciousness. You come round on the road outside Yarimura. You have lost all the money you were carrying, and up to six items (your choice) have been stolen. Cross them off your Adventure Sheet. Turn to **280**.

132

Which of these codewords do you have?

Defend	turn to **57**
Deliver	turn to **134**
Assist or *Dread*	turn to **242**
None of them	turn to **421**

133

You manage to evade your pursuers in the dark with ease. As for Luroc, there is neither sight nor sound of him. You doubt you'll ever see him again. You head off towards Yarimura.

Turn to **280**.

134

The Citadel of Velis Corin is now the base of King Nergan and the Northern Alliance. The guards salute you as King's Champion and hero of the people. You are escorted inside. Captain Vorkung, the king's aide, is there to greet you. He will provide you with a suite of rooms. You can stay there as long as you like, and restore any lost Stamina points.

The court sorcerer will cure you of any poison or disease you may be suffering from, such as the Blight of Nagil, but he cannot lift a curse.

If you have no money at all (including in the bank or in investments), Vorkung will give you 100 Shards to help you get back on your feet.

He tells you that the civil war goes on. Now that the Northern Alliance holds the citadel, the king hopes to push south and take Caran Baru, but all that is a long way off.

When you are ready, you leave. Turn to **152**.

135

Your ship, crew and cargo are lost to the deep, dark sea. Cross them off your Ship's Manifest. Your only thought now is to save yourself. Roll two dice. If the score is greater than your Rank, you are drowned (turn to **7**). If the score is less than or equal to your Rank, you manage to find some driftwood, and make it back to shore.

Lose Stamina points equal to the score of one die roll and, if you can survive that, turn to **436**.

136

You make a leap that is literally death-defying, but one of the cadavers pursuing you manages to snatch hold of your ankle at the same moment. You tumble to the ground, landing with your head between the bronze doors. An instant later they close, severing your neck. Still, it is a cleaner end than you might have suffered in Nagil's sepulchral hall.

Turn to **7**.

137

You realize that you are being subjected to some kind of spell or curse. It is affecting your judgment, filling you with the desire to kill Luroc. It is affecting him too, for he keeps glancing at you, and fingering his long dagger murderously.

You endeavour to control yourself and explain the situation to Luroc. He understands, but it won't be long before both of you fall under the spell and become completely enraged.

You will have to take what you can, and get out quickly or find a way of negating the curse. Choose three things only from the following:

1   500 Shards
2   **Dust of tranquillity**
3   **Battle-axe (COMBAT +2)**
4   **Casket of gems**
5   **Selenium ore**
6   **Silver holy symbol (SANCTITY +2)**

When you are ready, turn to **163**.

138

Your speech fills them with courage and loyalty. You sail slowly into the fog, which closes around the ship like a glove. You cannot see more than a few yards in front. A sailor checks the depth of the water with a plumb-line – his shouts, deadened by the fog, are the only sound you can hear.

Make a MAGIC roll at Difficulty 12.

Successful MAGIC roll   turn to **476**

Failed MAGIC roll   turn to **341**

139

Riders come toward you over the brow of a low hill. Their steeds are not horses but giant flightless birds whose powerful legs propel the group toward you with frightening speed. The riders hold long lances, and their mounts have vicious-looking beaks – an unpleasant combination.

One rider, a squat nomad in stinking leather armour, with a long greasy moustache, charges ahead of the rest, intent on impaling you with his lance.

Make a COMBAT roll at Difficulty 14.

Successful COMBAT roll   turn to **703**

Failed COMBAT roll   turn to **420**

140

You lose your way in the freezing tunnels, and wander for miles. Eventually, your light source burns out completely, and you are plunged into darkness.

A whistling wind springs up, and something rushes at you out of the blackness, howling like a banshee. You are struck senseless.

You come round on the shore of the lake, drained of your vital energy by some vampiric force. Reduce your Rank by one, and roll a die. The result is the number of Stamina points you lose, permanently. Turn to **320**.

141

The Sea Barrier is a great wall built across the entrance to the harbour. It is operated by huge winches, driven by hundreds of slaves. The barrier usually remains open, but in times of danger, it can be closed, making it impossible for ships to reach the port itself. It makes Yarimura well nigh impregnable against naval assault.

All shipping in and out of Yarimura must come through the offices of the harbourmaster. Here you can buy passage to far lands, or even a ship of your own, to fill with cargo and crew.

You can buy one-way passage on a ship to the following destinations:

Yellowport, cost 65 Shards	turn to **531**
Chambara, cost 65 Shards	turn to **205**

If you buy a ship, you are the captain, and can take it wherever you wish, exploring or trading. You also get to name it. Three types of ship are available.

Ship type	Cost	Capacity
Barque	250 Shards	1 Cargo Unit
Brigantine	450 Shards	2 Cargo Units
Galleon	900 Shards	3 Cargo Units

If you purchase a ship, add it to your Ship's Manifest, and name it as you wish. The quality of the ship's crew is poor unless you pay to upgrade it. If you already own a ship, you can sell it back to the harbourmaster at half the above prices.

It costs 50 Shards to upgrade a poor crew to average and 100 Shards to upgrade an average crew to good. Excellent crews are not available in Yarimura.

Cargo for your ship can be bought at the Silk Market, and sold at other ports for profit.

Put to sea	turn to **201**
Go to the Silk Market	turn to **252**
Return to city centre	turn to **10**

142

It is clear there is nothing here but the howling wind and the stench of decay. It is time to leave the Isle of Mystery, if you can. Turn to **407**.

143

To renounce the worship of Tambu, you must pay 40 Shards to the shamans by way of compensation.

'Fool! Those who incur the wrath of Tambu will never survive the steppes!' says a passing worshipper.

Do you want to change your mind? If you are determined to renounce your faith, pay the 40 Shards and erase Tambu from the God box on your Adventure Sheet.

When you have finished here, turn to **33**.

144

To the west, the Great Steppes stretch from horizon to horizon, tough plains grass marching as if for ever across the flatlands. To the east, the Gemstone Hills mark the end of the steppes. You are not far enough north for the cold to be a serious problem, but you still need to hunt for food.

Make a SCOUTING roll at Difficulty 12. If you succeed, you find a wild hare to eat. If you fail, you go hungry and must lose 1 Stamina point.

North	turn to **442**
South	turn to **145**
West, deeper into the steppes	turn to **44**
East to the Gemstone Hills	turn to **426**

145

If you have the codeword *Defend* or *Deliver*, turn to **619**. If not, read on.

You are in-between the Gemstone Hills and the Citadel of Velis Corin. A vast army has made camp near here, some miles north of the citadel. It is alive with activity — caravans of supplies and camp-followers are everywhere.

You learn that it is the army of the Northern Alliance, led by General Beladai. Beladai was the commander-in-chief of King Corin of Sokara's army, before Grieve Marlock usurped his throne. Now the new king-in-exile has made an alliance with the Horde of the Thousand Winds, the trau and the Mannekyn People of Sky Mountain. Together, they hope to take the citadel, and put the king back on the throne. They are readying themselves to march south, and lay siege to the citadel. But the citadel is supposed to be invincible.

Visit the camp	turn to **660**
Go south to the citadel	turn to **308**
North to the Gemstone Hills	turn to **426**
West into the plains	turn to **668**
North west into the plains	turn to **234**
Into the mountains west of the citadel	turn to **558**

146

The nomad looks you up and down. He seems satisfied by what he sees, and offers you a seat. His name is Luroc Bans, a man of the steppes who has taken up a new life in Yarimura.

'I like to steal from the townsfolk,' he says unashamedly, 'And I might have need of someone like you.'

The woman's name is Floril Dellas. She is a washerwoman, and she works for a rich merchant from Metriciens called Avar Hordeth, who owns a villa just outside town. According to the washerwoman, his treasure vault is stuffed full of wealth.

Luroc Bans says, 'Floril's given me a map of the place. I can get in there but we need a tough accomplice to help deal with whatever is guarding the treasure. Something is, but no one knows what. Once we've grabbed the loot, and got out, we split everything three ways. What do you say — you in or out?'

Join them	turn to **488**
Refuse	turn to **406**

147

The passage at the far end of the cathedral still lies open. Beyond it lies the Vault of the Shadar, now the lair of a pack of wolves. They leap out of the shadows to attack you. Treat them as one opponent.

Wolfpack, COMBAT 9, Defence 8, Stamina 18

If you lose, turn to **7**. If you win, you can take a **wolf pelt**.

Visit the Crypt of Kings	turn to **298**
Leave the City of Ruins	turn to **266**

148

The sarcophagus stands in the centre of the chamber, just as it did the last time you were here. You trace the mysterious carvings etched into its lid and wonder how long its occupant has lain here in this desolate region of the world.

> Lift the lid   turn to **527**
> Leave   turn to **226**

149

Your men drive the boarders back to the *Sea Centaur*, where you find Avar Hordeth, battered and weak, in his cabin.

He snarls, saying, 'You'll never take me alive!' and runs at you wielding his axe. You must fight him again.

Avar Hordeth, COMBAT 7, Defence 8, Stamina 3

If you win, turn to **114**. If you lose, turn to **7**.

150

You have no idea who they were, but their daggers were coated with some kind of poison. You also find some **lockpicks (THIEVERY +1)**, which you can take. Nothing else happens, so you return to the city centre. Turn to **10**.

151

You summon forth the thorns of the earth, and a hedge of viciously-spiked brambles rushes toward your opponent. Unfortunately, he has called up a wall of fire: the flames burn your wall of thorns to ashes in seconds and rush toward you. You attempt to dive out of the way, but the flames burn you in passing. Roll two dice and lose that many Stamina points.

> Down to zero Stamina   turn to **7**
> Still alive   turn to **81**

152

There is nothing else to do here but leave.

> North to the steppes   turn to **145**
> South into Sokara   turn to **400**

153

You recognize it as the legendary Hut of Gura Goru. Gura Goru is said to be an evil old crone, whose hut is a living thing, that can walk about on its legs.

Shout 'Gura Goru, over here!'	turn to **654**
Approach the hut	turn to **178**
Leave it alone	turn to **92**

154

Three figures erupt out of the water around you. They are fishmen, with frog-like heads and big, bulbous staring eyes on either side of their heads. Their bodies are covered in scales, and their arms and legs end in heavily webbed fingers and toes. A large dorsal fin runs the length of their backs. They brandish long spears and daggers made of serrated coral. The three fishmen take a step forward, blinking at you oddly.

Make a SCOUTING roll at Difficulty 9.

Successful SCOUTING roll	turn to **363**
Failed SCOUTING roll	turn to **258**

155

Blue Cap chuckles inanely. 'Yes sir!' he says. A few ear-crashing moments later and the panel of seemingly unbreakable ice is a pile of gleaming rubble.

'Payment now, please,' rumbles Blue Cap.

'How much?'

'Manthings pay two hundred Shards a job to Blue Cap.'

'Two hundred Shards for smashing one piece of ice!'

'Payment always the same, whatever job. Smash ice, dig tunnel all day – payment the same,' says Blue Cap. He hefts his pickaxe ominously.

Pay the money	turn to **359**
Can't or won't pay	turn to **562**

156

Your voice echoes hauntingly in the tunnel, adding to the effect of your song. The faery hound sinks back to the ground, and soon its

contented whimpers have turned to the regular breath of sleep.
You step over it and through the basalt door.

Turn to **108**.

157

Cross off a **candle** if you lit one, as it is now used up.

Return to the ship	turn to **191**
Head inland	turn to **41**

158

Gain the codeword *Deathless*.

Kaschuf falls at last, well and truly dead.

The villagers are overjoyed. The Lady Nastasya, whom Kaschuf
had imprisoned, is freed to take up her position as Duchess of
Vodhya. A fair is held to celebrate.

The duchess rewards you with 750 Shards and promises to
spread the word about your heroic deeds across the land. Increase
your CHARISMA by 1 point.

After much festivity, you take your leave. Turn to **398**.

159

You step into a small antechamber. Inside, the red glow is so bright
it hurts your eyes. You can feel it vibrating slightly, and this
vibration causes a low, thrumming hum like the sound of a
multitude of bees.

Two figures shamble toward you. Their half-rotten flesh, rust-
ing armour and putrid smell tell you they are undead. They fix
their dead-white eyes upon you, and utter a wordless cry of
bloodlust, gripping their pitted scimitars in quivering, skinless,
hands. The ruby light gives them an awful, hellish cast.

If your SANCTITY is 9 or more, turn to **416**. If not, turn to **659**.

160

A hulking brute of a man is lurking outside your house. He explains
in no uncertain terms that the Brotherhood of the Night has sent
him to collect protection money and that if you don't pay up, he
cannot be responsible for what happens. He asks you for 8 Shards.

Decide now whether you want to pay. If so, don't forget to cross off the 8 Shards. If you have the title Nightstalker, however, you don't have to pay anything.

Turn to **509**.

161

A darkening of the heavens heralds the gathering of the storm, above the mountain on the island. A ferocious wind sweeps the rain in sheets over your ship, and the waves rise and fall inexorably, lifting you up, and then dashing you down. Strangely enough, the fog that surrounds the Isle of Mystery is not dispelled by the high winds.

If you have the blessing of Alvir and Valmir, which confers Safety from Storms, you can ignore the storm. Cross off your blessing and turn to **296**.

Otherwise the storm hits with full fury. Roll one die if your ship is a barque, two dice if it is a brigantine, or three dice if a galleon. Add 1 to the roll if you have a good crew; add 2 if you have an excellent crew.

Score 1-3	Ship sinks	turn to **314**
Score 4-5	The mast splits	turn to **386**
Score 6-20	You weather the storm	turn to **296**

162

It backs away from you, bowing and scraping. Then it turns and dives into the river with a splash. You wait. And wait. After several minutes your worst fears are confirmed. It is not coming back. The water is as cold as ice, and as murky as mutton stew. It would be most unwise to dive after it.

You move on. Turn to **676**.

163

Luroc Bans suddenly gives an inarticulate scream, and charges at you, brandishing his long dagger! You feel an overwhelming urge to kill him too.

If you took the **dust of tranquillity** from the treasure hoard, turn to **275**. If not, turn to **209**.

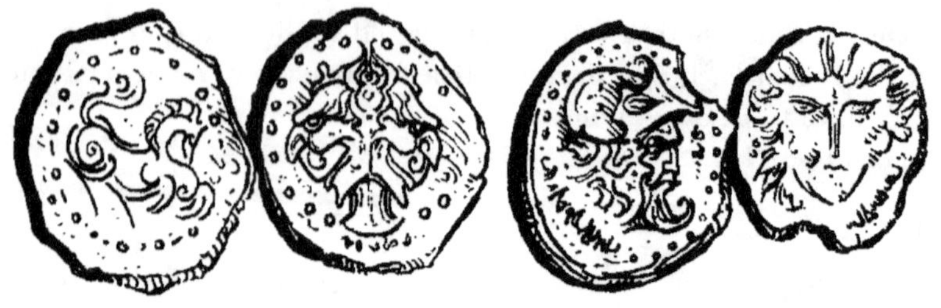

164

You arrive at the top of cliffs bordering the Great Steppes. It is a sheer drop of a thousand feet to the ground. Looking north, you see monstrous snow-clad peaks sloping up to the black vault of the sky.

Descend the cliffs — turn to **221**
Head into the mountains — turn to **264**

165

To renounce the worship of Nisoderu, you must pay 40 Shards to the temple by way of compensation.

A passing nun says disdainfully, 'If you are not pure enough to remain an initiate, then the sun will burn you, mark my words.'

Do you want to change your mind? If you are determined to renounce your faith, pay the 40 Shards and delete Nisoderu from the God box on your Adventure Sheet.

When you have finished here, turn to **89**.

166

The water comes up to your ankles, but the ground is solid enough. Roll a die.

Score 1-2	Finmen from the deep	turn to **154**
Score 3-4	Giant sea spider	turn to **265**
Score 5-6	Message in a bottle	turn to **188**

167

The redcaps have you cornered and you have no choice other than to fight them. They carry pikestaffs in their hands, and great talons grow from their fingertips. Their long, spiked teeth are dripping with saliva; coarse hair grows from their heads and falls over their shoulders like wire. Four of them close in with murderous intent. Fight them as if they were one opponent.

Redcaps, COMBAT 8, Defence 10, Stamina 16

If you win, turn to **603**. If you lose, turn to **7**.

168

You stumble and fall, and the guards catch you. You are over-whelmed by sheer force of numbers, disarmed, beaten savagely, and brought before Avar Hordeth.

He strips you of all the money and items you were carrying. Cross them off your Adventure Sheet. Later, you are taken to Yarimura, where he sells you to the city's small navy. You are put to work as a galley slave. Turn to **222**.

169

Luckily, your life has been spared. You wake up in the gutter of a street alongside other tramps and ne'er-do-wells. You have 1 Stamina point left, but all the money and possessions you were carrying have been taken. Erase them from your Adventure Sheet. Turn to **10**.

170

Record the codeword *Dotage*.

She falls at your feet. You release the prisoners, who cannot believe their good fortune. Among them you find Alissia, the daughter of the fort commander. She tells you the woman was Chizoka, from some strange sect called the Black Pagoda in Akat-surai.

You can take Chizoka's spear. It is a **naginata (COMBAT +1)**. You also find a seal she is carrying. Note the **seal of the Black Pagoda** on your Adventure Sheet.

Now that Chizoka is dead, the rest of the manbeasts don't know what to do. They mill around aimlessly.

You lead Alissia and the others to safety. They return to their homes, and you take Alissia to Fort Estgard in Sokara.

Turn to *The War-Torn Kingdom* **667**.

171

You soon discover the giant worm is all but impervious to injury.

Grey Worm, COMBAT 8, Defence 23, Stamina 8

If you turn around to flee it will get to bite a chunk out of your retreating back (lose 1-6 Stamina points).

Turn and flee	turn to **226**
Fight and win	turn to **429**
Fight and lose	turn to **7**

172

The inside of the pyramid is cool and dark. If you have the codeword *Dwarf*, turn to **646**. If not, read on.

You have come to a long hall, painted with murals depicting the life and times of Xinoc, a priest-king of the old Shadar empire. At the far end is another archway. Shadar runes are carved around it, full of dire warnings and curses for those who dare walk through it.

You can leave the pyramid by turning to **472**.

If you want to go through the archway ahead, make a MAGIC roll at Difficulty 14.

| Successful MAGIC roll | turn to **479** |
| Failed MAGIC roll | turn to **505** |

173 ☐

If there is a tick in the box, turn to **631** immediately. If not, put a tick there now, and read on.

Your lookout spots a drifting piece of sodden timber. Clinging to it is a man; he is holding on to the wood with the last of his strength. His face is bearded and scarred, and he is missing one ear. You know that captured pirates are often punished in this way. The man is, or certainly was, a pirate.

'Huh,' grunts your first mate, 'Once a pirate, always a pirate.'

| Pick him up | turn to **74** |
| Leave the pirate to his fate and sail on | turn to **236** |

174

The tunnels are natural, probably the course of an old underground river, now long dead.

Make a SCOUTING roll at Difficulty 13.

| Successful SCOUTING roll | turn to **466** |
| Failed SCOUTING roll | turn to **73** |

175

Sky Mountain rears up before you. Tiny black specks glide around the peak – it is said the tiny, winged Mannekyn People make their home there. You climb up the rocky flanks of the mountain.

Make a SCOUTING roll at Difficulty 13. Add one to the roll if you have some **rope**, or add 2 if you have **climbing gear**.

Successful SCOUTING roll	turn to **682**
Failed SCOUTING roll	turn to **34**

176

They seem impressed by your demeanour and you are signed on to the crew. After a time serving in the crew of the pirate captain who calls himself Scourge – the crew call him Barrelbelly – you distinguish yourself in a couple of sea battles. The captain offers to release you from service, and put you ashore at a port. You leave with 320 Shards, a suit of **leather armour (Defence +1)**, a **scimitar**, some **rope**, and a **flute (CHARISMA +1)**. Note them on your Adventure Sheet and choose where you will be put ashore.

Yarimura	turn to **10**
Yellowport	*The War-Torn Kingdom* **10**
Dweomer	*Over the Blood Dark Sea* **100**
Metriciens	*Cities of Gold and Glory* **48**
Chambara	*Lords of the Rising Sun* **100**

177

You snatch the necklace, which must be worth a thousand Shards. But the concubine sits up, her face a mask of pale rage in the dark. She screams, and all hell breaks loose.

Guards burst in, swords drawn. Desperately you try to make it back down the tower, but archers shoot you out of the sky. You plummet to your doom in the palace courtyard.

Turn to **7**.

178

As you approach the hut, much to your astonishment it lifts itself up out of the mire on its legs. It scuttles away like a crab and soon you have lost sight of it. Turn to **92**.

179

You summon forth a towering wall of water, and send it surging toward Vulcis Embers. The fiery wall he conjures meets the water in the middle of the arena with a hissing roar. Steam billows everywhere, but your wall of water extinguishes the flames and rolls on to overwhelm Embers. He is battered into unconsciousness. You are declared the winner. Turn to **228**.

180

They catch you and tear you to pieces. Death is swift. Turn to **7**.

181 ☐

If there is a tick in the box, turn to **622** immediately. If not, put a tick there now, and read on.

You find a barque beached on the shore, its hull breached. Huddled around a meagre fire are several desperate-looking men, cold and half-starved, wrapped in thin blankets and sails from the ship. They are burning some of the ship's timbers. As you approach, they glance up but barely acknowledge your presence, so lost in despair are they.

Leave them in their misery	turn to **669**
Try to rouse them into action	turn to **380**

182

Thieves' Kitchen is the most undesirable area of town. The scum of the plains have made this their home, along with dishonoured samurai and exiles from Sokara, Golnir and Uttaku. It is a ramshackle collection of huts, taverns and houses that are more like stockades than homes. The streets are dark and dingy; beggars and cutpurses infest every doorway and alley. Even the city patrol does not come here. It is said the local thieves' guild, called the Brotherhood of the Night, pays off the lord of the city with a fat fee to leave its members alone.

Visit a tavern	turn to **574**
Explore the streets	turn to **633**
Leave Thieves' Kitchen	turn to **10**

183

The supplies of rime ice have been depleted. The ice mine has shut down; all that remains is a jumble of rickety wooden buildings. There is nothing else here so you leave. Turn to **687**.

184

Tick the codeword *Dismal*.

You realize the dagger is coated with poison; the wound you took is burning painfully. Your head swims, and your vision blurs. Then you pass out.

You wake up tied to a chair in a dingy room. You have lost all your money and possessions. Cross them off your Adventure Sheet.

A tall, gangly fellow, dressed in dirty street clothes, regards you equably. His thin, pinched face has a sallow, unhealthy pallor. Behind him stand two large men, their arms folded.

The thin one speaks in a reedy voice. 'Hallo there. I'm Grilb Dante and you've been kidnapped. After all, you're a famous person. Everyone's heard about that affair over the Citadel of Velis Corin. You've made some powerful friends, and I'm sure they'll be happy to pay our ransom demand of 500 Shards. I couldn't believe it when you just strolled on to our turf without a care in the world. Talk about a gift horse! At last, Grilb, I said to myself, Lord Sig himself – may he be forever blessed – has seen fit to hand you 500 Shards on a plate as it were...'

He chatters on like this for some time. Which codeword do you have ticked?

Deliver	turn to **247**
Defend	turn to **211**

185

There is a blinding flash of light, and you feel a momentary sense of complete oblivion before you appear in mid-air. You crash into a heap on the ground. Picking yourself up, you look around, shivering because of the sudden cold. You have come to the Great Steppes. Turn to **668**.

186

You convince him to tell you what he knows about Kaschuf.

'He has bound his soul into a heart-shaped locket. It means he can never be slain while his life force is safe inside it.'

His voice fades to a conspiratorial whisper as he says, 'I know where he has hidden it. There is an uncharted island in the Violet Ocean, due north of ruined Tarshesh. Search there, find the locket, and open it. Then Kaschuf will be as mortal as you and I!'

Nervously, he hurries off.

Get the codeword *Dangle*.

You leave the village. Turn to **398**.

187

The rope goes taut in your hands, jerking you to a halt with stunning force. For a moment you black out. Lose 1-6 Stamina points (the roll of one die).

If still alive, you come round to find yourself being hauled up towards a tunnel in the cliff face. A hairy demon greets you with a laugh that sends a gust of reeking breath into your face.

'Nice of you to drop in,' it says.

You steady yourself against the tunnel wall, uncomfortably aware of the sheer drop just a single step behind you.

'Thanks. Who are you? And where is this?'

The demon stamps his huge red foot in quite immoderate mirth. 'As for my name, it's Kumba Karna, and I daresay that means little to you. But where you've landed — this'll shock — is the Under-world, the Land of Roots, the Place of Direful Dreams. In short, little mortal, you're in hell.'

Turn to **99** in *Into the Underworld*.

If you don't have *Into the Underworld*, then the demon says, 'And you don't belong here — yet!' He teleports you back to Yarimura. Turn to **10**.

188

A small bottle is bobbing in the water nearby. You pick it up, pull out the cork, and take the paper from inside. On it, a message reads, 'Don't open the bottle. And whatever you do, don't read this message.'

Instantly, you drop the bottle and its contents, terrified you may have incurred some kind of curse, but nothing seems to have happened. Puzzled, you return to your ship.

Later, the tide rises, and refloats your ship. You sail on. Turn to **471**.

189

The corpse is lying on a satchel. Gingerly, you heave the body over with a foot, and take the satchel. Inside, you find the **mirror of the Sun Goddess**.

The high priestess at the temple of Nisoderu in Yarimura asked you to retrieve the mirror. Nisoderu must have guided you to the mirror after she cursed the poor wretch who stole it. Looking at his corpse, the eyes pecked clean by birds, you muse on the dangers of incurring the wrath of gods.

Turn to **698**.

190

'But of course, my little friend,' says the genie.

He waves his hand, and you are instantly teleported to Yarimura. Turn to **10**.

191

You set sail away from Bazalek. 'What course, skipper?' asks the helmsman, always happy when he can look over his shoulder and see land dropping away astern.

Turn to **310**.

192

'Nice to see you again,' says Argon. He says he will arrange another resurrection clone for you, if you want, but this time it will cost you 150 Shards.

To arrange resurrection, pay the fee and write Sky Mountain, *The Plains of Howling Darkness* **244** in the Resurrection box on your Adventure Sheet. If you are later killed, turn to **244** in this book.

You can have only one resurrection arranged at any one time. If you arrange another resurrection later, the original one is cancelled (cross it off your Adventure Sheet). You do not get a refund.

When you are ready to leave, the Mannekyn People fly you to the base of Sky Mountain.

'Come back soon!' says Argon. Turn to **668**.

193

The fire comes from a beacon on an island in the middle of the bay. It is a large bonfire, lit by marines from Yarimura to guide merchant ships safely through the bay. The city relies heavily on trade, and Disaster Bay is notorious for wreckers and pirates who prey on the merchants. As you sail past it, you recall a time when another beacon had been lit as a decoy, set by wreckers to lure the unwary on to the rocks. Turn to **471**.

194

The temple of Amanushi is a dome, painted a night-dark blue and speckled with golden stars. Amanushi is the Walker-in-Shadows, the Master of the Night. He is the god of thieves, and assassins, and as such his temple is frowned upon by many Akatsurese. Normally, the temple would not be tolerated so openly, but Amanushi has been the patron god of the Clan of the White Spear since time immemorial, and here in Yarimura, he holds pride of place.

Become an initiate of Amanushi	turn to **334**
Renounce his worship	turn to **48**
Seek a blessing	turn to **447**
Leave the temple	turn to **58**

195 ☐

If there is a tick in the box, turn to **624** immediately. If not, put a tick there now, and read on.

You are on a kind of quayside, which sticks out from the sheer rock behind you. You gaze out on the yawning gulf of black night, hung with stars like jewels on black velvet. A silver barge, floating on air, is moored to the quay, as if awaiting a passenger.

Looking down, you see what can only be described as a celestial harbour. Ships with silver sails are docked there. You can also make out a huge doorway, set into the sheer rock face down below: an entrance into the underworld below Harkuna.

You have succeeded in reaching the gates of the underworld. Add 1 to your SCOUTING ability, permanently. If you are a Wayfarer, you also gain a Rank. Roll one die, and increase your unwounded Stamina total by the result, permanently.

You also find a niche in the rock wall. It is a shrine to the death god, Nagil. Inside is a gold rod with a large diamond fixed on the end. It is a **sacred rod of teleportation**. It has three charges. Note '**sacred rod of teleportation (x3 charges)** *The Plains of Howling Darkness* **685** (temples only)' on your Adventure Sheet. It can be used only when you are inside a temple (any temple) because it uses divine energy as a power source. When you want to use it, turn to paragraph **685** in this book.

If you want to board the silver barge, it will take you to the celestial harbour below. Turn to *Into the Underworld* **199**.

If you haven't got *Into the Underworld*, or you don't want to go there, your only means of getting out of here is the rod (or something like it). It will work here, as the shrine counts as a temple to Nagil.

The **verdigris key** opens the locked trapdoor. You descend some stairs into a square chamber in which there are several doors. They are doors of teleportation — step through and you will be taken to whatever place is displayed. Which door will go through?

Metriciens	*Cities of Gold and Glory* **48**
The base of Sky Mountain	turn to **85**
Dweomer	*Over the Blood-Dark Sea* **100**
Aku	*The Court of Hidden Faces* **10**
Chambara	*Lords of the Rising Sun* **79**
Caran Baru in Sokara	*The War-Torn Kingdom* **400**
The Isle of Mystery	turn to **121**

If you don't want to go, or don't have the relevant books, turn to **499** and choose again.

He falls at your feet. The other customers have been watching the fight, but once it is over, they turn back to their drinks, unconcerned — life is cheap in Thieves' Kitchen.

The fat woman has disappeared but you find 12 Shards on the body of the nomad.

A group of nomads starts watching you with unfriendly eyes. It is time to leave. Turn to **10**.

198

Record the codeword *Diamond*.

The High King looks you up and down. 'I didn't expect someone like you,' he says. 'Still, destiny has spoken.'

He commands you to kneel, and he touches your shoulder with his mace. Gain a Rank and roll one die. Add the result to your unwounded Stamina total, permanently.

Then he steps back and throws his arms wide.

'Awake, my paladins!' he commands.

The sleeping warriors begin to stir. They rise to their feet, clanking, and kneel at the feet of their liege lord.

'Now has the time come for our rebirth! Harkuna will be freed, and the Uttakin will feel the wrath of my revenge.'

Two of his paladins move one of the stone slabs aside. Underneath, a staircase descends into the depths. The paladins climb down, followed by the High King. He turns to you one last time.

'You cannot follow where we are going. It would be certain death. But come to me soon. You will find me at my seat, in Harkuna. Farewell, friend.'

With that he leaves.

When you look again, the staircase is gone. You make your way back through the tunnels, which are beginning to melt now that the High King is awake, and the spectral Ice Queen has been laid to rest. Turn to **687**.

199

If you have the codeword *Drake*, turn to **485** immediately. If not, read on.

The Tower of Bakhan is a tall, forbidding structure. You knock on the gargoyle-adorned doors, and are shown in to a dark, shadowy room. You sit at a table, at the far end of which squats a misshapen form, wreathed in voluminous robes, and indistinct in the darkness.

'I am Bakhan,' rasps a voice. As you watch, the robes begin to shift and rustle, as if changing shape. After a few minutes, the voice speaks again, sounding quite different this time. 'I have been cursed. Every hour, my form changes at random into hideous shapes and creatures that would blight your soul if you were to look upon them. But do not fear, for I will not hurt you.'

Bakhan has searched for ways to deal with curses for many years. If you are cursed, (such as the Curse of the Shadar) Bakhan can remove it for you, but it will cost you 100 Shards.

'You look a brave sort,' Bakhan croaks. 'I need a witch's hand and some parrot fungus if I am to lift my own curse. Bring me these things, and I will reward you.'

If you have a **witch's hand** and some **parrot fungus**, turn to **691**. If not, you leave. Turn to **10**.

200

You find a goat track leading up through the mountains.

Go north into the steppes   turn to **266**
South into the mountains   *Cities of Gold and Glory* **351**

201

You are sailing in the coastal waters around the city of Yarimura. To the east, the sea stretches away to the horizon.

Roll two dice.

Score 2-4   Storm   turn to **642**
Score 5-12   An uneventful voyage   turn to **580**

Wild horses rush out of the twilit gloom and thunder toward you. The herd is led by a huge black stallion, whose glossy flanks seem to glow in the pale radiance of a full moon.

Make a SANCTITY roll at Difficulty 14.

Successful SANCTITY roll	turn to **86**
Failed SANCTITY roll	turn to **694**

203

You unleash the wall of fire. Vulcis Embers also releases fire, and the two walls crash together in the middle of the arena, creating a veritable inferno. Vulcis Embers, however, is more accomplished than you in fire magic, for his fiery wall outlasts yours. You cannot maintain the spell, and flames rush toward you with such speed that you cannot avoid them completely.

Roll two dice and lose that many Stamina points as the flames burn you in passing.

Down to zero Stamina   turn to **7**
Still alive   turn to **81**

204

Far below, you see a harbour where ships with metal sails put out on the sea of night. The starfarers look like common sailors except that their clothes glitter in the celestial light. You come to a ledge. Beside the ledge, a silvery barge, covered in strange blocky glyphs, is floating in the air. It is unoccupied.

Climb back up   turn to **423**
Get on the barge   turn to **3**

205

A merchant from Golnir is prepared to take you to Imperial Chambara but you need *Lords of the Rising Sun* to travel there. If you have, cross off the 65 Shards and turn to *Lords of the Rising Sun* **79**. If not, turn to **141**.

206

The men absolutely refuse to sail into the Unbounded Ocean.

'There's no land out there, and the seas are infested with Demons of the Deep — if we go too far, we'll fall off the edge of the world!' says the first mate.

You have no choice but to reconsider your destination. Turn to **236** and choose again.

207

It is as if the horses were deliberately trying to trample you. You are able to avoid most of them, but one slams into you, knocking you to the ground. Lose 1-6 Stamina points.

If you're still alive, the herd thunders off into the darkening night.

You pick yourself up. Turn to **666**.

208

The men appear uncertain about your decision but they go along with it. You pass the beacon on your left in the distance. The crew is relying on you to navigate the ship safely through Disaster Bay.

Make a SCOUTING roll at Difficulty 14. You can add one to the roll if your crew is good or excellent quality. You can also add one if you have a **mariner's ruttier**.

Successful SCOUTING roll	turn to **471**
Failed SCOUTING roll	turn to **594**

209

You and Luroc have fallen under some kind of spell that makes you so enraged and full of hate, that you can think of nothing but killing each other.

You must fight Luroc Bans.

Luroc Bans, COMBAT 7, Defence 6, Stamina 11

Win	turn to **391**
Lose	turn to **7**

210 ☐

If the box above is empty, put a tick in it and turn to **128**. If it was already ticked, turn to **570**.

211

Several days pass. You are fed and watered, but Grilb is becoming anxious, and you begin to worry for your safety. Eventually, a letter arrives from Marlock City, in Sokara. Grilb, grim-faced, reads it to you.

'General Grieve Marlock does not deal with terrorists. Your captive is not my concern.'

General Marlock has abandoned you, despite the fact that you did his dirty work for him, disposing of Nergan Corin and Beladai. And just to save a lousy 500 Shards.

Grilb says, 'If you can pay the ransom, I'll let you go. If not....'

Your only hope is if you have 500 Shards in the bank at Yarimura. Turn to **600**, make a withdrawal, if you can, and then select the option 'Paying a ransom'.

212

You dart past them, and run for your life. They run after you, but you manage to make it out of Thieves' Kitchen, and they give up the chase. Turn to **10**.

213

The pedlar is a nomad trapper, heading for Yarimura. He'll sell you a **wolf pelt** for 75 Shards if you want to buy one. When you are ready, turn to **144**.

214

They explain the rules. As a Mage you will find that the mystical energy that radiates from the starstone floor of the arena will enable you to cast three types of wall of force spells: fire, water and thorns. The trick is to catch your opponent with a wall of energy that defeats his wall, and goes on to affect him directly. You must defeat two opponents to become Arena Champion.

Soon you find yourself facing your first opponent across the flat, marble expanse of the glowing starstone. Her name is Dialla Earth-daughter, a sorceress from the Isle of Druids to the south. A drum thunders, marking the start of the contest. You sense the power emanating from the ground, and you feel instinctively how to use it.

Wall of fire	turn to **4**
Wall of water	turn to **37**
Wall of thorns	turn to **60**

215

The snake demon dies, hissing horribly. If you were wounded in that fight, you have been poisoned. The venom is not fatal, but it has paralysed the muscles in one half of your face, and your left hand. Note you are poisoned and reduce your CHARISMA and COMBAT abilities by one until you can find a cure.

Gain the codeword *Dawn*.

At the far end of the hall, you find a large tomb plaque. It is inscribed: 'Here lies Xinoc the Priest-King, exalted under heaven.' There is a small hole in the plaque.

If you have an **obsidian key**, turn to **434**. If not, there is nothing you can do but leave.

Visit the Cave of Bells	turn to **657**
Visit the Vault of the Shadar	turn to **107**
Leave the City of Ruins	turn to **266**

216

You cross safely, but your men flatly refuse to even make the attempt. There is no point in berating them for their timidity; it is not given to all men to have the hearts of heroes. You set off along the riverbank. Turn to **467**.

217

He shrugs off your entreaties and hurries away, muttering under his breath. There is nothing else for you to do but leave the village. Turn to **398**.

218

Get the codeword *Defend*.

You have completed your mission, and lived to tell the tale. You return to the citadel, and are taken to see Orin Telana, the commander. He is more than pleased to see you.

'Beladai is dead, and his army is scattered to the four winds. You have done a great service for Sokara.'

Telana rewards you with one of the following items (your choice):

Sword of the Shadar (COMBAT +3)
Gold holy symbol (SANCTITY +3)
Enchanted flute (CHARISMA +3)
Sextant (SCOUTING +3)
Cobalt wand (MAGIC +3)
Gloves of Sig (THIEVERY +3)

When you're done, the commander tells you that Grieve Marlock, the ruler of Sokara wants to see you at his palace in Marlock City.'

It is time to leave the citadel.

North to the steppes	turn to **145**
South into Sokara	*The War-Torn Kingdom* **271**

<h1 style="text-align:center">219</h1>

As you slip the helmet over your head, dozens more of the manbeasts appear on the scene. Your vision blurs and your head begins to pound. It's clear that the helmet is doing something to your mind – and it hurts!

Make a MAGIC roll at Difficulty 14.

Successful MAGIC roll	turn to **401**
Failed MAGIC roll	turn to **677**

<h1 style="text-align:center">220</h1>

The merchants' guild is a domed building of red stone. Inside, rich tapestries and fine furnishings attest to the wealth and power of the guild in Yarimura. Here you can bank your money for safe-keeping – or invest it in guild enterprises in the hope of making a profit.

Make an investment	turn to **526**
Check on investments	turn to **355**
Deposit or withdraw money	turn to **600**
Return to the town centre	turn to **10**

<h1 style="text-align:center">221</h1>

You are scaling a sheer cliff face. There are many cracks you can use for purchase, but frost makes each step treacherous.

Make a SCOUTING roll at a Difficulty of 14. You can add 1 to the number rolled if you have **rope**, or 2 if you have **climbing gear**.

Successful SCOUTING roll	turn to **45**
Failed SCOUTING roll	turn to **556**

If you have the title Hatamoto, turn to **276** immediately. If not, read on.

You are set to work rowing on a Yarimuran warship. The next few months are hard indeed, though you do get a chance to heal a little (restore up to 6 points of Stamina). The life span of a Yarimuran galley slave is not long. Constant whippings, poor food, and an existence chained to a rower's bench weaken you considerably. Lose one Rank. Roll one die and subtract the score from your unwounded Stamina total, permanently.

After many battles at sea, your ship is captured by pirates from the Unnumbered Isles in the Violet Ocean. Turn to **27**.

If you are an initiate it costs only 10 Shards to purchase Nisoderu's blessing. A non-initiate must pay 25 Shards. Cross off the money

and mark SANCTITY in the Blessings box on your Adventure Sheet.
The blessing works by allowing you to try again when you fail a
SANCTITY roll. It is good for only one reroll. When you use the
blessing, cross it off your Adventure Sheet. You can have only one
SANCTITY blessing at any one time. Once it is used up, you can
return to any branch of the temple of Nisoderu to buy a new one.

When you are finished here, turn to **89**.

224

You are deep in the western steppes and night is falling. To the
west, you see something glitter on the horizon — the Rimewater.
To the south, the mountains of the Spine of Harkun rise up heaven-
wards.

You are not far enough north for the cold to be a serious
problem, but you still need to hunt for food. Make a SCOUTING roll
at Difficulty 11. If you succeed, you bring down a mountain goat
to eat. If you fail, you go hungry and must lose 1 Stamina point.

If you still live, in the morning you set off.

East	turn to **266**
North	turn to **29**
West to the Rimewater	turn to **320**
Climb the mountains to the south	turn to **100**

225

You ask the guards at the gate to let you through into Nerech. As
the gates swing open, a priest of Nagil, the God of Death, steps
forwards and reads the last rites over you.

'I'm not dead yet!' you shout, shoving the priest hard in the chest.

'As good as,' he mutters, in-between the chant of the Rites of
Nagil.

Turn back	*The War-Torn Kingdom* **472**
Venture forth	turn to **32**

226

You are travelling across snow-carpeted wastelands. To the north,
the Peaks at the Edge of the World rise up; these indomitable
mountains are completely impassable here. You put your position

as somewhere between the Pyramid of Xinoc and the Ruby Citadel.

If you have a **wolf pelt**, the fur helps to keep you warm. If you do not, lose 1 Stamina from the cold.

West	turn to **472**
East	turn to **535**
South	turn to **383**

227

You cut your arm. The witch, smiling evilly, passes her hand over your blood, as it flows from the cut. It turns into liquid gold and spatters to the ground. For every Stamina point you want to lose, you can gain 10 Shards.

When you are finished, she leaves, disappearing with Szgano into the night. Turn to **472**.

228

You have learnt much from your battle in the arena. You gain a Rank (note it on your Adventure Sheet). Roll one die and add the result to your total, unwounded Stamina score. Remember that an increase in Rank also increases your Defence. The spectators applaud your victory – note the title Arena Champion in the Titles box. Now turn to **274**.

229

The other warriors growl, but honour forbids them from interfering. The opening feints and leg-sweeps soon tell you that you are matched against a cunning fighter.

Make a COMBAT roll at a Difficulty of 14.

Successful COMBAT roll	turn to **80**
Failed COMBAT roll	turn to **379**

230

You are spotted halfway up the tower by an alert guard. You are caught like a fly in a trap. They summon archers, and you are shot out of the sky, to plummet to your doom in the palace courtyard. Turn to **7**.

The Horse Market is a large open corral, where traders sell the finest horses from the plains. Around its edge, stalls sell more traditional goods. If you have the Curse of Tambu, note this paragraph down (**231**) and turn to **12**. Otherwise, you can visit the market.

Armour	*To buy*	*To sell*
Leather (Defence +1)	50 Shards	45 Shards
Ring mail (Defence +2)	100 Shards	90 Shards
Chain mail (Defence +3)	200 Shards	180 Shards
Splint armour(Defence +4)	400 Shards	360 Shards
Plate armour (Defence +5)	—	720 Shards

Weapons (sword, axe, etc)	*To buy*	*To sell*
Without COMBAT bonus	50 Shards	40 Shards
COMBAT bonus +1	250 Shards	200 Shards
COMBAT bonus +2	—	400 Shards
COMBAT bonus +3	—	800 Shards

Magical equipment	*To buy*	*To sell*
Amber wand (MAGIC +1)	500 Shards	400 Shards
Ebony wand (MAGIC +2)	—	800 Shards

Other items	*To buy*	*To sell*
Flute (CHARISMA +1)	300 Shards	270 Shards
Lockpicks (THIEVERY +1)	300 Shards	270 Shards
Holy symbol (SANCTITY +1)	200 Shards	100 Shards
Compass (SCOUTING +1)	500 Shards	450 Shards
Rope	50 Shards	45 Shards
Lantern	100 Shards	90 Shards
Climbing gear	100 Shards	90 Shards
Wolf pelt	100 Shards	90 Shards
Bag of pearls	—	100 Shards
Silver nugget	—	200 Shards

When you are ready, turn to **10**.

232

You tell them you are out scouting for the Sokaran army but they ask you detailed questions you are unable to answer. You are arrested, and taken into the citadel for interrogation.

If you have the codeword *Drizzle* or *Assault*, turn to **661**. If you have neither codeword, read on.

The Sokarans are suspicious, and they torture you during interrogation. Lose 1-6 Stamina points (the roll of one die). If you still live, you have nothing to tell them so eventually they release you. Turn to **145**.

233

You have no idea what the runes say. You also know that you will never find your way back the way you came. Which tunnel will you go through?

Tunnel one	turn to **656**
Tunnel two	turn to **518**
Tunnel three	turn to **402**
Tunnel four	turn to **623**

234

You are walking across the plains, a featureless expanse of seemingly endless grasslands. Roll two dice.

Score 2-5	An old ruin	turn to **491**
Score 6-7	No event	turn to **144**
Score 8-12	A miserable pedlar	turn to **326**

235

Your attempt at the song is so bad, it only further enrages the Ice Queen. Turn to **110**.

236

You are sailing along the south coast of Nerech.

North east	turn to **120**
East	turn to **206**
South west along the coast	*The War-Torn Kingdom* **190**
South	*The War-Torn Kingdom* **136**

237

You spot the belfry tower where you dispelled the ghost of Khotep
the Sentinel. It is empty now, so you continue on your way. Turn
to **92**.

238

Your three assailants are wielding long, thin daggers. You must
fight them as one.

   Three Cutthroats, COMBAT 8, Defence 7, Stamina 17

   If you get wounded, turn to **184**. If you manage to defeat them
without losing a single point of Stamina, turn to **150**.

239

You vault nimbly on to the stallion's glossy black back. The steed
will take you wherever you want to go on the plains, and then it
will leave, galloping off into the sky.

City of Yarimura	turn to **280**
City of Ruins	turn to **266**
The Rimewater	turn to **320**
Tigre Bay	turn to **669**
The Ruby Citadel	turn to **535**
Near Beladai's Camp	turn to **145**
Get off, and stay here	turn to **666**

240

The marines and Hordeth retreat to the *Sea Centaur*. You and your
crew are too tired to pursue, and Hordeth pulls away.

   'I'll get you next time, you filthy swine!' he yells in parting.

   The *Sea Centaur* sails away, leaving you to continue your journey.
Turn to **236**.

241

Record the codeword *Drizzle*.

   'That is good,' pipes Lek.

   The trau in the corner gives an enormous grin.

   Beladai puts his hand on your shoulder, and bores his steely gaze
into your eyes.

'Do not fail us and may Tyrnai guide you,' he whispers. 'We will send a thousand of our best troops every night, under cover of darkness, as near to the gates as they can get undetected. As soon as the gates open, they'll charge.'

If you have the codeword *Deep*, turn to **709**. If not, you leave the camp. Turn to **145**.

242

Protector-General Marlock sent you to speak with the commander of the citadel. You show the guards your authorization from the general, and their attitude changes from one of disdainful contempt to polite attention. You are escorted into the citadel.

Turn to **295**.

243 ☐

If there is a tick in the box, turn to **193** immediately. If not, put a tick there now, and read on.

Through the grey skies, and sheets of rain, you can just make out a bright orange fire in the distance.

'That's the beacon. It's lit to guide ships through the rocky reefs of the bay. We should head straight for it — that way we should miss the danger spots, cap'n,' says the first mate.

You examine your charts of the area.

Make a SCOUTING roll at Difficulty 12. You can add one to the roll if you have a mariner's ruttier.

Successful SCOUTING roll	turn to **8**
Failed SCOUTING roll	turn to **46**

You awake, coughing and spluttering. You have come back to life in one of Argon's life-vats on the top of Sky Mountain.

The possessions and cash that you were carrying at the time of your death are lost. Cross them off your Adventure Sheet. Your Stamina is back to full, though. Also remember to delete the entry in the Resurrection box now that it has been used.

'Run into some trouble did we?' Argon asks as he helps you out of the vat.

Turn to **192**.

You step back involuntarily, as they reach for you with supernatural speed, night-black talons questing for your throat. Then they freeze.

'I smell faery mead!' says one.

'Well, it's going to be mine, then,' says the other.

'Oh, no!' says the first. 'It's my turn.'

You put the jug of **faery mead** on to the ground (cross it off your Adventure Sheet). The trau look at it, then they look at each other; giving each other a feral grin, they rush together and a shadowy battle commences.

It seems that they've forgotten about you. Where will you go now?

North to Yarimura	turn to **280**
West into the plains	turn to **234**
South	turn to **145**
Into the trau hole	turn to **94**

246

It is not a pleasant experience standing with the nomads as they watch their captive die. You know that to show distaste, however, would grievously offend them — and you have no desire to join the wretched man as he writhes and gasps towards his inevitable end.

The warriors give you jerky from their saddlebags, washed down with gulps of strong, sour kvass. Recover 1 Stamina point if injured and, if you are a Wayfarer, gain 1 point of CHARISMA for learning a little of the strange nomadic customs.

Their victim dies at last. The nomads give a grunt of approval, jump into their saddles and ride off. Turn to **52**.

247

Several days pass. You are fed and watered, but Grilb is becoming anxious, and you begin to worry for your safety. Then Captain Vorkung, the aide to King Nergan of Sokara, turns up. He speaks with Grilb and money changes hands.

'Farewell, my dear friend,' Grilb says to you in parting. 'Feel free to drop in any time!'

His two hired thugs laugh cruelly, and then they are gone.

'Ah, it is a sorry thing to see you in these straits, fallen prey to scum like that,' says Vorkung, untying your bonds. 'But King Nergan would never abandon the King's Champion, and saviour of the citadel. Nor would I.'

Captain Vorkung gives you a **sword** and **ring mail (Defence +2)** to help you get back on your feet. You enjoy a few ales with him in a local tavern before he has to head back to the citadel. You remain in Yarimura. Turn to **10**.

248

Blue Cap falls dead. You can take his **pickaxe** if you want.

You press on down the tunnel. After a while, you come to a large round chamber of dressed stone, hung with banners. Flat stone slabs are arranged around its edge. Upon them rest warriors, wearing golden armour and clasping long, two-handed swords in gauntleted hands. They appear to be asleep.

Turn to **75**.

249

You pause to rest. After a short while, you see the old butler, Kevar, drawing some water from the village well.

When you go to question him, he steps back, startled, and exclaims, 'No, no, I cannot speak with you, it is more than my life is worth!'

Make a CHARISMA roll at Difficulty 12.

Successful CHARISMA roll	turn to **186**
Failed CHARISMA roll	turn to **217**

250

You are restored to life at the temple of Nisoderu, Goddess of the Rising Sun, in Yarimura. Your Stamina is back to its normal score. The possessions and cash you were carrying at the time of your death are lost. Cross them off your Adventure Sheet. Also remember to delete the entry in the Resurrection box now it has been used.

The high priestess, sweating from the heat of a thousand candles that have been laid out around you in a specific ritual pattern, says, 'Nisoderu has seen fit to shine her light into the Land of the Dead, so that we could find your soul, and bring it back.'

When you are ready, turn to **89**.

251

As you draw nearer to the hill, something steps into your path. It looks like a man, but its limbs are strangely twisted, and its hands end in long black talons. It is covered in matted, grey fur, and wears little except an ornate iron helm, fashioned to resemble the head of bird, that covers its head completely. Two red specks glint from within the helm. The manbeast howls at the sky and comes for you.

If you have a **manbeast's helmet** and want to pull it over your head, turn to **219**. If not, turn to **83**.

252

You can buy goods at the Silk Market only if you own a ship which is docked at Yarimura. You can buy as much cargo as your ship has room for. You can also sell cargo here. All prices are for 1 Cargo Unit.

Cargo	To buy	To sell
Furs	100 Shards	85 Shards
Grain	270 Shards	250 Shards
Metals	600 Shards	560 Shards
Minerals	400 Shards	300 Shards
Spices	900 Shards	810 Shards
Textiles	325 Shards	275 Shards
Timber	110 Shards	90 Shards

Write your current cargo on the Ship's Manifest.

If you own a ship and wish to set sail, turn to **201**. Otherwise, you can go to the city centre. Turn to **10**.

253

The captain dismisses you as worthless garbage. The pirates casually toss you over the side without a thought. They sail away, leaving you behind.

By chance, you manage to find a piece of driftwood to hold on to. Roll a die and add one to the score. If the result is higher than your Rank, turn to **459**. If it is less than or equal to your Rank, turn to **98**.

254

You come out in to a large cavern. It looks empty, but then dozens of shadowy shapes detach themselves from the walls, and you are surrounded by many trau. They laugh cruelly as they seize you; one of them blows some kind of dust into your face. You drift into unconsciousness. Turn to **607**.

255

The crew will not follow you unless you are at least 7th Rank or higher. If you are not of high enough Rank, you will have to sail back south – turn to **201**.

If you are 7th Rank or higher, and still want to enter the cave, you must have Fabled Lands Book Twelve: *Into the Underworld*. If you haven't you'll have to turn back anyway – turn to **201**.

If you have it, turn to *Into the Underworld* **35**.

256

You are recognized by the guards as of sufficient rank within the hierarchy of Akatsurai to be allowed into the palace.

You are summoned to see Lord Kumonosu, daimyo of the Clan of the White Spear. His audience hall is a room of finely polished wood.

He acknowledges your position as Hatamoto in the personal guard of the Shogun of Akatsurai. Although he and the Shogun are enemies, he treats you well enough. Kumonosu gives you a sealed letter and asks that you take it to the Shogun. Note the **sealed letter** on your Adventure Sheet. You are shown out; you leave walking backwards, bowing the whole time.

If you have the codeword *Fog*, turn to **690**. If not, you leave the palace. Turn to **10**.

257

The water is so cold that it makes you groan like a dying man. A moment later you feel hands of mud and weed clutching at your ankles from the riverbed, and then you truly know the meaning of fear.

To cross safely you must cope not only with the strong current but also with the supernatural tendrils that are trying to pull you under. Make a SCOUTING roll and a MAGIC roll, both at a Difficulty of 14.

Both rolls successful	turn to **216**
One roll successful	turn to **413**
Both rolls failed	turn to **374**

258

You have no idea what these strange creatures are. One of them is lowering his spear towards you.

Attack them	turn to **520**
Wait to see what happens	turn to **634**

259 ☐

If there is a tick in the box, turn to **59** immediately. If not, put a tick there now, and read on.

Bakhan takes the ore and makes a selenium wand for you. Cross off the **selenium ore** and add the **selenium wand (MAGIC +4)** to your Adventure Sheet. Afterwards, she bids you a fond farewell. Turn to **10**.

260

You are reminded of an evening you spent among the One-Eyed Crow clan, down on the windswept plains. Their bard told a tale of an ancient folk hero who vanquished a vast invulnerable maggot by repeatedly striking it on the snout – the one part of the creature that was susceptible to injury.

Bearing this in mind, you keep up a barrage of painful blows on the worm's soft snout until it pulls back into the interior of its burrow.

Turn to **429**.

261

You sail for days until you sight land to the south. As you draw closer, one of the men recognizes the coastline – it's the Isle of Druids. Turn to *The War-Torn Kingdom* **136**.

262

You scatter the demon to the winds with your weapon. The creature drops a round lump of ore. Note the **selenium ore** on your Adventure Sheet.

With the demon gone, the storm quietens. Turn to **65**.

263

The battle begins. With a strange cry, Red Flame raises his arms and gestures in the air. To your amazement a wall of flames appears in front of him, and speeds away towards the finman with a roar. Simultaneously, the fish-scaled, webbed finman responds by opening his toothed maw and vomiting forth a stream of gushing water that forms into a wall of his own, and rushes, like a small tidal wave, to meet the wall of flame.

At the moment of impact, the flames are extinguished instantly, and the wall of water surges on to engulf Red Flame. He is lifted up, and dashed against the wall of the arena, where he lies unmoving.

Arena attendants run on to carry his body away, and the referees declare that the finman, whose name is unpronounceable by the human throat, is the victor.

If the finman can win two more bouts, he will have won the title of Arena Champion. If you bet and won, add the amount you bet to your total of Shards. If you lost, cross off the money.

Now turn to **13**.

264

You enter a region of high mountains whose peaks loom up like images glimpsed in a nightmare. The sky above is a swirl of white mist which occasionally parts to give glimpses of crystalline, star-dusted darkness. Food is hard to come by in this arctic wilderness, and there is no wood to make a fire.

Make a SCOUTING roll at a Difficulty of 16.

Successful SCOUTING roll	turn to **636**
Failed SCOUTING roll	turn to **317**

265 ☐

If there is a tick in the box, turn to **378** immediately. If not, put a tick there now, and read on.

There is a sudden violent splashing, and you are seized by long, insectoid limbs, and pulled under the sand before you have time to react! You have been grabbed and drawn into the lair of a giant sea spider, a creature that lurks buried under shallow sand, waiting to pounce on unwary prey that strays too near. The sea spider's many eyes regard you with glittering, black malice from the end of long, sinuous stalks, and its mandibles click together in anticipation of the meal you will provide. You will have to fight your way out of this one.

Sea Spider, COMBAT 7, Defence 6, Stamina 13

If you win, turn to **330**. If you lose, turn to **7**.

266

You are travelling across the southern steppes. To the south, the Spine of Harkun marches across the sky. To the north, endless grasslands stretch away. You come to a desolate ruin. Its cyclopean outer walls, crumbling now, tell of a once great city.

Go north	turn to **118**
Go west	turn to **643**
Go east	turn to **668**
Explore the City of Ruins	turn to **54**
Go south into the mountains	turn to **200**

267

Becoming an initiate of Nai gives you the benefit of paying less for blessings and other services the temple can offer. It costs 50 Shards to become an initiate. You cannot do this if you are already an initiate of another temple. If you choose to become an initiate, write Nai in the God box on your Adventure Sheet – and remember to cross off the 50 Shards.

Once you have finished here, turn to **614**.

Resurrection costs 200 Shards if you are an initiate, and 800 Shards if not. It is the last word in insurance. Once you have arranged for resurrection you need not fear death, as you will be magically restored to life here at the temple.

To arrange resurrection, pay the fee and write Temple of Nisoderu, *The Plains of Howling Darkness* **250** in the Resurrection box on your Adventure Sheet. If you are later killed, turn to **250** in this book. You can have only one resurrection arranged at any one time. If you arrange another resurrection later at a different temple, the original one is cancelled.

When you are finished here, turn to **89**.

269

Make a CHARISMA roll at Difficulty 13. Add one to the roll if your are a Troubadour.

Successful CHARISMA roll	turn to **156**
Failed CHARISMA roll	turn to **315**

270

Szgano is quickly subdued. The woman begins to scream with rage, and her eyes blaze with supernatural energy.

'Don't look in her eyes!' warns the old shaman. But it is too late; one of them has glanced at her. She sucks the soul out of him and he collapses, a withered husk of a man.

After a short ritual, the chief shaman runs her through the heart with the silver javelin. Her body quickly begins to shrivel. A column of fetid black smoke rises from the corpse into the moonlit sky and then fades away with a wail of despair.

Add 1 to your SANCTITY permanently for helping to rid the world of an ancient evil.

Afterwards, the shamans cut off her hands.

'Without her hands the Ruzbahn will be unable to open the gates of the underworld and return to the land of the living,' they explain.

You can take a **witch's hand** if you wish.

The shamans clean up and leave. Turn to **472**.

271

The Peaks at the Edge of the World dominate the skyline like the battlements of a castle of the gods. You find wide marble stairs hacked into the side of a mountain, which spiral upwards to a volcano that coughs black smoke into the heavens.

Ascend the stairs	turn to **14**
Return to the pyramid	turn to **472**

272

You are pushed and shoved into the middle of a circle formed by many of the nomads – men, women and children who mock and jeer at you. You shudder to think of your fate – the nomads of the steppes are renowned for their cruelty.

A burly fellow elbows his way into the circle. His piggy eyes regard you intently from within folds of fat. His stare seems most challenging.

'You maggot-ridden, dung-faced, flea-infested mound of horse manure!' he bellows at you. 'I, Yagotai the Brave, have slain dragons! I have slain demons of hell! I have already achieved more than one such as you could achieve in an entire lifetime, so worthless are you!'

The crowd laughs, and applauds wildly. Then they fall silent, all eyes upon you. Clearly, they expect you to reply. It is a contest of boasts and insults, an old nomad custom.

Make a CHARISMA roll at Difficulty 15.

Successful CHARISMA roll   turn to **393**
Failed CHARISMA roll   turn to **64**

273

You come to a dead end. In the flickering light, which reflects off the frosty walls in a kaleidoscope of blue flashes, you see a panel of ice blocking your way. You hammer at it, but it will not break.

There is a cough behind you.

Wheeling round, you come face to face with a huge, heavy-set miner, his face hidden by a blue-hooded cloak. At least you think it's a miner – his feet are bare, and they are covered in thick black hair. He growls in a guttural voice, 'Long time since...'

'Since what?'

'Long, long time. I not see a manthing for long time. I used to dig for them. Smash the ice!' The creature chuckles and hefts a heavy pickaxe in its hands. 'They loved old Blue Cap, they did. Yes. Good worker, they said.'

Ask Blue Cap to smash the panel   turn to **155**
Wait   turn to **590**

274

The City of Mystery is home to a community of mages. The city itself consists of a few houses and shops built around a temple to Molhern, and a huge colosseum, called the Starstone Arena.

Visit the arena   turn to **53**
Visit the market   turn to **111**
Go to the temple of Molhern   turn to **637**
Go to the White Warlock Tavern   turn to **455**
Visit the chief mage   turn to **403**
Leave the City of Mystery   turn to **90**

275

You sprinkle the dust over Luroc and yourself. Cross the **dust of tranquillity** off your Adventure Sheet. Instantly, a feeling of peace and calm washes over you both.

'Let's get out before we lose it completely,' says Luroc.

You race for the door, and slip away into the night.

Turn to **337**.

276

You are sold to a man from Akatsurai, and set to work on an Akatsuran warship. This is a ship of the Shogun of Akatsurai. Fortunately for you, the captain recognizes you. He has you freed immediately and is almost grovellingly apologetic.

You are treated royally in his cabin, where you can restore any lost stamina points. He also provides you with a **katana (COMBAT +1)**, a suit of **splint armour (Defence +4)** and 400 Shards. He sets you off in Yarimura.

Turn to **10**.

277

It is the music of the horse god, a spirit of the plains, nomadic and wild. He leads the dancing crowd past you. At the last minute he turns, and nods toward you in greeting. They dance on, into the distance.

Turn to **224**.

278

The sun glances low across a cliff sheathed in frost, casting little light and less warmth.

You are in the regions of the Long Night. North of here stand the mountains that mark the limit of the mundane world. Beyond, it is said, lies the sea of eternity.

You pass close by a low, snow-packed mound. A tunnel bores into it, deep and lifeless as the eye socket of a skull.

Investigate   turn to **405**

Continue on your way   turn to **226**

279

If you have the codeword *Drop*, turn to **311** immediately. If not, read on.

No one in the Severed Hand is prepared to talk to you. In fact, they take offence at your attentions, and you realize you had better leave before things turn ugly. Turn to **182**.

280

You are outside the walls of Yarimura, beside the Great Tatsu Gate, which is carved into the likeness of a huge dragon's head.

Visit the villa of Hordeth	turn to **307**
Explore Cliff Wood	turn to **325**
Enter the city	turn to **10**
Head north	turn to **398**
Head west into the Great Steppes	turn to **442**
Head south to the Gemstone Hills	turn to **426**

281

You are slogging across the frozen wastes of the steppes. To the west, you can just make out a river, glinting on the horizon, and northwards, a pyramid juts up, breaking the flat skyline. The shades of twilight are closing in, at the end of the day.

Roll two dice.

Score 2-5	Wild horses	turn to **202**
Score 6-7	No event	turn to **666**
Score 8-12	Running footsteps	turn to **583**

282

Your men are overwhelmed and you are forced to surrender. You are disarmed, beaten savagely, and brought before Avar Hordeth. He is sitting in his cabin, nursing a nasty head wound. He eyes you grimly, wincing as one of his crew tends to his injuries.

'You blasted heap of stinking dung!' he roars. 'I would kill you except that I've got a better idea.'

You are too weak to put up much of a fight. His men seize you, clap you in irons and throw you into the brig. You can hardly believe your misfortune. Of all the people to meet on the high seas!

Avar Hordeth takes all the money and items you were carrying. Cross them off your Adventure Sheet. He also seizes your ship – cross that off as well.

'That should make up for what you did to me, matey!' says Hordeth. You are taken to Yarimura, where Hordeth sells you to the city's small navy.

You are put to work as a galley slave, condemned to row under the lash. Turn to **222**.

283

You remember what you were taught about redcaps. They are found in old ruins where great battles have been fought in the past. The more blood spilt during the battle, the happier the redcaps are. They delight in carrying out murderous acts so they can dye their caps with the freshly spilt blood of their victims.

The only way to drive them away (short of killing them, that is) is with the holy texts of the gods. Make a SANCTITY roll at Difficulty 13 to remember the relevant text.

Successful SANCTITY roll	turn to **507**
Failed SANCTITY roll	turn to **432**

284

This time the golem does not give you three choices. Your only hope is to guess the password by luck. Add up the score of four dice – or three dice if you are an initiate of the Three Fortunes.

Score 3-5	turn to **425**
Score 6+	turn to **351**

285

You end up floating in the harbour, your throat cut, just another victim. You are dead. Cross off the possessions listed on your Adventure Sheet.

If you have a resurrection arranged then you can turn to the entry marked for it. If you have no resurrection then it really is the end; you should delete all ticks and codewords in all your Fabled Lands books and then start again (at **1** in any book in the series) with a new character.

286

As you step into the stone circle, you feel unclean. You have desecrated the temple of an ancient and unknown god. Lose all your blessings, if you had any.

If you have the codeword *Draw*, turn to **572**. If not, you are not welcome here, so you leave. Turn to **224**.

287

The captain's first mate recognizes you, but you have no idea who he is. He is amazed you don't know him.

'Don't you recognize your old friend Clarny Dukes,' he whines, distraught. 'You saved my life, when we were lost in the Desert of Bones. Don't you remember?'

You remember nothing. It must have happened during a period of your life of which you have no memory whatsoever. At any rate, you pretend to remember, and the first mate persuades the captain to let you live.

They put you ashore at their next port of call. Roll one die (if you don't have the relevant book in the series, roll again).

Score 1 or 2	Yarimura		turn to **10**
Score 3 or 4	Yellowport	*The War-Torn Kingdom* **10**
Score 5 or 6	Chambara	*Lords of the Rising Sun* **100**

288

Your ship, crew and cargo are lost to the deep, dark sea. Cross them off your Adventure Sheet. Your only thought now is to save yourself. Roll two dice. If the score is greater than your Rank, you are drowned (turn to **7**). If the score is less than or equal to your Rank, you manage to find some driftwood, and make it back to shore. Lose Stamina points equal to the score of one die roll and, if you can survive that, turn to **67**.

289

You have already mapped these tunnels, which run through the Spine of Harkun. Caves on either side of the mountains mark the entrance to the tunnels.

Go north   turn to **558**
Go south   *The War-Torn Kingdom* **3**

290

As soon as you pass through the arch, a huge slab of solid stone slams down over the portal, sealing you within. You are trapped inside a circular chamber. Its smooth walls rise up and up to the top of the pyramid, where small holes let in thin shafts of light. The floor is crawling with large stag beetles, and the dim, dusty room is filled with the unpleasant sound of their mandibles working back and forth. You look around but there is no way out.

As you are pondering your own death by starvation, the walls begin to glow and you are bathed in a soft, dirty-yellow light. Your clothes begin to grow. Or is it you that is growing smaller? In fact, you are shrinking fast, and your clothes and belongings fall around you. Within moments you are reduced to the height of only one foot. Turn to **586**.

291

Becoming an initiate of Tambu gives you the benefit of paying less for blessings and other services that the temple may have to offer. It costs 60 Shards to become an initiate. You cannot become an initiate of Tambu if you are an initiate of another temple.

If you choose to become an initiate, write Tambu in the God box on your Adventure Sheet – and remember to cross off the 60 Shards.

Once you have finished here, turn back to **33**.

292

A tall woman draped in a twist of silk steps out of the shadows to confront you. She looks like an angel, except that her wings are black.

'You were told never to return,' she says in a mild, sweetly musical voice.

'Unless I wished to dwell among the dead.'
She nods.
'That is so.'
Turn back and go on your way turn to **15**
Accompany Death's angel turn to **534**

293

You are too slow to realize that the figure in front is not the real threat. An arm snakes around your neck from behind and you feel the sharp prick of a dagger in your shoulder. Lose 1 Stamina point, then, if you still live, turn to **184**.

294

'This one'll do nicely,' says one of the dark figures and they reach for you with coal-black hands.

More trau boil up out of the ground behind you, and you are seized, trussed up, and dragged underground before you can say 'By Elnir's Thunder!'

If you are 8th Rank or higher, turn to *Into the Underworld* **50**.

If you are of lower Rank, or if you don't have *Into the Underworld*, turn to **607**.

295

The citadel is a vast complex of corridors and doors, a fortification of breathtaking sophistication. Huge cisterns are driven deep into the bedrock of the mountains and hold enough water for a year or more. The citadel also encloses a large open-aired field, given over to agriculture. Great nets are spread across the towers to defend against aerial attack from Mannekyn People. The garrison, the Knights of the Northern Shield, is the best Sokara has to offer.

The local gossip is that a large army, led by General Beladai is camped to the north. This army of the Northern Alliance consists of warriors of the Horde of the Thousand Winds, Mannekyn People, some trau and Sokaran troops still loyal to King Nergan, ruler of Sokara before Grieve Marlock and his new order took over.

The commander of the fort is Orin Telana, newly appointed by Grieve Marlock.

If you have the codeword *Drizzle*, turn to **670**. If not, but you have the codeword *Assist*, turn to **72**. If you have neither codeword, turn to **152**.

296

You are sailing close to the mist-shrouded Isle of Mystery.

West towards Disaster Bay	turn to **310**
South west along the coast of Nerech	turn to **50**
Into the fog around the Isle of Mystery	turn to **93**
East into the Unbounded Ocean	turn to **587**

297

After many days at sea, the lookout spots land ahead. You come to a small archipelago. Examining your charts, the first mate says, 'I think they're the Jawbone Isles, cap'n.' You find a suitable cove in one of the islands where you drop anchor.

Turn to *Lords of the Rising Sun* **150**.

298

If you have the codeword *Dawn*, turn to **610** immediately. Otherwise, read on.

The Crypt of Kings is a large marble mausoleum. Tall, fluted columns flank the entrance. Inside you discover many tombs set into its walls. Heavy blocks of stone seal the tombs, inscribed with the names and deeds of those buried there. Without a team of labourers, you cannot open them.

A slithering sound disturbs you. From the far end of the crypt, a serpentine shape coils towards you. It has the head and torso of man, but the body of giant snake. Eyes like black pearls stare from a face that is hooded like a cobra's head. Venom drips, hissing, to the floor from its fanged mouth.

Make a MAGIC roll at Difficulty 14.

Successful MAGIC roll	turn to **469**
Failed MAGIC roll	turn to **566**

299

If you are an initiate it costs only 10 Shards to purchase Juntoku's blessing. A non-initiate must pay 25 Shards. Cross off the money and mark CHARISMA in the Blessings box on your Adventure Sheet. The blessing works by allowing you to try again when you fail a CHARISMA roll. It is good for only one reroll. When you use the blessing, cross it off your Adventure Sheet. You can have only one CHARISMA blessing at any one time. Once it is used up, you can return to any branch of the temple of Juntoku to buy a new one. Turn to **58**.

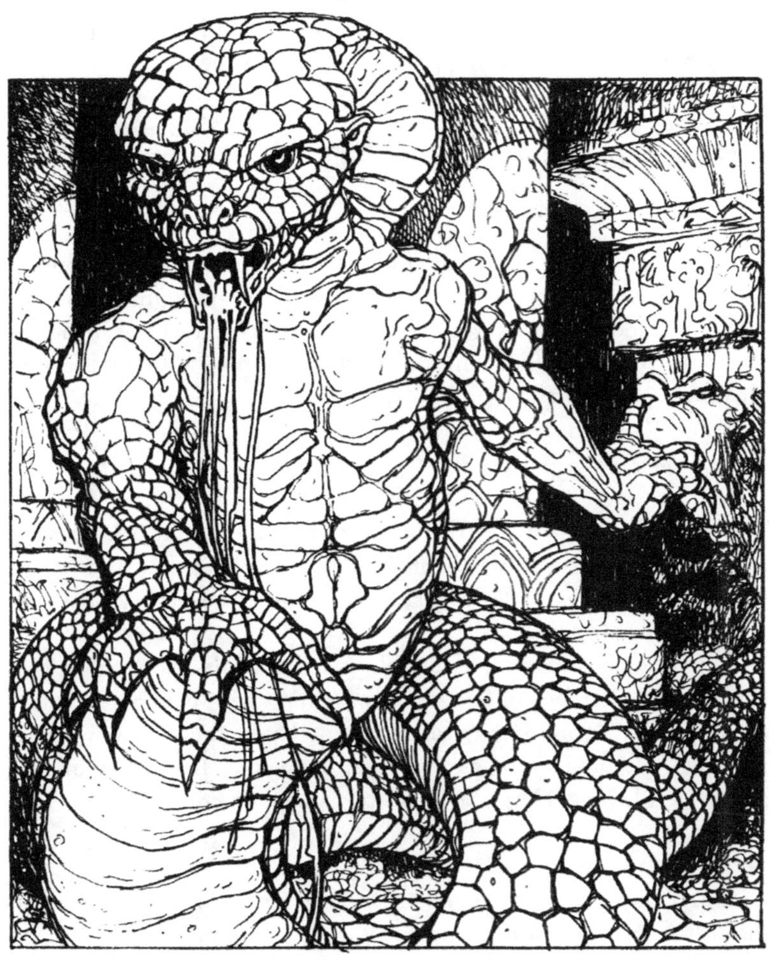

300

You struggle through the mountains until you come to Sky Mountain, which is twice the size of its neighbours. You follow a ridge that takes you on to its mighty slopes. Turn to **682**.

301

The black speck grows larger and larger until it becomes a huge bird, hurtling toward your ship like a thunderbolt. It is as big as a house, and its wingspan is as long as your ship with feathers as white as snow. It is a rukh, taloned and beaked like an eagle, and it swoops down, intent on plucking you from the deck.

Make a COMBAT roll at Difficulty 15.

Successful COMBAT roll	turn to **381**
Failed COMBAT roll	turn to **410**

302

You know that the ruin you find at the top is only an illusion, because you have been here before. You are recognized by the mages of the City of Mystery, and the illusion of a ruin is dispelled. The gate guards – enchanted, magical griffins with feathers of gleaming gold and eyes of onyx – welcome you to the City of Mystery. Turn to **274**.

303

You sprinkle the panel with the salts, and they melt a hole large enough for you to crawl through. It freezes back up, almost the instant you get to the other side. Cross the **uncanny salts** off your Adventure Sheet.

You press on down the tunnel. After a while, you come to a large round chamber of dressed stone, hung with banners. Around its edge, flat, stone slabs are arranged. Upon them rest warriors, wearing golden armour, and clasping long, two-handed swords in gauntleted hands. They appear to be asleep. Turn to **75**.

304

Your last blow sends Kaschuf's bald head spinning bloodily off his shoulders. His headless corpse slumps to the ground. But then, to your horror, the head and body rush together, and his wounds close up. Kaschuf stands before you again, completely whole. He bursts into laughter.

'Oh, you're a good fighter, I'll give you that, but they don't call me Kaschuf the Deathless for nothing!'

After a few more bouts that end with the same result you begin to tire. There seems to be no way to defeat him and you have no choice to flee for your life. Roll one die, and lose that many Stamina points as Kaschuf chops at you one last time.

If you still live, as you run down the hill, you hear him calling after you, 'Goodbye, milksop! Please come by again!'

Turn to **249**.

305

The crew absolutely refuses to sail the ship into the Unbounded Ocean.

'There's no land out there, and the seas are infested with Demons of the Deep — if we go too far, we'll fall off the edge of the world!' says the first mate. You have no choice but to reconsider your destination. Turn to **471** and choose again.

306

You sense magic in the air. Then you notice a ring of black dust has been sprinkled on the grass all around the pavilion — fire dust. On contact with the skin, it blazes like the sun. If you were to touch it, the guards would spot you instantly.

Avoiding the dust, you slit a hole in the back of the pavilion, and sneak in. Beladai is asleep, and you dispatch him easily.

As you are sneaking out the way you came, someone walks through the entrance, into the pavilion. Seconds later the alarm goes up, and the hunt for the killer is on! The news of Beladai's death, however, goes round the camp like wildfire, and the effect on the army's morale is devastating. The Northern Alliance is finished whether you escape or not.

If you have the codeword *Dim*, turn to **461** immediately. If not, roll two dice. If you score less than or equal to your Rank, turn to **615**. If you roll more than your Rank, turn to **47**.

307

If you have the codeword *Dead*, turn to **565** immediately. If not, but you have the codeword *Divest*, turn to **589**. If you have neither codeword, turn to **543**.

308

The Citadel of Velis Corin – or the Shield of the North as it is sometimes called – completely occupies the Pass of Eagles. The pass is the only way through the mountains of the Spine of Harkun. From this side, a massive wall stretches from one side of the pass to the other. The main entrance, in the middle of the wall, is a pair of huge steel doors, known as the Great Gate. Many towers rise up behind the wall, topped with flags and pennants fluttering in the wind. The citadel, gleaming white in the sun, looks completely invulnerable to a frontal assault from this side. A patrol of Knights of the Northern Shield rides out towards you.

Leave, and head north into the plains	turn to **145**
Wait for the guard patrol	turn to **132**

309

You have entered a long, dark and shadowy hall. Torches set into brackets on the wall give off a flickering, reddish light.

At the far end, sitting behind a massive oaken table, are five cowled figures. The one in the middle throws back his hood to reveal a shiny, black, featureless mask.

'Welcome,' he says in a thickly accented voice, 'to the Brotherhood of the Night.'

He explains that the brotherhood is looking for new members, and that you might be worthy of joining.

Apply for membership	turn to **616**
Leave	turn to **633**

310

You are sailing into Disaster Bay. Heavy rains begin to fall, and the skies darken, severely reducing visibility.

'These are dangerous waters, cap'n,' says the first mate. 'Some people say the reefs and rocks of the bay shift and change, making any chart unreliable.'

Roll two dice.

Score 2-5	Storm	turn to **645**
Score 6-9	Untroubled journey so far	turn to **533**
Score 11-12	A fire in the distance	turn to **243**

311

It was a mistake to come here. Several of the patrons recognize you as the one who betrayed Luroc Ban to Avar Hordeth. You turn to leave, but a couple of thugs barring your exit. You are set upon by several of Luroc's friends at once. Treat them as a single opponent.

Three Thugs, COMBAT 10, Defence 7, Stamina 19

If you win, turn to **430**. If you lose, turn to **169**.

312

You notice something odd about the tracks it has left in the mud. They are not the hoof-prints of a horse, but of a kelpie, a shape-changing water sprite known for luring travellers into the depths.

Attack it   turn to **555**

Leave   turn to **676**

313

The golem grudgingly allows you to pass. Inside the fortress you find a **sword (COMBAT +5)**. Add this to your list of possessions and then hasten back to the ship by turning to **191**.

314

Your ship, crew and cargo are lost to the deep, dark sea. Cross them off your Adventure Sheet. Your only thought now is to save yourself. Roll two dice. If the score is greater than your Rank, you are drowned. If the score is less than or equal to your Rank, you manage to find some driftwood, and make it back to shore. Lose Stamina points equal to the score of one die roll and, if you can survive that, turn to **524**.

315

Your cracked and tuneless serenade only further enrages the hound.
Turn to **62**.

316

You sail for days until you are able to match the stars with your sea
charts. It seems you have sailed far to the south, beyond the Isle of
Druids and into the Violet Ocean.

Turn to *Over the Blood-Dark Sea* **55**.

317

For days you slog on, hungry and half-blind with the glare of low,
slanting rays of sunlight that glance off the ice. You are bone weary
but it is too cold to snatch more than a few minutes' sleep. Each
footstep plunges you thigh-deep in snow. Avalanches are a constant threat. You should never have ventured into this merciless
wasteland.

Lose 1-6 Stamina points (the roll of one die) and, if still alive,
make a SCOUTING roll at a Difficulty of 18.

Successful SCOUTING roll	turn to **636**
Failed SCOUTING roll	turn to **452**

318

If you have the codeword *Dead*, turn to **98** immediately. If not,
read on

You cling on, only your hardy toughness keeps you alive. Fortunately for you, a passing merchant ship picks you up.

The captain, a certain Avar Hordeth, from Metriciens, in Golnir,
is happy to take you to Yarimura, his next port of call.

If you have the codeword *Divest*, turn to **51** immediately. If not,
read on.

After an uneventful journey, you disembark at the harbour in
Yarimura. Turn to **10**.

319

You uncork the vial and hold it under the shaman's nose. His eyes
snap open and he gives you a red-rimmed stare.

'Go where the dead spirits go,' he says in a throaty growl. 'Find the deep tunnels below the ice. Wrap up warm, mind, or your veins will with rubies fill and with feet of marble you'll take your last step. Placate the foreign chief's guardian fetch with bard-song, learned of old.'

Perhaps it was a wasted effort bringing the old shaman round. He seems to be babbling nonsense. Moreover the **uncanny salts** have dissolved into the cold night air; cross them off your Adventure Sheet. You return to the camp to find a warm place by the fire where you can get some sleep. Turn to **394**.

320

If you have the codeword *Diamond*, turn to **687**. If not, read on.

You have come to the ice-bound shores of the Rimewater. The lake is completely frozen over, and the ice has a strange sheen to it. Three sluggish rivers, thick with half-frozen water debouch into the lake from the north. On the southern shore of the lake sits a small complex of buildings, from which smoke spirals into the clear, crisp sky – the ice mine.

Visit the ice mine	turn to **373**
Go north to the river plain	turn to **91**
Head into the mountains	*The Court of Hidden Faces* **35**

321

The night passes peacefully, if not comfortably. Turn to **144**.

322

He collapses into the gutter, unconscious. After the unpleasant task of searching his body you find, on the roll of a die:

Score 1 or 2	**Lantern**
Score 3 or 4	5 Shards
Score 5 or 6	**Rope**

When you are finished, turn to **182**.

323

The crew seems surprised to see you.

'We thought you'd never be coming back alive, cap'n!' says the first mate.

You sail your ship back through the fog bank that surrounds the isle, and into open waters. Turn to **296**.

324

You realize this is an ancient temple, sacred to gods as old as the hills. Stepping into the circle, you recite the proper mantra so well that you receive a Blessing. Mark COMBAT in the Blessings box on your Adventure Sheet. The blessing works by allowing you to try again when you fail a COMBAT roll. It is good for only one reroll. When you use the blessing, cross it off your Adventure Sheet. You can have only one COMBAT blessing at any one time.

If you have the codeword *Draw*, turn to **572**. If not, you leave. Turn to **224**.

325

Cliff Wood is a pleasant tract of woodland. Birds sing in the trees, and the air is fresh and bracing.

You find a cottage in a clearing in the wood. The old nomad woman who lives there offers to read your fortune with regard to a particular question for 10 Shards.

Ask about the High King	turn to **635**
Ask about the Ruby Citadel	turn to **55**
Ask about City of Ruins	turn to **353**
Leave the wood	turn to **280**

326 ☐

If there is a tick in the box, turn to **213** immediately. If not, put a tick there now, and read on.

You find a feeble old man sitting by the dirt track you are following. His eyes are almost sightless, and his hands quiver and shake with ague. As you near, he pushes out a basket in front of him, trying to sell you his wares. All he has for sale is an ancient scroll, engraved with gold letters and strange glyphs. He wants 5 Shards for it.

Buy the scroll	turn to **31**
Leave	turn to **144**

327

You do not hear the voices again. Eventually, the storm subsides, leaving you soaked, and half-frozen. Lose 1 point of Stamina.

Before you can make camp for the night, you have to hunt for food. Make a SCOUTING roll at Difficulty 11. If you succeed, you find a small, flightless bird to eat. If you fail, you go hungry and must lose another Stamina point.

If you are still alive, turn to **65**.

328

On the other side of the bridge waits an armoured knight mounted on a huge black lion. As he sees you he lowers his visor and readies his lance.

'Prepare to joust,' grates his voice from inside the metal helm.

'I have no steed!' you protest.

'A misfortune,' he admits. 'You should have come better pre-pared.'

He comes charging along the bridge. If you have a **rope**, turn to **538**. If not, turn to **446**.

329

Acquire the codeword *Dragon*.

You send a clear, pure note into the roseate air. It matches the harmonic resonance of the giant ruby exactly, and it begins to shake ominously. The man in black is thrown into panic; his staff wavers and a blast of icy blackness shoots past you.

'No, no!' he cries but it is too late.

The whole citadel begins to shudder and shake, and a block of translucent rock crashes to the floor, followed by a torrent of others. The man in black is buried in seconds.

You notice the block that imprisons the tattooed man has shat-tered, freeing him. He gestures oddly, and is surrounded instantly with a glowing field of blue energy, that protects him from the collapsing ruby.

You, however, are not so protected. Roll one die, and add 2. If you score less than or equal to your Rank, turn to **441**. If you roll greater than your Rank, turn to **679**.

The sea spider collapses, oozing a foul-smelling black ichor into the water.

Its lair is an underground cave full of water that comes up to your waist. It would be totally submerged at high tide. There you find the skeletal remains of some poor unfortunate sailor, the last meal of the spider. In a pouch, you discover a **gold compass (SCOUTING +2)**. Note it on your Adventure Sheet.

You climb out to find your crew searching for you.

'We thought you were a goner for sure, cap'n,' says one of them.

You make it back to your ship, and set sail at high tide.

Turn to **471**.

The trau reach for you with coal-black hands, intent on seizing you and dragging you down into the underworld. But they cannot abide piety and godliness. You are too saintly for their needs, and they fall back, cursing.

'Aaach, this one smells like temple incense,' growls one.

They disappear into the hole as fast as they came, and the stone slab slams firmly shut with a resounding crash.

Where will you go from here?

North to Yarimura	turn to **280**
West into the plains	turn to **234**
South	turn to **145**

332

You find 15 Shards and a **compass (SCOUTING +1)**. Unfortunately, you have also contracted the disease he died from. You come out in a nasty red, blotchy rash. Note that you are diseased (with the Red Ague), and lose 1 point from your CHARISMA and COMBAT abilities until you can a cure. If you find a cure, you can restore the lost points. Turn to **698**.

333

You take the ship north until you are passing the Peaks at the Edge of the World to the west – awesome mountains that rise majestically into the clouds. To the north, you find that the sea comes up against huge cliffs, towering into the heavens. A strong current threatens to pull your ship into a gigantic cave at the base of the cliffs. The sea churns violently at the cave mouth, throwing up great waves.

On either side of the cave mouth, two enormous statues stand waist-deep in the sea. They are stone warriors of cyclopean size, weather-beaten and pitted – they have been standing there for

hundreds of years, perhaps even thousands. Their faces look out across the world, as if observing distant events far off to the south.

'The Silent Sentinels,' whispers one of the crew in awed tones.

'Aye,' says another, 'the Guardians at the World's Edge. Best to turn back now, captain.'

'Some say that's the Mouth of Harkun, the elder god from whose bones the world was formed, and that it leads to the land below the world! Turn back, cap'n, please!' says your first mate.

Turn back	turn to **201**
Entreat the men to enter the cave	turn to **255**

334

Becoming an initiate of Amanushi gives you the benefit of paying less for blessings and other services that the temple can offer. It costs 50 Shards to become an initiate. You cannot do this if you are already an initiate of another temple. If you choose to become an initiate, write Amanushi in the God box on your Adventure Sheet — and remember to cross off the 50 Shards. Once you have finished here, turn to **194**.

335

You have encountered the ghost-ship before, and you know it is only an illusion, set here to frighten the gullible away from the Isle of Mystery. You sail straight through it, and the pirate-ship fades away, the illusion dispelled. Turn to **296**.

336

You are sailing in Tigre Bay. It is bitterly cold; ice floes dot the surface of the bay. Roll two dice.

Score 2-4	Storm	turn to **512**
Score 5-8	An uneventful voyage	turn to **438**
Score 9-12	A black speck in the sky	turn to **301**

337

Tick the codeword *Divest*.

You and Luroc make it safely back to Yarimura, where he takes his leave.

'It'll go down as one of the greatest stings of all time!' he boasts. 'I look forward to working with you again some day.'

If you took the **casket of gems**, its contents are worth 850 Shards. Add this amount to your money and cross off the casket.

The experience has taught you much — add one to your THIEVERY rating, permanently, and then turn to **10**.

338

Hordeth's last blow sends you reeling back, and in the press of combat, you and he are separated. You collapse, but one of your men binds your wounds in the nick of time – you come round with one Stamina point. It is clear to both sides, however, that you lost the duel with Hordeth, and this will effect the morale of your crew.

The main battle is still unfinished. Roll three dice if you are a Warrior, or two dice if you belong to any other profession. Add your Rank to this roll. Then, if your crew is poor quality, subtract 2 from the total. If the crew is good quality, add 2. If the crew is excellent quality, add 3.

Score 0-15	You are defeated	turn to **282**
Score 16-18	You fight them off	turn to **240**
Score 19+	Outright victory	turn to **149**

339

The despondent men ignore your feeble attempts to raise their flagging spirits.

'Just go away,' one of them mutters.

You shrug your shoulders and leave. Turn to **669**.

340

If you have the codewords *Dragon* or *Edifice*, turn to **499** immediately. If not, turn to **584**.

341

After a while, the ship slips out of the fog into bright sunshine. With a shock of recognition, you realize you have sailed in a big circle and have come back to where you started from.

Turn to **296** and choose again (you can try to sail into the island again, if you like).

342

Note your ship is docked in Tigre Bay. The coastline is harsh and rocky. Hardy sedge-grass is all that grows along the shore.

Put out to sea	turn to **336**
Leave the ship here and go inland	turn to **669**

343

You recall a man, tortured by the nomads, who told you with his dying breath of these great metal doors. What was the ritual he described? Oh yes. You place your hand on your heart and bow three times.

You wait. There is no sound but the sigh of the wind across the plains. You are about to turn away when the doors slowly swing inwards.

Enter	turn to **513**
Leave	turn to **15**
Climb the cliffs	turn to **221**

344

At the merest mention of the name, he jumps to his scrawny legs like a startled stick-insect and bolts off to hide in his tent. When you try to coax him out, he peers out from behind the tent flap and tells you to go before he places a hex on you.

There is no point in upsetting the poor old devil any more than you have done. You walk back to the camp and ask a nomad where you can sleep. Turn to **394**.

345

He can tell you about:

Surviving on the steppes	turn to **671**
The Ruby Citadel	turn to **433**
The City of Ruins	turn to **649**
The Fane of the Four Winds	turn to **612**

346

The river plain is no longer bound by an icy fog. Since the thawing of the Rimewater, the rivers are flowing faster, though massive ice floes still float on the waters.

Head west to Tigre Bay	turn to **669**
Head north east to the pyramid	turn to **472**
Go south to the Rimewater	turn to **320**
Head east	turn to **281**
Go south east	turn to **29**

You stoop and start shifting the rocks. In this cramped space it is hard work, made no easier by the stale air. You are soon sweating inside your jerkin in spite of the cold.

At last you clear a hole that is big enough to squeeze through. You are astounded at what lies before you. It is a burial chamber heaped with trinkets of silver and blue jade.

Before you can start to fill your pockets, there comes a heavy slithering sound from the main tunnel. A giant serpentine shape heaves its bulk across the hole, blocking off your escape route. You pound and jab at its leathery flank to no avail – it seems impervious to injury.

At last, exhausted, you slump to the floor of the chamber. There is no escape. Surrounded by treasure, you can only wait for a lingering death by asphyxiation or dehydration. Turn to **7**.

You sense the figure in front is not alone. Instinctively, you dodge aside as two more dark figures appear behind you.

'Curse it!' yells the first figure. 'Can't you fools do anything right? Get him!' All three of them, wiry looking villains dressed in black leather armour, lunge for you.

Fight them   turn to **238**

Run for it   turn to **212**

349

If you have the title Nightstalker, turn to **450** immediately. If not, read on.

The thugs guarding the entrance to the building look you up and down. 'Another enterprising rogue, come to pay his respects to the brotherhood,' one of them says to his friend. They laugh, but none the less move aside to let you through the door.

Enter the building	turn to **309**
Leave	turn to **633**

350

If you have the codeword *Deep* or *Dim*, turn to **289**. If not, read on.

You come to a network of underground tunnels that run under the mountains.

It is pitch dark, and you must have a source of light, such as a **lantern** or **candle**, to proceed. If not, you will have to go back – turn to *The War-Torn Kingdom* **3**. If you have a source of light, you can explore the tunnels by turning to **174**.

351

The golem pretends to accept your answer, only to crush your head between its granite hands when you go to step past.

If you have a resurrection deal, turn to the entry marked for it on your Adventure Sheet. Otherwise your only option is to start again with a new character after first deleting all ticks and codewords in your Fabled Lands books. You can start again at **1** in any book in the series.

352

The woman, who is from Akatsurai, spots you. 'You have not been processed!' she says in surprise.

'We'll see who gets processed here, you she-devil,' you reply through gritted teeth.

She smiles evilly and takes up a long-bladed spear, spinning it about her head and body in a display of breath-taking martial skill.

She-devil, COMBAT 8, Defence 6, Stamina 10

If you lose, turn to **7**. If you win, turn to **170**.

353

Cross off the 10 Shards. The woman stares into a ball of blue-coloured glass for some minutes, then whispers, as if in a trance, 'There is wealth ahead of you – or death. Seek for a way forward in the pyramid. You will suffer a calamity but do not despair, all is not lost!' Then she slumps forward, suddenly asleep.

You leave the wood. Turn to **280**.

354

Lochos Veshtu set you the task of stealing into the daimyo's bedchamber. If you want to attempt it now, turn to **493**. If not, turn to **665**.

355

To find out how well your investments have done, roll two dice. Add 1 to the dice roll if you are an initiate of the Three Fortunes. Also add 1 if you have the codeword *Almanac*, add 2 if you have the codeword *Brush*, and add 3 if you have the codeword *Eldritch*.

Score 2-4	Lose entire sum invested
Score 5-6	Loss of 50%
Score 7-8	Loss of 10%
Score 9-10	Investment remains unchanged
Score 11-12	Profit of 10%
Score 13-14	Profit of 50%
Score 15-16	Double initial investment
Score 17+	Profit of 150%

Turn to **526**, where you can withdraw or leave the sum written in the box there after adjusting it according to the result rolled.

356

You tell them you are working for a merchant in Yarimura, travelling south to set up a trade route with the merchants' guild of Sokara. They believe it and let you pass.

Head north	turn to **145**
Enter the citadel	turn to **295**

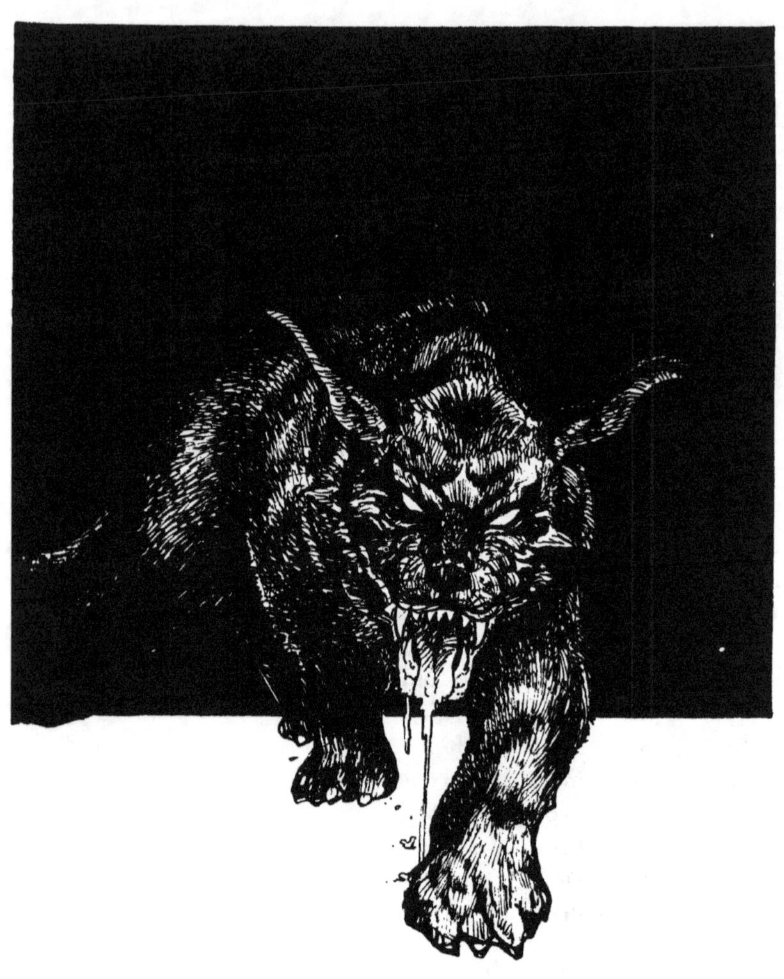

357

You are sold to the navy and put to work as a galley slave, condemned to row under the lash. Turn to **222**.

358

Your ship is thrown about like flotsam and jetsam. When the storm subsides, you take stock. Much has been swept overboard – lose 1

Cargo Unit of your choice. Also, the ship has been swept way off course and the mate has no idea where you are.

'We're lost at sea, cap'n!' he moans.

Turn to **390**.

359

Cross off the 200 Shards from your Adventure Sheet. Blue Cap snorts with satisfaction and lumbers off into the dark.

You press on down the tunnel. After a while, you come to a large round chamber of dressed stone, hung with banners. Flat, stone slabs are arranged around its edge. Upon them rest warriors in golden armour. They clasp long, two-handed swords in their gauntleted hands. They appear to be asleep. Turn to **75**.

360 ☐

If there is a tick in the box, turn to **593** immediately. If not, put a tick there now, and read on.

You come to a door of solid basalt. In front of it sits a shadowy shape, with eyes of ruby red. It stands up on four black legs, and growls a throaty, booming growl, baring rows of razor-sharp teeth. It is a faery hound, a trau guard-dog, and it looks about to pounce.

You have heard stories that these black hounds can be soothed to sleep with beautiful music or song.

Try to sing it to sleep	turn to **269**
Fight it	turn to **62**

361

The high priestess greets you. You explain how you found the mirror of the Sun Goddess at great risk to yourself, but that you lost it after a terrible calamity befell you. But she doesn't seem bothered.

'Indeed, though you say you lost it, Nisoderu chose to guide it back to us. A woman from the south, called Lauria, returned it to us. I'm afraid she has already collected the reward. And we having nothing left to give — after all, we have only your word that you ever saw it, let alone recovered it.'

You leave, somewhat disgruntled. Turn to **58**.

362

You reach the very highest peaks of the world. Your lungs strain for every breath at this altitude. Each step is hard-fought and requires herculean effort.

If you have the codeword *Calcium* then you can breathe the thin air. If not, you lose 2-12 Stamina (the roll of two dice).

Make your way south	turn to **264**
Press northwards	turn to **423**

363

Your knowledge of the creatures of the wild tells you that these are finmen, a race of underwater beings that is thought to be quite intelligent, and mostly peaceful in its dealings with mankind.

One of them lowers his spear towards you.

Attack them	turn to **520**
Wait to see what happens	turn to **634**

364

Darkness falls and the nomad warriors make their camp. Crouching around their cookpot, they throw only occasional curious glances towards their sobbing captive.

Free the poor wretch	turn to **129**
Continue on your way	turn to **52**

365

You ask the gate guard to let you through into Nerech. He looks you up and down, and eyes you askance for a moment. Then he says, 'Give us yer boots, then. They're a nice pair, and it's sad to think they would go to waste.'

He grins ghoulishly at you.

Turn back	*The War-Torn Kingdom* **259**
Venture forth	turn to **32**

366

You find him tending to the finest of the riding beasts.

'These are the fineitri, which means cousins in our tongue,' he says. 'From them we get fur to make rope, hides for our tents and clothing, bone for our bows and meat to fill our bellies.'

You gaze into the strange, sad, half-human face of the beast.

'They are your cattle, then?'

He gives a snort. 'Much more than cattle, as those who do not wander understand the term. We respect the fineitri and must slay them only according to a sacred ritual that ensures the beast's spirit goes safely on to the next world. According to our myths, the first fineitri and the first man were brothers.'

With some effort you stifle a yawn. The rigours of the day are catching up with you. Making your apologies to the chief, you go off to find a place to sleep. Turn to **394**.

367

You recognize Kaschuf. During your seafaring days on the Violet Ocean you came across an uncharted island. There you found a heart-shaped locket, with Kaschuf's bald face and piercing green eyes painted inside. And when you opened it you released something. You tell Kaschuf your tale, and the effect is extraordinary. He goes white with terror!

But Kevar hops from foot to foot in glee and croaks, 'You found his soul in that locket! And released it! Kaschuf is no longer deathless! He can be killed...'

'The fight's not over yet, old man,' bellows Kaschuf, as he glares savagely at you. 'I could still win!'

Kevar claps his hand over his mouth. You must fight.

Kaschuf, COMBAT 8, Defence 8, Stamina 20

If you win, turn to **158**. If you lose, turn to **7**.

368

`Wait!' one of them shrieks.

It flies down, and looks in your face. Then it says, `I know you!'

It is Pikalik, the Wing-warrior. You bought him in the slave market in Caran Baru, and then set him free. The others become friendly, and fly you up to their lair, a maze of caves running through the topmost peak, accessible only by air.

The journey is quite exhilarating, though it takes seven or eight Mannekyn People to carry you. Pikalik takes you to their leader. You are shown into a richly adorned cave, deep in the rock.

Turn to **428**.

369

The hut pulls up short. `Not this time!' shrieks a voice from inside the hut. `Gura Goru never falls for the same trick twice.'

With that, the hut scuttles away in the opposite direction.

Turn to **92**.

370

`I see,' says the genie, `It's always wealth — you mortals are all the same.'

He waves his hand. Thousands of Shards begin to pour on to the raft as if from nowhere. You quickly realize that the raft will sink under all that weight, but it is already too late. The raft breaks up under the heavy coins, ditching all the money and you into the sea. The genie, laughing uproariously, disappears with a pop. You are left holding on to a single log of the raft, with a fortune in Shards somewhere in the deeps.

Now, however, your only thought is how you will survive. Roll one die and add one to the score. If the result is higher than your Rank, turn to **459**. If less than or equal to your Rank, turn to **318**.

371

The battle is swift and bitter. You have to face two of them. Fight them as if they were one opponent.

Hooded Men, COMBAT 7, Defence 7, Stamina 15

If you win, turn to **99**. If you lose, turn to **7**.

372

You have stepped into the lair of a necromancer. Bodies lie on slabs awaiting reanimation, and potions bubble and boil in alembics and cauldrons. A man, dressed in black robes and holding a staff, turns to face you. His pallid face is cruel and pinched, with the look of madness in his eyes.

Behind him, at the far end, a block of ruby rock encloses another, trapped within it like a fly in amber. He wears baroque clothes of almost preposterous ornateness, and every inch of his skin that you can see is covered in tattoos of equal complexity. He is frozen in time and space, but appears to be alive.

The man in black speaks, 'What is this? An intruder! Begone, you absurd buffoon!'

He levels his staff at you.

Make a MAGIC roll at Difficulty 13.

Successful MAGIC roll	turn to **482**
Failed MAGIC roll	turn to **550**

373

You walk into a large, functional stone building. Inside, a roaring fire gives a welcome relief from the freezing air outside. Several burly men sit around a long table, eating. By the door, a portly, red-bearded fellow sits behind a desk. He looks up as you enter.

'Welcome to the ice mine, sir. I am Jalalul the Red, overseer of the mine, by appointment of the Court of Hidden Faces,' he says politely.

He tells you that the entire lake is formed out of solid ice, and that this ice has the peculiar property of melting at an incredibly slow rate. Indeed, a block of rime ice may last for as long as a month.

Naturally, there is money to be made out of this. The miners dig tunnels into the lake, and take the ice across the mountains by caravan to the southern cities of the decadent Uttaku. There, the masked nobles pay well for the ice, so that their sherbet, wines and sorbets are nicely chilled.

The mine also provides tours of the tunnels – many lords and ladies of Uttaku come here to walk amid the frosted walls. The tour costs 10 Shards.

Buy some rime ice	turn to **579**
Go on a tour	turn to **22**
Leave the mine	turn to **320**

374

You are caught fast by the tendrils and dragged down into the embrace of the river mud. Your men are too appalled to do anything but watch as you die a slow death by drowning.

If you have a resurrection deal, turn to the entry marked for it on your Adventure Sheet. Otherwise your only option is to start again with a new character after first deleting all ticks and code-words in your Fabled Lands books. (You can start again at **1** in any book in the series.)

375

Gain the codeword *Deliver*.

Beladai's men are fighting their way into the courtyard, but resistance is stiff as the garrison rapidly reinforces the gate. A dozen soldiers rush up the stairs of the winch-house to try to close the gates. You hold them off long enough for Beladai's army to get into the citadel but you take a mortal sword thrust in the process. The citadel will fall to the Northern Alliance, but you will not live to see the victory celebrations.

Turn to **7**.

376 ☐

If there is a tick in the box, turn to **418** immediately. If not, put a tick there now, and read on.

You are walking down an alley when a dark figure steps out in front of you.

Make a SCOUTING roll at Difficulty 13.

Successful SCOUTING roll   turn to **348**
Failed SCOUTING roll   turn to **293**

377

At this height, everything looks huge – including the stag beetles. To you, they have become hideous giant insects, the size of your arm! And to them, you have become a viable meal. The ancient Shadar builders of this pyramid certainly knew how to deal with tomb-robbers.

The structure's very age, however, may have saved you. You spot a hole in the wall where some of the masonry has fallen away. It is just big enough for you to crawl through. You make a run for it as the beetles close in.

Roll one die and add one. If the result is less than or equal to your Rank, turn to **412**. If it is greater than your Rank, turn to **708**.

378

You find a partly submerged cave that contains the rotting body of a giant sea spider. There is nothing else of interest.

You leave, and head back to your ship. High tide comes, refloating your ship, and you sail on.

Turn to **471**.

379

You are knocked to the ground, expertly pinned, and given a vicious beating. Lose 2-12 Stamina points (the roll of two dice). If still alive, you are barely conscious of the nomads stripping you of your possessions. They leave your money, having no use for coinage.

By the time you can get to your feet, the nomads have ridden off. Their captive hangs dead in his bonds. Delete all possessions from your Adventure Sheet and turn to **52**.

380

Make a CHARISMA roll at Difficulty 13.
Successful CHARISMA roll   turn to **475**
Failed CHARISMA roll   turn to **339**

381

You manage to throw yourself aside. The rukh snatches one of your crew, and he is carried off into the endless sky, screaming horribly. After calming the rest of the crew, you sail on. Turn to **438**.

382

If you have the codeword *Drink*, turn to **30**. If not, read on.

A black stallion stands on the bank of the River of Destiny, lapping at the water.

Make a SCOUTING roll at Difficulty 15.

Successful SCOUTING roll	turn to **312**
Failed SCOUTING roll	turn to **95**

383

This far north, winter's icy grip lasts almost the whole year round. The hard, frosted grass crunches underfoot, and a cold, drizzling rain plunges you into a dark despair.

Roll two dice.

Score 2-5	A rotting corpse	turn to **702**
Score 6-7	No event	turn to **698**
Score 8-12	Bird-riders	turn to **139**

384

If you are an initiate it costs only 15 Shards to purchase Molhern's blessing. A non-initiate must pay 25 Shards. Cross off the money and mark MAGIC in the Blessings box on your Adventure Sheet.

The blessing works by allowing you to try again when you fail a MAGIC roll. It is good for only one reroll. When you use the blessing, cross it off your Adventure Sheet. You can have only one MAGIC blessing at any one time.

Once it is used up, you can return to any branch of the temple of Molhern to buy a new one.

When you are finished here, turn to **274**.

385

A golden tower slowly materializes before you, hanging some fifty feet above the plain. Sunlight reflects off the tower, making it look like a gigantic blazing torch and bathing the snow with golden light. The tower begins to flicker indistinctly, as if it were a mirage. A hazy, insubstantial golden stairway descends from the tower to the ground. You try to walk up it, but your feet pass through the first step as if it wasn't there.

If you have a **pathfinder's gem**, turn to **417**.

If not, turn to **567**.

386

The mast splits in two and your ship is thrown about like flotsam and jetsam. When the storm subsides, you take stock. Much has been swept overboard – you lose 1 Cargo Unit, if you had any, of your choice. Also, the ship has been swept way off course and the mate has no idea where you are.

'We're lost at sea, cap'n!' he moans. Turn to **390**.

387

The dead reach out to take your arms. 'Join us,' they say. 'Why struggle in the harsh sunlit world, when darkness and eternal peace are here to be enjoyed throughout eternity?'

You duck, grab a silver chalice from the table next to you, and race back towards the surface with the gibbering horde of sheeted dead in full pursuit.

'Stay, stay!' they implore. It is a sound to curdle the blood.

At last the wan daylight of the steppes comes in sight. But the bronze doors are closing! Can you make it in time? Roll two dice and add your Rank.

Score 3-12	turn to **136**
Score 13+	turn to **581**

388

If you are an initiate it costs only 10 Shards to purchase Tambu's blessing. A non-initiate must pay 25 Shards. Cross off the money and mark SCOUTING in the Blessings box on your Adventure Sheet. The blessing works by allowing you to try again when you fail a SCOUTING roll. It is good for only one reroll. When you use the blessing, cross it off your Adventure Sheet. You can have only one SCOUTING blessing at any one time. Once it is used up, you can return to buy a new one.

When you are finished here, turn to **33**.

389

Roll one die to see what you find amid the offerings.

Score 1 or 2	**Shadar spear (COMBAT +2)** and a **flute (CHARISMA +1)**

Score 3 or 4   **Plate armour (Defence +5)** and a
                      wolf pelt
Score 5 or 6   **Faery mead** and a **silver holy symbol**
                      (**SANCTITY +2**)

However, you have desecrated the shrine of Tambu, and have incurred his wrath. Lose one point of SCOUTING permanently. Now turn to **118**.

390

The sea stretches away in all directions. There is not a jot of land in sight. 'I think we may be lost on the Unbounded Ocean,' whispers the first mate. The crew mutter among themselves, for the Unbounded Ocean has a reputation for demons and other such manifestations of evil.

Make a SCOUTING roll at Difficulty 14.

Successful SCOUTING roll   turn to **602**
Failed SCOUTING roll   turn to **557**

391

Luroc falls dead at your feet. As he does, the spell you were under passes. You hear someone clapping, and you look round to see Avar Hordeth, flanked by many guards, applauding. The guards rush you, and you are overwhelmed by sheer force of numbers, disarmed, beaten savagely, and brought on your knees before Avar Hordeth. He is a thick-set man with a sly slant to his features. He eyes you grimly.

'You stinking thief!' he says. 'I could kill you, but that was a most entertaining interlude, watching you fight. I think I've got a better idea.'

Hordeth takes all your money and items. Cross them off your Adventure Sheet. Later, you are taken to Yarimura, where Hordeth sells you to the city's small navy. You are put to work as a galley slave, condemned to row under the lash. Turn to **222**.

392

Avar staggers back, groaning. In the press of the melee, you and he are separated, but it is clear to your crew and to the enemy that you were winning. This is good for the morale of your crew, and bad for the enemies' morale.

The main battle is still unfinished. Roll three dice if you are a Warrior, or two dice if you belong to any other profession. Add your Rank to this roll. Then, if your crew is poor quality, subtract 2 from the total. If the crew is good quality, add 2. If the crew is excellent quality, add 3.

Score 0-10	You are defeated	turn to **282**
Score 11-15	They are beaten off	turn to **240**
Score 16+	You get the upper hand	turn to **149**

393

The nomads are overawed by your boasts of strange adventures and tales of lands they have never seen. And you cow Yagotai with a range of insults from the gutters of cities and ports that are fresh and amusing to them. They welcome you into their camp, where you are fed and looked after well. Restore any lost Stamina points.

There is also a nomad market here.

Armour	To buy	To sell
Leather (Defence +1)	50 Shards	45 Shards
Ring mail (Defence +2)	100 Shards	90 Shards

Weapons (sword, axe, etc)	To buy	To sell
Without COMBAT bonus	50 Shards	40 Shards
COMBAT bonus +1	250 Shards	200 Shards
COMBAT bonus +2	500 Shards	400 Shards

Other items	To buy	To sell
Flute (CHARISMA +1)	200 Shards	180 Shards
Compass (SCOUTING +1)	500 Shards	450 Shards
Rope	50 Shards	45 Shards
Wolf pelt	50 Shards	45 Shards
Parrot fungus	150 Shards	135 Shards

When you are finished, if you have the codeword *Azure*, turn to **500**. If not, the next day you continue on your way:

Go north	turn to **15**
Go east toward Yarimura	turn to **280**
Go south	turn to **234**
Head west deeper into the steppes	turn to **17**

394

Wrapped in heavy blankets provided by the nomads, you lie down and are soon lulled off to sleep by the bard's droning song. Morning brings a crisp cold wind from the north, but you are well rested and your hosts see to it that you are given the best of their food. Recover 1 Stamina point if injured. It is time to bid farewell to the One-Eyed Crow clan. Turn to **65**.

395 ☐

If there is a tick in the box, turn to **563** immediately. If not, put a tick there now, and read on.

You hand over the copy you made of the carvings on the Shadar Runestone. Runciman is pleased with your performance and his mages instruct you in the arcane arts. Add one to your MAGIC ability permanently.

When you are ready, turn to **274**.

396

You wait until nightfall to make your move. First, you will have to sneak into the stockade and find Beladai's tent.

Make a THIEVERY roll at Difficulty 14.

| Successful THIEVERY roll | turn to **483** |
| Failed THIEVERY roll | turn to **638** |

397

The golem stands with folded arms, waiting for you to give the wrong password so that it can pummel your bones to a fine powder. Which of these three options will you pick?

Azure	turn to **18**
Emerald	turn to **351**
Scarlet	turn to **313**

398

You are far to the north. The lands here are covered with snow most of the year round, but well forested with hardy fir trees. Smoke curls into the frosty sky from a nearby village. Further north, the Peaks at the Edge of the World dominate the horizon, grim and indomitable. They are completely impassable in these parts. To the west, the steppes stretch away as far as the eye can see. Eastward, rocky cliffs lean over the cold, grey sea.

Visit the village	turn to **548**
Head west into the steppes	turn to **15**
Head south to Yarimura	turn to **280**

399

Your foot slips, your fingers close on thin air – with a sickening lurch you go plummeting down into the void.

If you possess a **rope**, turn to **187**. If not, nothing can save you and you are doomed to fall for ever through illimitable darkness – turn to **7**.

400

You are outside the Citadel of Velis Corin, or the Shield of the North as it is sometimes known. It rises up before you, great white bastions and towers gleaming in the sun. It fills the Pass of Eagles completely. From this side of the Spine of Harkun, it is less fortified – its purpose is to keep out the barbarians of the north.

Try to enter the citadel	turn to **2**
Go south	*The War-Torn Kingdom* **271**
Head west	*The War-Torn Kingdom* **276**
Go east	*The War-Torn Kingdom* **60**

401

You feel as if the helm were trying to seize control of your mind, but you manage to overcome the insidious enchantment, and the pain dies away to a nagging itch.

Roll one 1 die and add 2. If the result is more than your MAGIC rating, you can increase it by one permanently.

Looking through the eyeholes of the helm you see that the

manbeasts are ignoring you – plainly they are too stupid to realize you are not one of them.

The tall hill turns out to be the lair of the manbeasts. It is honeycombed with caves, and you wander through them, unmolested. You come to a large cavern. At the far end, about twenty people are locked up behind a steel portcullis. One of the prisoners has been strapped to a table, and a woman dressed in black and yellow silken robes is fastening a dog-shaped beast helmet over his head, oblivious to her victim's cries for mercy. As the helmet slides into place, he begins to shudder. To your disgust, his limbs contort and twist, and grey fur begins to sprout all over him. Soon he will have become a mindless manbeast, his mind destroyed and his body enslaved.

Turn to **352**.

402

As you step up to the arch of the tunnel, you notice that the air in the entrance shimmers with a bluish light. As you pass through it, you feel a momentary sense of dislocation. You continue on for hours, until you come to a ladder leading upward. You climb up through a hole in the ground, emerging from the side of a grassless hill. Then the hole closes up behind you! You cannot go back.

Turn to *The War-Torn Kingdom* **110**.

403

The chief mage lives in a ramshackle building on the edge of town. He is a kindly old man, rheumy eyed but keen of brain, called Runciman.

If you have the codeword *Dove*, turn to **395** immediately. If not, read on.

The job of chief mage is mostly ceremonial, and isn't taken that seriously in the City of Mystery, but he still has to carry out certain tasks. At the sight of you, he visibly brightens.

'Aha!' he exclaims. 'You look like a capable young adventurer. We've need of someone like you.'

He explains that the mages of the Isle of Mystery are researching the arcane arts of the Shadar, an ancient race that ruled Harkuna thousands of years ago. They want you to find the Runestone, a Shadar stone stelae carved with sigils.

'Make a copy of the runes, and bring it to me,' says Runciman. 'In return, we can help you improve your magical knowledge. The Runestone is known to be somewhere on the steppes.'

If you take up the quest, record the codeword *Draw*. When you are ready, you leave. Turn to **274**.

404

Tambu is pleased. Cross off the item from your Adventure Sheet. He bestows upon you a Blessing. Mark SCOUTING in the Blessings box on your Adventure Sheet. The blessing works by allowing you to try again when you fail a SCOUTING roll. It is good for only one reroll. When you use the blessing, cross it off your Adventure Sheet. You can have only one SCOUTING blessing at any one time, so if you already have one, you don't get another. Also, you are cured of any effects of poison or disease (such as the Blight of Nagil) that you may be suffering from, and any curses you are under (such as a Shadar curse) are lifted.

Make another offering	turn to **456**
Leave	turn to **118**

405

The tunnel is unlit. To enter the mound you must possess a **candle**, **lantern**, or other light source. (If you light a **candle**, cross it off because it can be used only this once.)

Enter the mound	turn to **598**
No light source	turn to **226**

406

'Pity,' says Luroc Bans, 'You realize I can't let you leave alive.'
He overturns the table, and draws a long, barbed knife. The
woman backs away. You must fight him.

Luroc Bans, COMBAT 7, Defence 6, Stamina 11

If you win, turn to **197**. If you lose, turn to **7**.

407

If you own a ship, and it is anchored nearby, turn to **323**. If you
don't have a ship, turn to **629**.

408

You fall helplessly under the spell of the flute, and join the mad
throng, no longer the master of your own destiny. The next few
weeks are a confused time, of which you can remember nothing.
Cross off all your money and possessions. Instead, you have a
silver flute (CHARISMA +2), a **witch's hand**, some **parrot
fungus, rope** and a **Shadar spear (COMBAT +1)**.

You come to your senses to discover that you have travelled
many leagues. You are alone, and strangely sad, now that you have
lost the music. Turn to **398**.

409

If you have the codeword *Citrus*, turn to **532** immediately. If not,
read on.

You have been here before. Kaschuf the Deathless cannot be
killed by normal means, and you have still not found a way of
defeating him.

If you want to talk to his butler, old man Kevar, turn to **249**.
Otherwise, you might as well leave Vodhya – turn to **398**.

410

The rukh's claws pluck you from the deck as if you were a rabbit in
a field. You are carried up and up; the pale, upturned faces of your
crew grow more and more distant, until your ship is nothing but a
speck on the ocean.

You will never see them again. Cross the ship, cargo and crew off your Ship's Manifest.

The rukh screeches deafeningly; its wingbeats are like thunder. It flies for hours until it comes to a remote mountain peak. There it tosses you unceremoniously into a nest made of tree trunks where a young rukh is cawing for food. The parent flies off, but you must fight the chick, which is twice your size!

Young Rukh, COMBAT 6, Defence 5, Stamina 21

If you lose, it eats you: turn to **7**. If you win, turn to **678**.

411

You have only one choice – to lead your men in a concerted attack up the beach, and try to defeat the wreckers in battle. Otherwise you will be picked off one by one. As for the ship – you can see that it will be lost. With a vengeful battle cry, you try to rally your crew.

'Up and at 'em, lads!' you shout, and, waist deep in the water, you charge at the beach.

Make a CHARISMA roll at Difficulty 11. Add 1 to your roll if you are a Warrior, and one if you are 4th Rank or higher. Subtract one if you have a poor crew, and add one if you have a good or an excellent crew.

Successful CHARISMA roll	turn to **561**
Failed CHARISMA roll	turn to **497**

412

You dodge past the lurching beetles, avoiding their antlers. One of them, however, takes a chunk out of your leg. Lose 1-6 Stamina (the roll of one die).

If you still live, you throw yourself into the hole, and crawl forward. You come out in a small, square chamber, deep within the pyramid. Turn to **496**.

413

You break free of the tendrils and, with a last effort, manage to swim back to the bank. Your men haul you to safety and the first mate gives you mouth-to-mouth resuscitation. Unfortunately his dentures come loose and you nearly choke on them. Lose 1-6 Stamina points (the roll of one die).

Make another attempt to swim across	turn to **257**
Walk along to the bridge	turn to **328**
Return to the ship	turn to **191**

414

Lose the codeword *Dirty*.

You wait until nightfall before approaching the villa. Its white, marbled walls seem to glow in the moonlight. Four guards patrol the perimeter.

'Psst!' a voice hisses from the darkness, and Luroc Bans steps up beside you. He is dressed completely in black, and is carrying a grappling iron.

'We go in over the walls – there's an inner courtyard. Floril will meet us inside. She should have got the keys to the vault by now. Just follow me.'

Follow Luroc	turn to **626**
Pull out	turn to **667**
Pull out and warn Avar Hordeth	turn to **601**

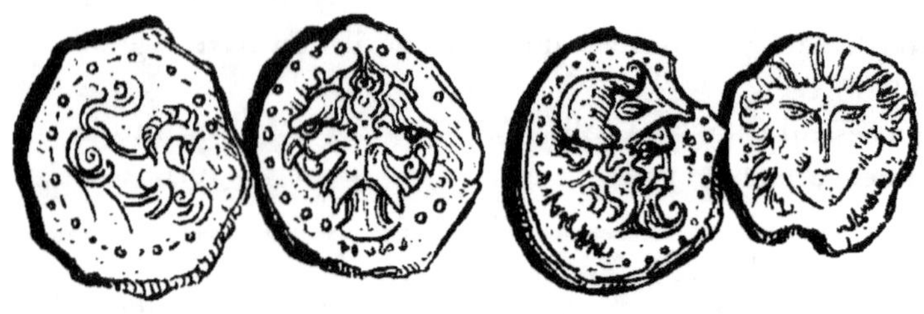

415

The crew absolutely refuses to sail into the Unbounded Ocean.

'There's no land out there, and the seas are infested with Demons of the Deep – if we go too far, we'll fall off the edge of the world!' says the first mate.

Turn to **580** and choose again.

416

The undead warriors shrink away from you, mewling piteously. You step past them into the main hall. Turn to **372**.

417

Looking through the gem you are able to see clearly the exact position of the stairway, and you ascend. At the gates of the tower, a man with golden skin, and amber eyes, greets you.

'Welcome to the Bazaar of the Golden Ones, traveller,' he says in a musical voice. Inside, you find a market like none you have ever seen.

Armour	To buy	To sell
Leather (Defence +1)	50 Shards	45 Shards
Ring mail (Defence +2)	100 Shards	90 Shards
Chain mail (Defence +3)	200 Shards	180 Shards
Splint armour(Defence +4)	400 Shards	360 Shards
Plate armour (Defence +5)	800 Shards	720 Shards
Heavy plate (Defence +6)	1600 Shards	1440 Shards

Weapons (sword, axe, etc)		
Without COMBAT bonus	50 Shards	40 Shards
COMBAT bonus +1	250 Shards	200 Shards

	To buy	To sell
COMBAT bonus +2	500 Shards	400 Shards
COMBAT bonus +3	1000 Shards	800 Shards
COMBAT bonus +4	2000 Shards	1600 Shards
COMBAT bonus +5	4000 Shards	3200 Shards
COMBAT bonus +6	8000 Shards	6400 Shards

Magical equipment	*To buy*	*To sell*
Amber wand (MAGIC +1)	500 Shards	400 Shards
Ebony wand (MAGIC +2)	1000 Shards	800 Shards
Cobalt wand (MAGIC +3)	2000 Shards	1600 Shards
Selenium wand (MAGIC +4)	4000 Shards	3200 Shards
Celestium wand (MAGIC +5)	8000 Shards	6400 Shards

Other items	*To buy*	*To sell*
Flute (CHARISMA +1)	200 Shards	180 Shards
Silver flute (CHARISMA +2)	400 Shards	360 Shards
Centaur flute (CHARISMA +3)	800 Shards	720 Shards
Lockpicks (THIEVERY +1)	300 Shards	270 Shards
Magic lockpicks (THIEVERY +2)	600 Shards	540 Shards
Gloves of Sig (THIEVERY +3)	1200 Shards	880 Shards
Holy symbol (SANCTITY +1)	200 Shards	100 Shards
Silver holy symbol (SANCTITY +2)	400 Shards	360 Shards
Gold holy symbol (SANCTITY +3)	800 Shards	720 Shards
Compass (SCOUTING +1)	500 Shards	450 Shards
Cross-staff (SCOUTING +2)	800 Shards	720 Shards
Sextant (SCOUTING +3)	1200 Shards	1000 Shards
Rope	50 Shards	45 Shards
Lantern	100 Shards	90 Shards
Climbing gear	100 Shards	90 Shards
Wolf pelt	100 Shards	90 Shards
Witch's hand	500 Shards	450 Shards
Parrot fungus	150 Shards	120 Shards

Banner of the Shadar	800 Shards	500 Shards
Selenium ore	700 Shards	600 Shards
Faery mead	200 Shards	150 Shards
Scroll of Ebron	500 Shards	350 Shards
Uncanny salts	100 Shards	90 Shards
Sacred rod of teleportation	–	1500 Shards

When you are finished, you leave the tower. Turn to **567**.

418

You wander around the dingy streets. Hooded faces stare at you from doorways, and dark figures lurk in every corner. A small boy runs past, and turns to watch you in astonishment. Incredibly you are unmolested. It seems the locals are so amazed by your brazen fearlessness, that they assume you to be mad, or a mighty wizard or hero, best left alone! Turn to **182**.

419

The *Sea Centaur* draws alongside. On the poop deck, you see Avar Hordeth, dressed for battle.

He spots you, and points you out to his men. 'I knew it! There's the thieving devil who stitched me up! Get them, men!' he orders.

His marines throw grappling hooks with experienced efficiency, and soon your two ships are locked in a struggle to the death. Marines and sailors swarm aboard, and a desperate fight ensues.

During the confused melee, you come face to face with Avar Hordeth himself. He is wearing armour, and wields a two-handed axe.

'I've been dreaming of this,' he says through gritted teeth. 'And now I'll take my revenge by splitting your skull with my axe!'

You'll have to fight him.

Avar Hordeth, COMBAT 8, Defence 8, Stamina 12

If you reduce him to 3 or fewer points of Stamina, turn to **392**. If you lose, turn to **338**.

420

You mistime your move, and he drives his lance into your gut. Lose all your Stamina points, save one.

Barely alive, you sink to the ground in agony. The bird-riders spit contemptuously at your performance — they had hoped for more sport. They ride away in disgust, leaving you to die. It will be very hard to survive the cruel steppes in your current condition.

Turn to **698**.

421

If you have the title Protector of Sokara or an **officer's pass**, the knights greet you civilly, and escort you into the citadel — turn to **295**.

If not, they surround you, and demand to know what you are doing here.

Make a CHARISMA roll at Difficulty 15.

Successful CHARISMA roll	turn to **356**
Failed CHARISMA roll	turn to **232**

422

After a time of aimless drifting, you come out on to the open sea. High winds, a strong current, and heavy rains sweep you and the raft to a destination over which you have no control.

The raft is washed up on a thin sliver of beach, under towering cliffs. Judging by the landscape, this is Nerech, the Land of the Manbeasts.

Turn to **688**.

423

You find yourself at the top of cliffs that seem to form the shore of a great sea of darkness. Far, far off in the black void you mark a few faint whirlpools of light, each seemingly made up of a thousand stellar pinpricks.

Climb down the cliffs	turn to **651**
Return south through the mountains	turn to **362**

424

'He sings of the victory of One-Eyed Crow, our first ancestor, over Grey Worm. Grey Worm made himself invulnerable, you see, by rolling in the magic dust of the gods' footprints. But he forgot that he hadn't got any of the dust on his nose, so One-Eyed Crow pecked him on his nose again and again until he fled. He hid in a hole in the ground, which is where worms have lived ever since.'

He gives you a wide half-mad grin. Spittle drools down his chin and his head slowly sinks to his chest. You rise, intending to leave him to sleep off his potion, but suddenly he grasps your arm and says: 'Worm has a big burrow these days!'

With that he falls asleep. You return to the camp to get some rest yourself. Get the codeword *Drape* and turn to **394**.

425

With apparent reluctance the golem admits you to the fortress, where you are allowed to stuff your pockets with gold and precious gems worth 1000-6000 Shards (roll one die and multiply by 1000).

With your newfound wealth dripping from both hands, you hasten back to where your men are waiting and tell them to make ready to put to sea. Turn to **191**.

426

You are strolling through an area of low, rolling hills — the Gemstone Hills. They are lush and green, and covered in woods. It is strangely quiet. There are no birds singing in the trees, and you see no woodland animals.

Make a MAGIC roll at Difficulty 12.

Successful MAGIC roll	turn to **39**
Failed MAGIC roll	turn to **102**

427

To renounce the worship of Nai, you must pay 40 Shards to the priesthood by way of compensation.

A samurai watches and sneers, 'Now that you have lost the goodwill of Nai, you will be easy meat for your enemies.'

Do you want to change your mind? If you are determined to renounce your faith, pay the 40 Shards and delete Nai from the God box on your Adventure Sheet.

When you have finished here, turn to **58**.

428 ☐

If there is a tick in the box, turn to **192** immediately. If not, put a tick there now, and read on.

A scholarly-looking gentleman comes out of the back.

'So you're the one Pikalik told me about,' he says in a thin, reedy voice.

He tells you his name is Argon the Alchemist. He takes you to his sanctum, a laboratory full of vats and alembics. Several contain half-formed Mannekyn People.

'They are my creations, you see,' says Argon. 'I grow them all, here, in the life-vats. I think of them as my children, and because you helped one of my people, I will help you.'

Argon will create a duplicate clone of your body in one of his vats. 'If you are slain, your spirit will leave your body, and fly to your clone, and you will live again!'

Write Sky Mountain, *The Plains of Howling Darkness* **244** in the Resurrection box on your Adventure Sheet. If you are later killed, turn to **244** in this book. You can have only one resurrection arranged at any one time, so if you already had a resurrection deal from a temple, the temple one is cancelled. You do not get a refund.

When you are ready to leave, the Mannekyn People fly you to the base of Sky Mountain.

Turn to **668**.

429 ☐

With the worm out of the way you have the chance to investigate the blocked-off opening in the tunnel wall.

If the box above is empty, put a tick in it and turn to **82**. If the box was already ticked, turn to **148**.

430

You defeat all three of them. Your display of martial skill has cowed the locals. Several slink out, the rest do their best to pretend you aren't here. You find 11 Shards on the bodies of the thugs, before you leave. Turn to **182**.

It will be tricky finding a solid path through the marsh to reach the light.

Make a SCOUTING roll at Difficulty 13.

Successful SCOUTING roll   turn to **490**

Failed SCOUTING roll   turn to **521**

You cannot remember the rituals for dealing with these creatures. Turn to **167**.

You learn that a great wizard called Targdaz the Magnificent is imprisoned within the citadel. A necromancer called Shazir from 'the lands of the southern devils', as the shaman puts it, inhabits the citadel now. He forces Targdaz to do his bidding.

'It is known that Targdaz has promised a great reward to any who can free him,' says the shaman. With that he falls silent, indicating that the audience is at an end.

Turn to **33**.

The key fits into the hole, and then disappears. It is lost for ever. Cross the **obsidian key** off your Adventure Sheet.

The plaque swings open with a click, and a rush of cloying, sickly air blows out of it into your face. Coughing, you step into the tomb.

Inside, you find a heavy stone sarcophagus, around which has been arrayed the goods and materials for Xinoc to use in the afterlife. Much of it is decayed and rotten now, but not the more durable of items. You find a triangular key. Note the **pyramid key** on your Adventure Sheet. You also find a **Shadar sword (COMBAT +4)**, some **heavy plate (Defence +6)**, a jar of **uncanny salts**, and a **ring of defence +4 (three uses)**. Note that the ring can be used three times only. You can invoke the ring before a fight, and it will add 4 to your Defence for the duration of that combat only. You also find some rainbow-coloured **parrot fungus**, inside an old jar of oil.

When you are finished, you return to the central square.

Visit the Cave of Bells   turn to **657**
Visit the Vault of the Shadar   turn to **107**
Visit the Crypt of Kings   turn to **298**
Leave the City of Ruins   turn to **266**

435

The priestess seems surprised to see you. 'Where is the mirror of
the Sun Goddess you promised to find for us? All we know is that
a nomad from the Horde of the Thundering Skies is said to possess
it. Please, go and search for it.'

She has nothing else to say, so you return to the temple proper.
Turn to **89**.

436

You are washed up on to a pebble beach. Cliffs tower above you.
You have probably been washed up on Nerech, the Land of the
Manbeasts. Turn to **688**.

437 ☐

If there is a tick in the box, General Beladai refuses to talk to you until you have completed your mission – turn to **145** immediately. If not, put a tick there now, and read on.

Beladai is surprised to see you. 'It is vital for us all that you infiltrate the citadel,' he says. 'Do your best to open the gates. If you are having trouble penetrating the citadel, perhaps this will help. We took it from a patrol yesterday.'

He gives you an **officer's pass**. Note it on your Adventure Sheet.

If you have the codeword *Deep*, turn to **709**.

If not, you leave – turn to **145**.

438

From here, you can sail:

West to the Cragdrift Sea	*The Isle of a Thousand Spires* **50**
South, along the coast	*The Court of Hidden Faces* **250**
Go ashore in Tigre Bay	turn to **342**

439

You sail for days, until the food and water begin to run out. You have to put yourself and the crew on half rations, and then quarter rations. You are dying of thirst. Lose 4 Stamina points.

If you still live, several of the crew have died. Reduce your crew rating by one level – i.e. excellent becomes good, good becomes average and average becomes poor. If the crew is already of poor quality, there is no further effect.

Finally, you spot land. You recognize the coastline of the Great Steppes, and the harbour city of Yarimura.

Turn to **580**.

440 ☐☐☐

If there is a tick in all three boxes, turn to **183** immediately. If not, put a tick in an empty box, and read on.

Since the ice melted, operations at the mine have all but ceased. A miserable looking Jalalul, the overseer of the mine, sits inside the main building. He has lost much weight, but he's not out of business yet. The stores of ice stockpiled in the warehouse will take months to melt, and, since it is the only rime ice left, he can command a good price for it. A satchel of **rime ice** costs 150 Shards. You cannot carry more than two satchels. If you buy any, cross off the money and add the **rime ice** to your Adventure Sheet.

There is nothing else here, so you leave.

Turn to **687**.

441

You manage to run outside safely. The Ruby Citadel collapses in on itself with a thundering roar, but the tattooed man calmly walks out, chunks of ruby rock bouncing off his blue energy shield. His hawk-nosed face is made all the more strange by the bizarre tattoos that cover him entirely.

'I am Targdaz,' he says, 'the Magnificent.' He tilts his head back as he says 'magnificent', as if challenging you to gainsay him. 'Anyway,' he goes on, 'I'm grateful...' He pauses for a moment, and looks away, struck by a sudden thought. Then he yells, 'By the Fiery One! Of course!'

He turns away, gestures, and a large palanquin of black and gold appears in mid-air, floating in front of him. He jumps in, and yells: 'Take me to the Hall of Ebron and no further!'

The palanquin moves off. You notice footprints appearing in the snow, as of invisible bearers, carrying the palanquin away. Then it accelerates to an impossible speed, and races out of sight. The last thing you hear is Targdaz muttering, 'Must tell Hetepek....'

You examine the footprints, and give an involuntary shudder: they are not human.

Musing about the strange behaviour of wizards, especially ungrateful ones, you carry on your way.

If you are a Troubadour, turn to **28**. If not, turn to **499**.

442

You have entered a cold, barren land of howling winds and pitiless rains. Roll two dice.

Score 2-5	A gruesome punishment	turn to **210**
Score 6-7	No event	turn to **52**
Score 8-12	A gathering of the tribes	turn to **473**

443

A strange ship emerges from the fog bank. It is barely seaworthy, a floating wreck with rotting rigging, and mouldy timbers. But it is the nature of the crew that draws your attention – ghostly forms, undead pirates, spectral figures that leap and dance, wielding rusty cutlasses. A tattered red pennant flies from the mast.

Your crew is filled with dread. 'Ye gods,' wails the first mate. 'It's a ghost ship – if they catch us, they'll take our souls down into the cold, dark deeps!'

The spectral ship surges towards you in silent pursuit as the hot sun beats down.

Make a run for it	turn to **492**
Prepare to fight	turn to **546**

444

The rogues loitering at the door of the brotherhood building applaud as you approach the guild. They are well aware of your daring exploits.

You are taken to see Lochos Veshtu of Aku, Master of Knaves. He seems pleased you have succeeded in your task, though you cannot be sure because his black mask hides his face.

He announces that you are a full member of the brotherhood and gives you the title Nightstalker. Note it on your Adventure Sheet in the Titles box. This allows you to use the building as a safe house to store equipment and to rest, but you will have to pay a fee to the Brotherhood.

He also provides a little training in roguery, and you gain a Rank. Roll one die, and add the score to your unwounded Stamina total, permanently.

When you are ready to leave, turn to **633**.

445

Lose 1-6 Stamina points (the roll of one die). If you still live, the Mannekyn People stay well out of your reach, and you are forced to climb back down while they hurl rocks, and lively abuse at you. Strangers do not seem welcome on Sky Mountain.

You reach the bottom, at which point the Mannekyn People fly off and leave you alone. Turn to **668**.

446

The knight rides in, impales you on his lance and then jumps gallantly from the saddle. Lose 2-12 Stamina points (the roll of two dice). If you survive you must now fight him on foot.

Sir Leo, COMBAT 8, Defence 20, Stamina 35

Fight him and win	turn to **571**
Run back to the ship	turn to **191**

447

If you are an initiate it costs only 20 Shards to purchase Amanushi's blessing. A non-initiate must pay 35 Shards. Cross off the money and mark THIEVERY in the Blessings box on your Adventure Sheet.

The blessing works by allowing you to try again when you fail a THIEVERY roll. It is good for only one reroll. When you use the blessing, cross it off your Adventure Sheet. You can have only one THIEVERY blessing at any one time. Once it is used up, you can return to any branch of the temple of Amanushi to buy a new one.

When you are finished here, turn to **58**.

448

If you have the codeword *Defend* or *Deliver*, turn to **376**. If not, turn to **418**.

449

'Next!' you cry boldly. The nomads look at you in astonishment for a moment, and then start laughing. You are invited to their camp, which comprises a circle of wagons.

The bird-riders are of the Wingless Hawk tribe, part of the Horde of the Thundering Skies. You are treated as an honoured guest for some time, and are well fed and looked after. You can restore any lost Stamina points.

Soon, they move on to seek new pastures for their giant elephant-birds.

Gain the codeword *Drifter* and turn to **698**.

You are recognized as a member of the brotherhood and shown in. If you have the codeword *East*, turn to **650** immediately. If not, read on.

You must pay your membership fee of 5 Shards. If you cannot or won't pay, you are promptly shown out again — turn to **633**.

ITEMS PROTECTED BY BROTHERHOOD

If you pay, you can leave possessions and money here to save having to carry them around with you. You can also rest here safely, and recover any Stamina points you have lost. Record in the box anything you wish to leave. When you are ready, you can leave by turning to **633**.

451

The *Sea Centaur* pursues you. Roll two dice, and add your Rank. Also add one if you have a good crew, and add 2 if you have an excellent crew.

Score 2-10	The *Sea Centaur* catches up	turn to **419**
Score 11+	You outrun it	turn to **236**

452

You cannot feel your limbs. Your blood is thick with cold. Hunger turns from a gnawing pain into a sensation of hollowness and enervation. Darkness flutters at the edge of your vision: you could imagine it is the robe of Nagil as he quickens his pace behind you in the snow.

Lose 2-12 Stamina points (the roll of two dice). If still alive, make a SCOUTING roll at Difficulty 18.

Successful SCOUTING roll	turn to **317**
Failed SCOUTING roll	turn to **7**

453

Your ship is thrown about like flotsam and jetsam. When the storm subsides, you take stock. Much has been swept overboard – you lose 1 Cargo Unit, if you had any, of your choice. Delete it from the Ship's Manifest. Turn to **438**.

454

The man, whose name is Szgano, leads you north to the Pyramid of Xinoc.

At the top of the pyramid, the light from several burning torches casts a greenish glow over the scene. Five robed and hooded men stand around a woman who is stretched out on the flat top of the pyramid. The hooded figures chant ominously, and one wields a long, silver-tipped javelin. The woman is manacled with silver chains, and she wrestles and twists against her bonds, screaming and cursing in a most unladylike manner.

You and Szgano race up the steps carved into the side of the pyramid, and confront them.

'Hold!' you shout. 'I will not let fiends butcher an innocent woman.'

The captive stops struggling and looks at you with hope-filled eyes that are as green as emeralds. Her hair is as white as snow, although she cannot be much more than twenty years old. Her skin is pale like the moon. She is quite beautiful.

The man with the javelin throws back his hood, revealing the wind-ravaged face of an old nomad shaman.

`You stupid outlander!' he bellows. `Innocent? She is the Ruz-bahn, the vampire witch! Many of the babes of our tribe have been taken by her to feed her monstrous appetite and to keep her young. Szgano there is nothing but her slave, a dupe, sworn to serve her.'

`Lies, lies!' shouts Szgano, `She is Ruzbahn all right. But that's just her name, and she is my betrothed. These stinking necromancers want to sacrifice her to their dark god, because she has white hair and green eyes.'

`Not so,' counters the shaman. `This ritual is the only way to destroy the Ruzbahn — a silver spear, on ground consecrated to the old gods.'

You stand unsure for a moment.

`Bah! We have no time for this,' says the shaman, who turns his back on you. He signals to his companions, who draw wicked daggers and advance on Szgano, eyeing you warily.

`Save me, save me!' implores the woman huskily.

`Silence, witch!' shouts the shaman, clasping a hand over her mouth.

Fight the shamans	turn to **371**
Help the shamans	turn to **270**

455

The White Warlock Tavern is frequented by mages and priests of Molhern. The tavern costs you 1 Shard a day. Each day you spend here, you can recover 1 Stamina point if injured, up to the limit of your normal unwounded Stamina score.

You also hear a Troubadour singing a mythic tale about the High King. Five hundred years ago the High King ruled Old Harkuna, and he defended it vigorously against invaders from Uttaku. The Uttakin used black sorcery to imprison the king beneath the Rimewater, where he and his paladins were frozen in ice. His wife, and only true love, Leanora, was an Uttakin princess, but the Masked Lords of Uttaku, angry at her love for the king, slew her, and bound her ghost to serve as the merciless guardian jailer of the High King. Now she is a terrible spectre, the Ice Queen, whose heart is as frozen as the lake she haunts. Or so they say.

When you are ready, you leave the tavern. Turn to **274**.

456

As an initiate of Tambu, you know you can make an offering here
in the hope of winning Tambu's favour. The object must be of
value and have an ability bonus (CHARISMA, COMBAT and so on) of
at least +1.

+1 item	turn to **641**
+2 item	turn to **404**
+3 item or better	turn to **568**
Leave	turn to **118**

457

The chief shaman is a short fat fellow who is dressed in furs and
covered in strange tattoos. If you are an initiate, or if you donate
10 Shards to the temple, he will speak with you.

Initiate or donate 10 Shards	turn to **345**
Leave	turn to **33**

458

The shaman throws back his head and stares directly upwards as if
reading his answer from the ice-bright pattern of the stars. 'A
foreign lord lies sleeping there, under the hard waters. His dreams
are dreams of life. When life becomes an intolerable nightmare,
then he will awaken.'

The legends of Old Harkuna say that the High King will return
in the country's hour of need.

'Is there any other way to wake him?' you ask.

He thrusts a vial of **uncanny salts** into your hand. Note this on
your list of possessions. The salts smell pungent, like smelling salts.

The shaman suddenly falls into a drug-induced sleep.

Use the **uncanny salts** to wake him	turn to **319**
Leave and get some sleep	turn to **394**

459

After several days, you pass out from lack of food, water, and sleep. You slip beneath the waves and drown.

Turn to **7**.

460

You manage to evade your pursuers. The manbeasts are ferocious, but seem rather stupid, and make bad trackers. Turn to **32**.

461

The Sokaran troops that have come through the tunnels are waiting to attack. At the sight of the camp in chaos they charge. The army of the Northern Alliance is already in disarray, and the fresh attack causes absolute panic. In the confusion, you easily escape. Turn to **218**.

462

The Temple of Juntoku is built to look like a gigantic granite helmet. Juntoku is the 'Warrior that Never Sleeps', the war god of Akatsurai. He is worshipped as a great general, and leader of men. He is not a god of battle, but of the art of war.

Become an initiate of Juntoku	turn to **96**
Renounce his worship	turn to **23**
Seek a blessing	turn to **299**
Leave the temple	turn to **58**

463

You ask about the spectre that visited you one night in your cabin, aboard ship on the Violet Ocean, and of its request that you go to the fane. At the mention of the name Tayang Khan, the shaman makes a sign of warding.

'Do not mention that name here!' he shrills, spraying spittle in your face.

He indicates that the audience is over.

Turn to **33**.

464

The man in black hesitates as you send a clear, resonating note into the rosy air. But nothing happens, and he smiles an evil smile, levelling his staff at you once again.

Turn to **550**.

465

You cannot harm the ghostly figure, no matter what you try. It plunges its spectral hands into your chest and drains the life out of you, gibbering madly as it does so. Instantly, you black out.

When you come to, you are lying on a mound of earth in the middle of the marsh — the tower is nowhere to be seen. You have been drained of some of your life energy. Lose 1 Rank and roll one die. Subtract the result from your unwounded Stamina total permanently. (If you are only of the 1st Rank anyway, there is no effect).

You resume your journey. Turn to **92**.

466

Get the codeword *Deep*. You are able to map the main tunnels. They run under the Spine of Harkun, from north to south. You have discovered a secret way to cross the mountains without having to go through the Pass of Eagles. Caves on either side of the mountains mark the entrance to the tunnels.

Go north   turn to **558**
Go south   *The War-Torn Kingdom* **3**

At the centre of the island stands a fortress with featureless grey walls and a single gate. The drawbridge is down and the portcullis raised, but on the other side stands a massive golem with thews of adamantine rock.

'You must give the password,' booms the golem.

The boxes above are used to record how many times you have got this far. Tick one now.

If this is your first visit, turn to **516**. If your second, turn to **397**. If your third (or more), turn to **284**.

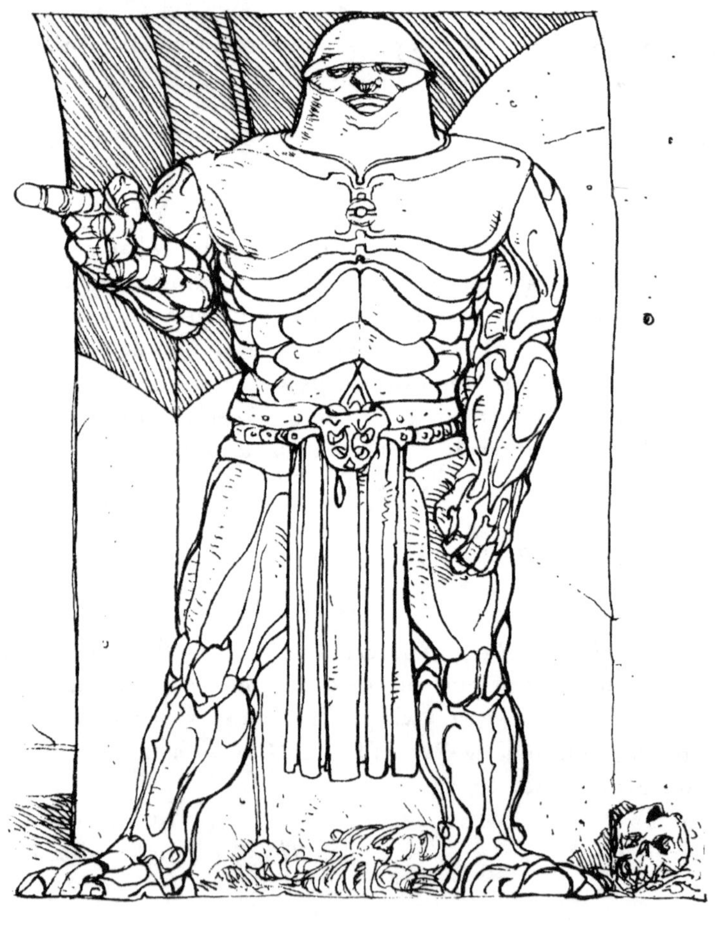

468

You tell the guard your name. He recognizes you and explains that Avar Hordeth is not at home, but your room is set aside for you as promised. You can leave possessions and money here to save having to carry them around with you. You can also rest here safely and recover any Stamina points you have lost. Record in the box anything you wish to leave.

<table>
<tr><td>ITEMS IN HORDETH'S VILLA

</td></tr>
</table>

Each time you return, roll two dice.

Score 2-11   Your possessions are safe

Score 12   A thief. Lose one possession (your choice) if any, that you left here

You can return to Yarimura by turning to **10**.

469

You know from arcane bestiaries that this is a snake demon, bound by long-dead Shadar priests to guard their tombs. You recite a spell which is said to be effective against such demons. The beast recoils for a moment, and a green bile bursts from its eyes and ears. It shrieks in agony, but it does not die. Enraged, it closes in.

Snake Demon, COMBAT 7, Defence 7, Stamina 10

If you win, turn to **215**. If you lose, turn to **7**.

470

The merchant ship is a large galleon with a complement of marines on board. It is called the *Sea Centaur*; your first mate tells you it is owned by Avar Hordeth – the man you robbed in Yarimura.

The *Sea Centaur* changes direction and bears down on you.

Make a run for it   turn to **451**

Sail to meet it   turn to **419**

471

You have successfully navigated the dangerous waters of Disaster
Bay. Up ahead, your lookout spots an island.

'That be Bazalek Isle,' says your mate, 'No one who has landed
there has ever got back alive — I'd advise against it, unless you've a
map or something, cap'n.'

North along the coast to Yarimura	turn to **201**
East towards the Isle of Mystery	turn to **120**
Out into the Unbounded Ocean	turn to **305**
Drop anchor and explore Bazalek Isle	turn to **673**

472

You are crossing the frozen northern steppes. Snow carpets the
ground. Rising up out of the white wastes, a great pyramid stands.
It is panelled with a strange, yellowish marble, and an ornately
carved gateway is set into one of its faces, flanked by two idols.
Curiously, it is untouched by the snow, and when you draw nearer
you realize it is giving off a faint warmth, enough to melt any ice
or snow that falls upon it. Steps cut into the sides of the pyramid
lead up to its flat top. Beyond the pyramid are the Peaks at the
Edge of the World, massive mountains of mind-boggling size.

Approach the gates	turn to **21**
Go north to the peaks	turn to **271**
Go west to the River of Destiny	turn to **91**
Go east	turn to **630**
Go south	turn to **281**

473

Many horse nomads ride up and surround you. Their inscrutable
faces glare down at you without pity and they herd you with the
points of their spears to their camp. Thousands of the nomads have
gathered here for a meeting of all the tribes of the Horde of the
Thousand Winds. Turn to **272**.

474

Your eloquent appeal sways the nomad chiefs, who invite you to
join the camp as their guest. You soon learn that they are people

of the One-Eyed Crow clan on their way to join the Horde of the Windswept Ice, to which they belong.

As darkness deepens between the nomads' tents, fires leap and roar in the chill wind. A bard starts to sing of ancient glories and some of the young men of the clan jump up to dance in the firelight.

Stay and listen	turn to **553**
Go to talk to the clan chief	turn to **366**
Seek out their shaman	turn to **523**
Go to sleep	turn to **394**

475

You convince them that the ship can be repaired — all you need is some wood.

The first mate stands up, along with several others. He tells you the barque is called the *Mermaid's Desire*, and that they lost their captain in the storm that beached the ship. Clearly, they look to you for leadership.

'We've got the tools to repair her,' says the mate, 'but where's the wood?'

You decide to lead them in search of timber, though the landscape is bleak and desolate.

Make a SCOUTING roll at Difficulty 14.

Successful SCOUTING roll	turn to **559**
Failed SCOUTING roll	turn to **681**

476

You realize the fog is the product of sorcery, and that it is intended to turn ships back from the isle. You are able to guide the ship through, using your sorcerous instinct.

Eventually, you come out of the fog into a small cove where you can drop anchor. The island is covered in a hot, steamy jungle from which rises a forested mountain.

The men will not go ashore, but they will wait here for you to explore the Isle of Mystery, if you want. If you go ashore, note that your ship is docked at the Isle of Mystery.

To head inland, on your own, turn to **564**. To sail back to the sea, turn to **296**.

477

You make your way down a long tunnel to a hall which is lit by a thousand white candles and lined with tables. Here you are greeted by men and women who are clad in shrouds that they wear like togas; their faces are pale as marble, their eyes like dull grey jewels.

There is a presence in the deep darkness at the distant end of the hall. 'Who goes there?' booms a voice that fills you with awe — the voice of Nagil, Lord of the Dead.

If you have the title Chosen One of Nagil, turn to **103**. If not but you are an initiate of Nagil, turn to **551**. If neither, turn to **387**.

478

At the top, you find only the large, sprawling ruin of a mountain stronghold. Broken towers and shattered walls are all that is left.

A voice rings out, as if from nowhere, 'By Molhern! It's you!'

The ruin seems to waver and dissolve in front of your eyes, to be replaced by a thriving fortified settlement! At the gate tower stands Pyletes the Sage. You took the Book of the Seven Sages from the scorpion men and returned it to Pyletes in Yellowport, Sokara. It seems like an age ago now, but he hasn't forgotten you.

He opens the gates for you, and explains that the Isle of Mystery is inhabited by magicians who worship Molhern, the god of knowledge and magic. They like to live in solitude, and shield their island with illusions.

'But an illuminate is always welcome,' says Pyletes.

You enter the City of Mystery. Turn to **274**.

479

You know enough magical lore to ward off any ill effects of the Shadar curse. Turn to **290**.

480

The sun flares cold and crimson behind a bank of cloud. The gloom helps your task as you slowly work your way closer across the bone-cold ground. Now you can hear the captive's whimpered cries as the crows peck at his limbs.

Make a THIEVERY roll at a Difficulty of 12.

Successful THIEVERY roll   turn to **364**
Failed THIEVERY roll   turn to **515**

481

Make a SANCTITY roll at Difficulty 13.

Successful SANCTITY roll   turn to **331**
Failed SANCTITY roll   turn to **294**

482

You sense a disharmony in the vibrations of the citadel. Your magical intuition gives you an idea — it ought to be possible to set up a musical vibration of your own, and the resonant harmonics might just shatter the thrumming ruby and bring it down on the necromancer.

If you have a **flute** or **whistle**, whether or not they have a bonus, turn to **632**.

Otherwise, you will have to try to sing the right note. Make a CHARISMA roll at Difficulty 15. You can add one to the roll if you are a Troubadour.

Successful CHARISMA roll   turn to **329**
Failed CHARISMA roll   turn to **464**

483

Silent as a shadow, you slip over the stockade wall. You crawl through the night towards a large purple pavilion of silk. It is the largest, so you reckon it must be Beladai's tent. Still unseen, you make it to within a few feet of the tent.

Make a MAGIC roll at Difficulty 14.

Successful MAGIC roll	turn to **306**
Failed MAGIC roll	turn to **638**

484

You sail for days. Suddenly the ship surges forward, out of control! To your horror, a gigantic whirlpool appears in the middle of the ocean, sucking you down with relentless speed. Soon you are hurtling around on sheer walls of water. The sky is a small blue window that looks down at you through the towering columns of the sea!

'We are being sucked into the land below the world by the Demons of the Deep!' howls one of your men.

Turn to *Into the Underworld* **75**.

485

Bakhan welcomes you to her tower. If you have some **selenium ore** turn to **259**. If not, all Bakhan can do for you is to lift a curse, if you are suffering from one. This she will do free of charge, as you saved her from her own curse. Cross off any curses you have recorded and adjust your abilities to normal. When you are finished, turn to **10**.

486

If you have the codeword *Dangle*, turn to **409** immediately. If not, read on.

The doors are opened by an old man with long white hair hanging to his shoulders. He steps aside and gestures for you to enter, looking at you with frightened eyes. You step into a hall of grey stone, with blood-red banners hung on the walls.

'Don't mind old Kevar, my butler,' booms a voice from the back of the hall. 'He's a bit simple but it's difficult to get good staff these days.'

With that the voice dissolves into laughter. A man steps from the shadows at the back of the hall. He is tall, built like a blacksmith, and completely bald. His eyes are a bleak, piercing green. He is dressed in ornate red and black lacquered armour, and holds a huge battle-axe.

'My name is Kaschuf, called the Deathless. I guess you to be another one of those fools come to rescue the Lady Nastasya.'

He falls into paroxysms of laughter once more. He wipes a tear from his eye and then straightens up. 'Well, let's get on with it. I've no time for you unless you're here for a fight.'

Fight Kaschuf	turn to **87**
Leave the village	turn to **398**

487

A giant grey worm suddenly slithers out of the darkness ahead, opening its maw wide to swallow you. You can smell the harsh acidic stink of its digestive juices, like warm rancid bile.

If you have the codeword *Drape*, turn to **260**. If not, turn to **171**.

488

Acquire the codeword *Dirty*.

You shake hands with Luroc and Floril, and the deal is sealed. Luroc arranges a night to meet you outside the villa of Avar Hordeth, south of Yarimura. When you go there, he will be waiting for you.

You leave the tavern. Turn to **10**.

489

The mast splits in two and your ship is thrown about like flotsam and jetsam. When the storm subsides, you take stock. Much has been swept overboard – you lose 1 Cargo Unit, if you had any, of your choice.

Also, the ship has been swept way off course and the mate has no idea where you are.

'We're lost at sea, cap'n!' he moans.

Turn to **390**.

490

You find a safe path to the glowing light. As you draw nearer, you realize it is coming from the belfry of a sunken tower, only the tip of which is jutting out of the marsh. You step inside the ruin, through what was once a window.

Inside, it is dank and musty, and bone-numbingly cold. An ornate bronze brazier burns with a sickly green light that flickers eerily in the gathering gloom of evening. Oddly, it gives off not a welcoming warmth, but an icy chill.

A hunched, spectral figure, dressed in what once were rich, ornately-stitched robes, but are now little more than rags, squats before the wan, emerald flames. It turns its phantasmal face to gaze upon you with eyes as black as the pits of hell.

The ghostly figure rasps in a sepulchral whisper, 'Who dares disturbs Khotep, Sentinel of the glorious Shadar Empire!'

It rises into the air on an ethereal wind, and glides toward you, reaching out for with blackened, withered claws.

Make a SANCTITY roll at Difficulty 12.

Successful SANCTITY roll   turn to **541**
Failed SANCTITY roll   turn to **465**

491 ☐

Night is falling and it becomes ever more colder as the last of the sun's warmth leaves the steppes. You stumble across an ancient ruined tower. There is little left of the roof but you manage to huddle in a corner which shelters you from the cold wind.

If there is a tick in the box, turn to **321** immediately. If not, put a tick there now, and read on.

You sleep uninterrupted for a few hours but you are woken by a rustling sound. At first you see nothing but then you manage to make out two small red lights a few feet away from you, then another two, then four more.

You realize they are not lights but fiery red eyes just as a fireball is thrown to the floor by one of the creatures. The fireball lights up the whole ruin – you can see you are surrounded by redcaps, a particularly unpleasant type of goblin.

Make a MAGIC roll at Difficulty 12.

Successful MAGIC roll   turn to **283**
Failed MAGIC roll   turn to **167**

492

As your ship pulls away, the ghost pirates seem to give up the chase, as if they were unable to follow you too far from the fog-bank. The men cheer with heartfelt relief.

Head west towards Disaster Bay   turn to **310**
Sail south west along the coast of Nerech   turn to **50**

493

Lord Kumonosu's bedchamber is at the top of the tallest tower of the palace. That night, you assay the task of climbing it.

Make a THIEVERY roll at Difficulty 15. If you have some **rope** add one to the roll. If you have some **climbing gear**, add two (but the pluses are not cumulative).

Successful THIEVERY roll   turn to **693**
Failed THIEVERY roll   turn to **230**

494

You are set upon by a gang of ruffians who are intent on robbing you. Make a COMBAT roll at Difficulty 15.

Successful COMBAT roll   turn to **692**

Failed COMBAT roll   turn to **131**

495

You know enough arcane lore to decipher the plaques above the tunnel entrances. They read 'Dweomer', 'Imperial Chambara', 'The Bronze Hills' and 'The Pyramid'.

You realize that finding your way back the way you came will be virtually impossible. You will have to go through one of the tunnels.

Dweomer   turn to **656**

Imperial Chambara   turn to **518**

The Bronze Hills   turn to **402**

The Pyramid   turn to **623**

496

Gain the codeword *Dwarf*.

The room is empty, except for a key made of obsidian lying on the stone floor. Note the **obsidian key** on your Adventure Sheet.

You find a ventilation shaft you can crawl through and emerge from the pyramid, alive but rather small. Outside, however, the magical effect wears off after a few hours and you are soon back to normal size. Turn to **472**.

497

You wade up the beach, but not enough of your men have come with you. Panic has set in, and most of them are diving into the water with cries of 'Every man for himself!'

Desperately, you try to take on the wreckers, but there are too

many and it is not long before your men are cut down. You fall
under a punishing blow to the back of the head, and everything
goes black. Lose 3 Stamina.

If you still live, turn to **582**.

498

That night you decide to make your move. You will have to get to
the Great Gate undetected, and then into the winch-house, where
a huge cog-wheel mechanism is turned to open and shut the gates.

The corridors of the citadel are regularly patrolled, but the
lighting is poor, and there are many niches and shadowy corners
where a stealthy person can hide.

Make a THIEVERY roll at Difficulty 14.

Successful THIEVERY roll   turn to **674**
Failed THIEVERY roll   turn to **530**

499

The Ruby Citadel is no more. All that remains are the shattered
fragments of its former glory, destroyed by your cunning. There
is nothing here, except for a locked verdigris trapdoor in the floor
of what was once the main hall.

If you have a **verdigris key**, you can turn to **196**. If not, there
is nothing for you to do but leave.

Go west   turn to **630**
Go east   turn to **15**
Go south   turn to **17**

500 ☐

If there is a tick in the box, turn to **699** immediately. If not, put a
tick there now, and read on.

You are taken to see one of their princes, in a large blue and
white striped tent. Inside, a man sits on the floor at a low table. At
the sight of you he leaps to his feet.

'By Great Tambu!' he cries. 'It's you!'

He is Akradai, Prince of the Azure Sky tribe. You saved him
once, in Yellowport, Sokara. He was under a curse, and you
released him from it. He promised then that he would reward you.

Akradai gives you 500 Shards, and his shamans will cure you of any disease or poison you may be suffering from (but they cannot lift a curse).

They also prepare you a magical elixir, used by the nomads to hone their sense of direction, a **potion of nature**. Potions can be used just before a Difficulty roll to add one to the relevant ability and can be used once only. A **potion of nature** will add one to your SCOUTING ability.

The next day, you continue on your way.

Go north	turn to **15**
Go east toward Yarimura	turn to **280**
Go south	turn to **234**
Head west deeper into the steppes	turn to **17**

501

If you didn't have enough money in the bank to cover the ransom demand, turn to **285**. Otherwise, your captors take the money and run. You are released in Yarimura – turn to **10**.

502

Your intuition tells you something is not right. Suddenly, the ruined stronghold wavers and fades before your eyes to be replaced by a thriving fortified settlement. The blind man has turned into a rather well-dressed, corpulent fellow, who isn't even blind. The whole thing was an illusion.

'Ah, well, I see that you can see,' he says.

He explains that the Isle of Mystery is inhabited by magicians who worship Molhern, the god of knowledge and magic. They like to live in solitude, and shield their island with illusions.

'You might as well go in, now that you've seen through our little trick,' mutters the man.

You stroll through the main gate in to the City of Mystery.

Turn to **274**.

503

The dragon turns all three heads, and breathes an inferno of flames over you. You are instantly burnt to a crisp. Turn to **7**.

You try to make a joke about the situation, but they take it as an insult to the fighting quality of their tribe, and their faces suddenly set in hard lines, like stone. They seize you, take all your money and possessions (cross them off your Adventure Sheet) and tie your hands behind your back. Then they set you running, and chase after on their huge birds, which they encourage to kick and peck at you. Lose 3-18 Stamina points (the roll of three dice).

If you still live, eventually they tire of their sport and ride off, leaving you half-alive and bleeding. You manage to loosen your bonds, but your situation is desperate, alone on the steppes with nothing.

Turn to **698**.

The runes above the arch glow ominously as you walk through. You have incurred a curse. Note you have the Curse of the Shadar, and subtract one from your MAGIC and COMBAT abilities until you can find a way to lift the curse. Turn to **290**.

After a time of aimless drifting, you come out on to the open sea. You are swept toward a destination over which you have no control. After a few days, you begin to feel weak from lack of food and water. Fortunately, a merchant ship picks you up.

If you have the codeword *Dead*, turn to **98** immediately. If not, read on.

The captain is happy to take you to his next port of call.

If you have the codeword *Divest*, turn to **51** immediately. If not, read on.

After an uneventful journey, you disembark at the harbour in Yarimura. Turn to **10**.

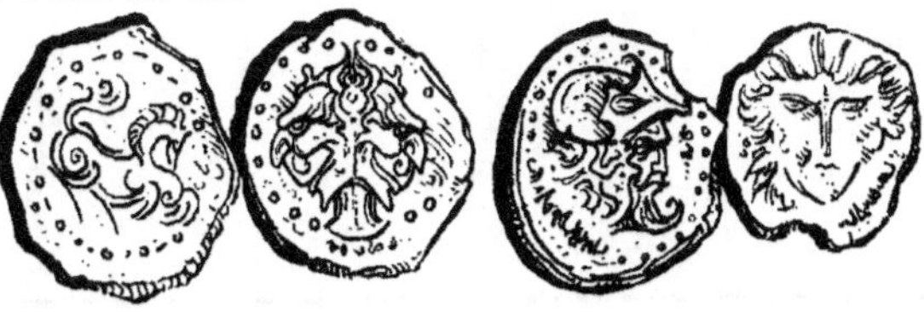

507

You recite some holy scriptures and the redcaps immediately retreat, wailing mournfully. As they flee, one drops a small sack. Inside you find a **Shadar scroll** and some **faery mead**. The scroll is mundane, but may have some value to a collector of Shadar antiquities. Note them on your Adventure Sheet.

The rest of the night passes peacefully. Turn to **144**.

508

The shaman points north, then south; east, then west. 'Search all four corners of the plain, and in-between you'll find the fane,' he cackles.

You suck your teeth, finding the reply confusing but no more cryptic than you'd expect from any shaman or wizard. Since the old man now seems to be getting tired, you return to the camp to find a bed for the night. Turn to **394**.

509

You can leave possessions and money here to save having to carry them around with you. You can also rest here safely, and recover any Stamina points you have lost. Record in the box anything you wish to leave. Each time you return, roll two dice — unless you paid the protection money or you have the title Nightstalker, in which case the house is automatically safe.

Score 2-7   Your possessions are safe
Score 8-12   Lose everything you left here
Turn to **10** when you are ready.

ITEMS IN TOWNHOUSE

<h1 style="text-align:center">510</h1>

It is not long before you get completely lost. You struggle on in a dream-like state, unsure where you are going, and where you've been. Roll a die, and add one.

If the result is less than or equal to your Rank, turn to **123**. If it is greater than your Rank, turn to **254**.

<h1 style="text-align:center">511</h1>

The storm demon laughs at your attempt to invoke the power of Elnir. The thunder and lightning intensifies. Turn to **536**.

<h1 style="text-align:center">512</h1>

A darkening of the heavens heralds the gathering storm. A ferocious wind sweeps the rain in sheets over your ship, and the waves rise and fall inexorably, lifting you up, and then dashing you down.

If you have a blessing of Safety from Storms, you can ignore the storm. Cross off your blessing and turn **438**.

Otherwise the storm hits with full fury. Roll one die if your ship is a barque, two dice if it is a brigantine, or three dice if it is a galleon. Add 1 to the roll if you have a good crew; add 2 if you have an excellent crew.

Score 1-3	Ship sinks	turn to **540**
Score 4-5	The mast splits	turn to **453**
Score 6-20	You weather the storm	turn to **438**

513 ☐

If the box above is empty, put a tick in it and turn to **477**. If it was already ticked, turn to **292**.

514

A merchant ship is heading towards you. If you have the codeword *Dead*, turn to **569** immediately. If not, but you have the codeword *Divest*, turn to **470** immediately. If you have neither codeword, read on.

The merchant ship is a large galleon, called the *Sea Centaur*.

Your first mate says, 'That's the ship of Avar Hordeth. He's from Metriciens originally, but he has a villa in Yarimura. He's one of the richest merchants around – his treasure room is said to be awash with gold and jewels. And some say he didn't get it all honestly, if you catch my drift, cap'n.'

You sail on. Turn to **236**.

515

You are seen by one of the nomad warriors, who grabs you and hauls you to your feet. They stare at you – about a dozen of them, as hard-eyed a bunch of men as you've ever had to face.

Run for your life	turn to **664**
Wait to see what they do	turn to **56**

516

The golem waits for the password, but is at least sporting enough to give you three choices.

Glass	turn to **425**
Zinc	turn to **18**
Ice	turn to **351**

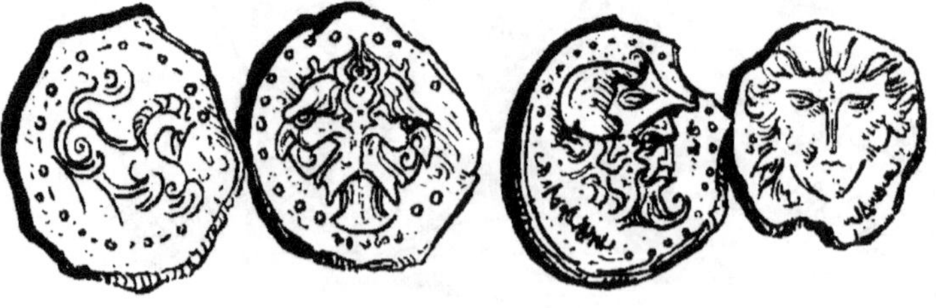

517

Becoming an initiate of Molhern gives you the benefit of paying less for blessings and other services the temple can offer. It costs 50 Shards to become an initiate. You cannot do this if you are already an initiate of another temple.

If you choose to become an initiate, write Molhern in the God box on your Adventure Sheet and cross off the 50 Shards.

Once you have finished here, turn to **637**.

518

As you step up to the arch of the tunnel, you notice that the air in the entrance shimmers with a bluish light. As you pass through it, you feel a momentary sense of dislocation. You continue on for hours, until you come to a ladder leading upward. You climb up.

Turn to *Lords of the Rising Sun* **75**. If you haven't got that book yet, turn back to **495** and choose again.

520

You utter a battle-cry and ready your weapon to strike. Immediately, all three give a warbling cry of fear and dive into the waters, swimming away into the depths.

Shrugging your shoulders, you head back. High tide comes, refloating your ship, and you sail on.

Turn to **471**.

521

You lose your footing, and fall into the marsh. The thick, viscous mud starts to drag you under. Coughing and spluttering, you reach for the branch of a blackened, gnarled tree.

Roll one die and add 2. If you score less than or equal to your Rank turn to **597**. If you score greater than your Rank, turn to **7**.

522 ☐

If there is a tick in the box turn to **277**, immediately. If not, put a tick there now, and read on.

You have heard tell of this centaur. Among the plains people he is called the Horse that Sings, the living incarnation of the nomad spirit, the wanderlust. But you are steeped in magical lore, quite capable of resisting the beguiling music. As the ensorcelled dancers pass by you, the centaur stops playing. The people slump to the earth, exhausted.

Horse that Sings canters over to you.

'Few mortals can refuse the call of the flute,' he says in a lilting voice, like wind in the trees. 'Here,' he says, smiling whimsically, and he hands you his flute.

Note the **centaur flute (CHARISMA +3)** on your Adventure Sheet.

The centaur rides away. Another flute appears in his hands, and the carnival begins again. Exhausted dancers rise to their feet, filled with supernatural energy, to follow their master once more.

Turn to **224**.

523

The shaman's tent is pitched beyond the boundary of the camp, on a patch of ground surrounded by animal skulls. He disdains the use of fire, chewing his meat raw from the bone. When he looks up you notice that his eyes are glassy, his pupils dilated, and you wonder if he has ingested a hallucinogenic potion.

You squat beside him. He acknowledges you with a disinterested grunt. What will you speak to him about?

The bard's song	turn to **424**
The Fane of the Four Winds	turn to **508**
The Rimewater	turn to **458**
Tayang Khan	turn to **344**

524

You are washed up on to a pebble beach. A wall of fog hangs out to sea, encircling the island you have been washed up on in a thick miasma of cloying mist. Inland, it is clear of fog. A hot sun beats down on a hazy, buzzing jungle. A tree-covered mountain rises up out of the vegetation. You have been washed up on the Isle of Mystery.

Turn to **564**.

525

A storm gathers, plunging the day into gloom. A howling wind descends upon you, and the heavens open in a deluge of rain. Thunder and lightning shatter the sky. You cannot see more than a few feet in front of you, and there is nowhere to take shelter. Amid the fury of the storm you fancy to hear voices, calling. Or is it the wind?

Follow the voices   turn to **628**

Huddle down and sit out the storm   turn to **327**

526

Lose the codewords *Almanac*, *Brush* and *Eldritch* if you have them.

You can invest money in multiples of 100 Shards. The guild will buy and sell commodities on your behalf using this money until you return to collect it.

'Don't forget that you can lose money as well,' mutters a sullen merchant who leaves penniless.

> *MONEY INVESTED*

Write the sum you are investing in the box here — or withdraw a sum invested previously. Then turn to **220**.

527

You set your shoulder to the lid and push, straining with all your might. After several seconds it moves slightly, producing a deep scraping noise. A gust of dry air wafts up....

All at once the lid shoots straight up. You stumble forward and find yourself lying across the lap of the casket's dreadful occupant, who is now sitting bolt upright with the heavy stone lid held above his head as though it weighed no more than a plank of wood. He leans his grinning grey face close to yours and speaks in a gravid whisper: 'Despoiler. The gods will give you no merit for such deeds.'

Lose a point of SANCTITY. Reeling from his rank breath, you bolt from the tomb and run headlong across the wintry landscape until you drop from exhaustion. Fortunately, the cadaver has not pursued you. Turn to **226**.

528

When you fit the key into the hole, it is sucked in with a hiss, and disappears. Cross the **pyramid key** off your Adventure Sheet.

The stone slab retracts upward with a rumble. The chamber

beyond is still crawling with stag beetles but the walls have lost their yellow glow. Any equipment that you had to leave here the last time is still there. Note this paragraph down (**528**). You can reclaim your gear. Simply turn to **586**, cross off the stuff you want that is written in the box there, and transfer it to your Adventure Sheet. When you have finished, turn back here.

When you are ready to leave, the slab slams down again, and with the pyramid key gone, seals the chamber once and for all. Turn to **472**.

529

'As you wish,' says the genie. He waves a hand in the air. Bolts of red energy leap from his eyes and seem to burn their way through your brain. You pass out.

When you awake the genie is gone, but you realize you have learned some new tricks. Add one to the attribute of your choice (i.e. CHARISMA, COMBAT, SCOUTING etc), permanently.

Unfortunately for you, you are still drifting aimlessly across the seas. You are out of water, and will soon be dead of thirst.

Roll a die and add one to the score. If the result is higher than your Rank, turn to **459**. If it is less than or equal to your Rank, turn to **318**.

530

You are caught red-handed by alert guards, and it is not long before more have arrived. There is no escape, this time, nor mercy. Summary justice is swiftly carried out. A sign saying 'Thus die all traitors' is slung around your neck. Then you are hung in a cage from the battlements above the Great Gate, to die slowly of starvation, as a warning to the army of the Northern Alliance. Turn to **7**.

531

A merchant is prepared to take you to Yellowport but you need *The War-Torn Kingdom* to travel there. If you have, cross off the 65 Shards and turn to *The War-Torn Kingdom* **10**.

If not, turn back to **141**.

532

The doors are opened by the butler, Kevar. His long white hair is even longer now. Kaschuf himself, tall, strong, and as bald as ever steps forward. 'Haven't I seen you somewhere before? No matter, I'll carve you to pieces, just like all the others!'

Kaschuf goes white with terror when you tell him that you have released his soul from a locket you found on an uncharted island.

Kevar hops from foot to foot in glee and croaks, 'Kaschuf is no longer Deathless! He can be killed! He can be killed!'

'The fight's not over yet, old man,' bellows Kaschuf, as he glares savagely at you. 'I could still win!' Kevar freezes and claps his hand over his mouth.

You must fight.

Kaschuf, COMBAT 8, Defence 8, Stamina 20

If you win, turn to **158**. If you lose, turn to **7**.

533

You examine your charts. The crew are relying on you to navigate the ship safely through Disaster Bay.

Make a SCOUTING roll at Difficulty 14. You can add one to the roll if your crew is good or excellent quality. You can also add one if you have a **mariner's ruttier**.

Successful SCOUTING roll	turn to **471**
Failed SCOUTING roll	turn to **594**

534

She takes you by the hand. You give an involuntary gasp; her touch is so cold it burns. Then the feeling passes. She leads you deep into the earth, to a feasting hall where you are welcomed as one of the honoured dead. If you have the title Chosen One of Nagil, you are given a seat at the god's right hand. If not you are set among the shrouded knights along the tables.

This is the end. You have achieved a glorious fate for any worshipper of the Death God. Now it is time to go back and start afresh with a new character. Erase all ticks and codewords in your Fabled Lands books. You can start at **1** in any of the books in the series, using a character of the appropriate Rank given in the rules.

535

You are travelling across the icy wastes of the northern steppes. To the north, near the Peaks at the Edge of the World, you see a reddish glow reflecting off the snow, in the distance. Could it be the Ruby Citadel?

Investigate the glow	turn to **340**
Go west	turn to **630**
Go east	turn to **15**
Go south	turn to **17**

536

The creature swoops down from its cloud to attack you. Its flickering, coruscating body is hard to strike.

Storm Demon, COMBAT 8, Defence 10, Stamina 15

If you win, turn to **262**. If you lose, turn to **7**.

537

The high priestess, enveloped in ceremonial silks, welcomes you warmly, as the one who retrieved their holy relic. You can stay at the temple if wish, and rest, restoring any lost Stamina points. She can also cure poison and diseases, such as the Blight of Nagil. When you are ready to leave, turn to **58**.

538

Tossing one end of the rope to the bosun and the other to the first mate, you plant yourself directly in the knight's path. Your doughty crewmen immediately see what you have in mind. Rushing to either side, they pull the rope taut so that the lion trips. Its head slams into the planks of the bridge with stunning force and the rider goes sailing through the air overhead to land in a clattering heap. But a moment later he staggers to his feet and woozily draws his sword, still determined to challenge your right to pass.

Sir Leo, COMBAT 8, Defence 20, Stamina 6

Fight him and win	turn to **571**
Retreat to the ship	turn to **191**

539

'You may not pass,' booms the jackal head. It breathes and you are blown like a leaf in the wind, for hundreds of yards. Lose 1-6 Stamina points (the roll of one die).

You pick yourself up. Turn to **266**.

540

Your ship, crew and cargo are lost to the deep, dark sea. Cross them off your Adventure Sheet. Your only thought now is to save yourself. Roll two dice. If the score is greater than your Rank, you are drowned (turn to **7**). If the score is less than or equal to your Rank, you manage to find some driftwood, and make it back to shore. Lose Stamina points equal to the score of one die roll and, if you can survive that, turn to **585**.

541

You stand firm, resolute in your faith. The phantom figure shrinks back, cowed by your divine power.

'I only seek to perform my allotted task, for am I not the Sentinel of the Empire?' it moans, suddenly contrite under your divinely inspired gaze.

'The Shadar empire sank beneath the seas of time a thousand years ago, and you should have gone with it,' you reply.

The phantom seems to hesitate, and then says, 'I see that it is true. Perhaps, at last, I can rest.'

With that, it fades away with a ghostly wail. Instantly, the cold, green flames wink out, and you are left alone in the ruined tower.

Amid the debris you find an old banner, emblazoned with a golden sun, and a green gem worth 100 Shards. Record the codeword *Dispel* and note the **banner of the Shadar**, and 100 Shards on your Adventure Sheet.

You go back the way you came. Turn to **92**.

542

The Nomad's Rest costs you 1 Shard a day. Each day you spend here, you can recover 1 Stamina point if injured, up to the limit of your normal unwounded Stamina score.

You hear a fireside tale about a tomb-robber who tried his luck at looting the City of Ruins, an ancient Shadar capital. He carried a flag or banner of the Shadar, and this was some protection — but not enough, for he was driven quite mad by the gibbering ghosts that are said to inhabit the ruin.

When you are ready, turn to **10**.

543

If you have the codeword *Dirty*, turn to **414**. If not, but you have the codeword *Drop*, turn to **468**. Otherwise read on.

The villa of Avar Hordeth is a white-marbled structure built in the Atticalan style — fortified walls surrounding an inner open courtyard. As you approach, an armed guard stops you at the gate.

`Avar Hordeth is not at home,' he says gruffly, `Go away.'

You have little choice but to do just that — there's not much you can do in broad daylight. Turn to **280**.

544

You have a mission from Orin Telana, commander of the citadel, to assassinate General Beladai. If you want to make the attempt tonight, turn to **396**. If not, you leave the camp — turn to **145**.

545 ☐

If there is a tick in the box, turn to **369** immediately. If not, put a tick there now, and read on.

Thinking fast, you tie the rope between two gnarled stumps of dead marsh trees. The hut hurtles towards you with frightening speed, and an eerie howling fills the air — Gura Goru, spurring her hut onwards. But its legs are caught by the rope, and the whole thing comes crashing to the ground.

A scream of rage spills from the hut, along with a shower of objects — a cooking pot, some rags, firewood and the like.

You find a **cross-staff (SCOUTING +2)** and a **verdigris key**, that fall at your feet. Note them on your Adventure Sheet.

Gura Goru is shrieking at the hut to get up, so you make a run for it while you still can. Turn to **92**.

546

You can either sail straight towards the ghost pirates, and take the offensive (turn to **605**) or call on the gods to repel the undead ship (turn to **662**).

547

The dragon turns the attention of all three heads upon you, as if noticing you for the first time.

'Wait,' it rumbles, bathing you in a blast of warm, sulphurous air, 'I sense that you are indeed blessed. Though not dead. Hmm. Odd. Still, I have my duty.'

The dragon shuffles aside, opening the way to the Stairs of the Land Below the World.

'By the way, once you go through the arch, you cannot get back this way,' adds the celestial dragon.

Descend into the dark	turn to **653**
Go back down the way you came	turn to **684**

548

If you have the codeword *Deathless*, turn to **672**. If not, read on.

The village is called Vodhya. The people stare at you in amazement as you walk into the main square. They seem a pale, unhealthy lot, dogged by some terrible worry, their faces drawn and pinched. Then they pull their furs around them and hurry off, slamming doors and windows, until you are all alone, save for a young boy that gazes at you wide-eyed.

Above the village is a tall hill upon which squats a dark and windswept keep, which dominates the land. You ask the boy what's going on.

He just turns and looks up at the grim, iron-grey keep and whispers dolefully, 'The Lady Nastasya, Kaschuf's got her... and he won't stop hurting us until she promises to marry him. But she won't, no she won't. How could she marry the one who killed her father?'

Leave Vodhya	turn to **398**
Go up to the Keep of Kaschuf	turn to **42**

549

You are washed up on the beaches near the city of Yarimura. With nowhere else to go, you head into the city.

Turn to **10**.

550

You charge the man in black, hoping to bring him down before he uses his staff. But a ball of liquid blackness shoots from the end of his staff towards you, growing larger all the time. It envelops you completely.

In an instant, you are flung through time and space to another part of the world.

Turn to **613**.

551

You are invited to sit at the table and share the food and drink of the dead. It has no taste — or, if any taste at all, it is just the taste of the air in long-sealed tombs. None the less it gives you sustenance. If you are injured, restore your Stamina to its normal unwounded score.

A handsome cadaver beside you leans over to touch your arm. 'It is time you were leaving,' he says in a whisper like dry leaves. 'If you linger too long among us you will join our company for ever.'

You rise and bow to them, giving just a quick respectful glance to the Olympian figure on the throne at the end of the hall. 'My divine lord, ladies, gentlemen... I thank you for your hospitality.'

'Return to the living world now,' resounds the voice of Nagil. 'If you come back to this hall it must be to stay.'

You bow and hurry back to the surface. The bronze doors close behind you without a sound. Turn to **15**.

552

At the top, you find only the large, sprawling ruin of a mountain stronghold. Broken towers and shattered walls are all that is left now. A disconsolate old man appears, blind, and dressed in rags.

'All gone now,' he mutters, 'all gone. It was a city of magicians, until they messed with magics best left untouched by man. Leave while you still can, adventurer.'

Make a MAGIC or SANCTITY roll (your choice as to which) at Difficulty 13.

Successful MAGIC or SANCTITY roll	turn to **502**
Failed MAGIC or SANCTITY roll	turn to **142**

553

The song tells of ancient heroes of the clan. The youths' dance re-enacts those heroes' mightiest deeds. The effect is almost hypnotic, as young men daubed in ritual body-paint leap to and fro above the fire.

If you are a Troubadour, get the codeword *Drape*. If you belong to any other profession the songs mean little to you.

Now turn to **394**.

554

If you are an initiate it costs only 10 Shards to purchase Nai's blessing. A non-initiate must pay 25 Shards. Cross off the money and mark COMBAT in the Blessings box on your Adventure Sheet.

The blessing works by allowing you to try again when you fail a COMBAT roll. It is good for only one reroll. When you use the blessing, cross it off your Adventure Sheet. You can have only one COMBAT blessing at any one time. Once it is used up, you can return to any branch of the temple of Nai to buy a new one.

When you are finished here, turn to **58**.

555

The kelpie turns and counter-charges, sprouting two long, pointed horns from its head.

Kelpie, COMBAT 6, Defence 8, Stamina 12

If you win, turn to **625**. If you lose, turn to **7**.

556

You slip and fall, plunging with a short cry towards the hard icy ground below. It would mean certain doom if not for the fact your fall is broken by a deep snowdrift. As it is you lose 3-18 Stamina points (the roll of three dice); you can subtract 1 from this if you are an initiate of the Three Fortunes.

If still alive, you pick yourself up and decide what to do next.

Climb the cliffs   turn to **221**

Leave   turn to **15**

557

If you have *Into the Underworld*, turn to **484** in this book. If not, but you have *Lords of the Rising Sun*, turn to **297**. If you have neither, but you do have *Over the Blood-Dark Sea*, turn to **316**. If you have none of the above, but you do have *The War-Torn Kingdom*, turn to **261**. If you have none of the books listed, turn to **439**. (Note that all the paragraphs listed above refer to *this* book, *The Plains of Howling Darkness*.)

558

You are at the base of the mountains of the Spine of Harkun, west of the Pass of Eagles. The mountains rise up before you, an impassable barrier. You find a small cave mouth in a cleft of rock.

Enter the cave   turn to **35**

Leave   turn to **145**

559

You scour the land for miles around. Eventually, you spot an owl in the air, which you tell the men to follow.

'Why are we following an owl?' grumbles the mate.

You explain that this particular owl makes its nest in a tree, so there must be a wood nearby. Sure enough, you cross the crest of a hill to find a forest of fir trees, marching north to the Peaks at the Edge of the World.

The men are able to chop enough timber to make repairs, and soon the *Mermaid's Desire* is sea-worthy. They elect you captain. Note the *Mermaid's Desire* on your Ship's Manifest. It is a barque with a capacity of 1 Cargo Unit. The ship has no cargo and the crew quality is poor.

Turn to **342**.

560

You approach the entrance to the Brotherhood of Night, the thieves' guild.

If you are a Rogue, turn to **349**. If not, read on.

'Whaddya want?' growls one of the men lounging on the steps. 'Get lost, or we'll lose you in the harbour, if you get my drift.'

You are clearly unwelcome here. Turn to **633**.

561

Your men are inspired by your brave leadership, and with a bloodthirsty roar, they follow you up the beach. A bitter struggle ensues, a desperate contest fought on slippery rocks and in salty surf. The rain courses down, and lightning flashes across the sky. You come up against a huge, red-bearded giant of a man wielding a massive iron club. You'll have to fight him.

Wrecker, COMBAT 6, Defence 6, Stamina 15

If you win, turn to **658**. If you lose, you're killed, robbed, and thrown into the sea to feed the fishes – turn to **7**.

562

Blue Cap roars angrily, and attacks you with the pickaxe.

Blue Cap, COMBAT 8, Defence 6, Stamina 22

If you lose, turn to **7**. If you win, turn to **248**.

563

Runciman recognizes you as the one who found the Runestone of the Shadar for him. He has no further tasks for you, however, or help to give. Turn to **274**.

564

You are forcing your way through jungle vines, and strange, luxuriant foliage. Steam rises from the moist earth, and brightly coloured birds sing in the trees. The ground begins to rise; you have started to climb the mountain in the middle of the isle.

'Turn back! Turn back!' squawks a large red and gold parrot, before it takes to the air and flies away.

Turn back	turn to **407**
Press on up the mountain	turn to **122**

565

Since Avar Hordeth's unfortunate demise at sea, his villa has fallen to rack and ruin. Everything valuable has been looted.

Turn to **280**.

566

You have no idea what the thing is! Not that it matters much, for anyone can tell it is extremely hostile.

Snake Demon, COMBAT 9, Defence 9, Stamina 18

If you win, turn to **215**. If you lose, turn to **7**.

567

After a while, the stairs retract into the tower, which winks out with an audible pop. It is gone, leaving no traces. Turn to **226**.

568

You have won the favour of Tambu, Great Spirit of the Steppes. Note the title Blessed of Tambu in the Titles box on your Adventure Sheet.

Make another offering	turn to **456**
Leave	turn to **118**

569

The merchant ship, a brigantine, flies the colours of the merchants' guild in Yarimura. Your first mate tells you it used to be a ship in the fleet of Avar Hordeth. Since his death, it seems his ships have gone to the guild. It gives you a wide berth, and sails away. Turn to **236**.

570

You find the remains of a poor wretch who had been left lashed to a rock for the carrion birds to peck at. All that is left when you come along are yellow bones and a rust-coloured patch of dried blood.

If you are a Troubadour, turn to **652**. If not, turn to **52**.

571

The knight has fallen and lies there barely moaning. With luck he
will live. His feline mount gives you a smouldering sidelong look,
growls, and slinks away.

You can take the knight's **sword (COMBAT +2)** and his **heavy
plate (Defence +6)**.

The way is clear, but your men haven't the courage to accompany you further.

'We'll guard your back, skipper,' says the bosun lamely.

Return to the ship	turn to **191**
Press on alone	turn to **467**

572

Erase the codeword *Draw* and gain the codeword *Dove*.

You recognize the stelae as the Shadar Runestone whose runes
Runciman, the chief mage on the Isle of Mystery, asked you to
copy. You perform your task, and leave. Turn to **224**.

573

You rap upon it and the stone slab slides upward, revealing a
yawning, black hole. Two dark figure, blacker than night itself and
wreathed in shadow, jump out. All you can make out are their red,
glowing eyes, and huge silvery grins like crescent moons that split
their shadowy faces. You realize they are trau, delvers in the dark,
the faery goblin-folk of the underworld.

'Ooh, a mortal. What fun!' says one in a deep voice.

If you have some **faery mead**, turn to **245**. If not, turn to **481**.

574

You wander into the Severed Hand inn. Many of the patrons do
indeed seem to have lost their hands — a common punishment for
theft in the city. It goes quiet when you enter, but everyone
quickly returns to their business.

People sit huddled in the shadowy corners of the inn, talking in
low tones.

Approach some locals	turn to **63**
Leave the tavern	turn to **182**

At last you reach end of the stairs. You have come to the flat top of one of the highest peaks of all. Northward is only blackness, the yawning, star filled emptiness of the gulf between the worlds, spoken of only in myth and legend.

Standing before you is something else from legend. It is a dragon of enormous size, with three heads. From its three mouths smoke and flames belch forth into the sky – it was the dragon's triple breath that made you think this peak was a volcano. On the other side of the dragon, you see an archway that frames stairs that descend into the blackness beyond.

One of the dragon's heads turns its lambent amber eyes upon you. Its voice is like an earthquake.

'I am the Celestial Dragon of the North, Son of Great Tambu. None but the blessed may descend the Stairway of the Land Below the World.'

If you have the title Blessed of Tambu, turn to **547**. If not, you can leave, turn to **684**, or attack the dragon, turn to **503**.

576

After a time of aimless drifting, you come out on to the open sea. One day, you spot a bottle bobbing in the waves. You pluck it from the waters, and pop the cork.

To your amazement, a great stream of scarlet smoke roars out of the bottle. The smoke condenses into a huge, fat-bellied genie, wearing a loincloth, and a bejewelled turban. His skin is bright red.

The genie speaks in a rumbling baritone, 'Ah, free at last! Thank you, small one, for freeing me. Now, as is customary in these affairs, I will grant you a wish as a reward. What do you desire?'

Ask to be teleported to Yarimura	turn to **190**
Ask for a king's ransom in gold Shards	turn to **370**
Ask for knowledge of a skill of your choice	turn to **529**

577

Lose 2-12 Stamina points (the roll of two dice). If you are still alive, your courage earns the nomads' respect and they lower their weapons, offering you comradeship.

Turn to **246**.

578

You realize you have made a mistake. The hut hurtles towards you with frightening speed, and an eerie howling fills the air — Gura Goru, spurring her hut onwards. There is nowhere to run to, and its thorned legs batter you to the ground.

Roll two dice and lose that many Stamina points.

If you are killed, turn to **7**. If you still live, Gura Goru races off, laughing cruelly.

Turn to **92**.

579

Blocks of ice are stored in a vast warehouse nearby. A satchel of **rime ice** costs 50 Shards. You cannot carry more than two satchels. If you buy any, cross the money off and add the **rime ice** to your Adventure Sheet.

Go on a tour	turn to **22**
Leave the mine	turn to **320**

580

You are sailing close to Yarimura.

Sail south towards Disaster Bay	turn to **310**
Enter the harbour of Yarimura	turn to **141**
East into the Unbounded Ocean	turn to **415**
Head north into uncharted waters	turn to **333**

581

You put on a burst of speed, diving between the bronze doors an instant before they slam shut. Crouching on the icy ground, you gulp grateful lungfuls of the fresh clean air and listen to the faint pounding of the horde on the other side of the doors.

You stuff the chalice that you stole into your travelling pack. It is worth 1500 Shards; add this sum to your cash.

Then you are jolted to your feet by a deep resonant voice that seems to speak to you out of the cold ground: 'Do not violate my realm again, mortal, unless you wish to abide with me for ever. The next time I'll send one of my handmaidens to greet you.'

You have been warned – by none other than the Lord of Death himself. Now turn to **15**.

582

You wake to the desolate cry of a seagull, calling into the empty skies. You are alone on a rocky island in the middle of the sea. Scattered around are the dead bodies of your crew, looted and left for the birds. Your ship and cargo is gone, and you have been robbed. Lose all the items and money you were carrying with you. Cross them, and your ship, cargo and crew, off your Adventure Sheet. No wonder they call it Disaster Bay!

All is not lost, however. You are marooned, but there is plenty of wood and rigging from the wreck of your ship for you to build a raft. After a day's hard work, you have built a serviceable raft. You push out into the sea. Roll one die.

Score 1 or 2	turn to **422**
Score 3 or 4	turn to **506**
Score 5 or 6	turn to **576**

If there is a tick in the box, turn to **604** immediately. If not, put a tick there now, and read on.

The evening is drawing in and the moon rises, bleeding its light on to the snow. You are huddled around your camp-fire when a man runs at breakneck speed into the firelight. He is a nomad of the steppes, with a pale, wan complexion.

He drops to his knees before you and says, 'Help me! Help me! They have taken her to the top of the pyramid. They will surely kill her.'

Follow him to the pyramid   turn to **454**
Refuse to help   turn to **666**

584

You have come upon the Ruby Citadel. It is a bizarrely structured tower, seemingly carved from a single ruby of gargantuan size. Legend has it that it fell from the skies in the time of the Elder Gods. Some say it was a palace of a minor godling, cast down during the War of the Gods, when Harkun himself was slain, and fell from the heavens. Harkun's body created the world, and his blood the rivers. The citadel glows redly, casting a rosy hue over the snow. It is a beautiful sight.

Enter the Ruby Citadel   turn to **159**
Leave   turn to **535**

585

You are washed up on to the beaches of Tigre Bay. Turn to **669**.

586

You cannot carry any of your possessions, except for any **keys** you might have, which you can just about manage. Nor can you wear any armour. Cross off all your money and possessions (except keys) on your Adventure Sheet and transfer them to the box below.

When you are done, turn to **377**.

587

The crew absolutely refuses to sail into the Unbounded Ocean.

'There's no land out there, and the seas are infested with Demons of the Deep — if we go too far, we'll fall off the edge of the world!' says the first mate.

You have no choice but to reconsider your destination. Turn to **296** and choose again.

588

If you have the codeword *Drizzle*, turn to **437**. If not, read on.

King Nergan asked you to talk to Beladai, and see what assistance you could give him. The guards at the stockade take you to Beladai's tent, a large pavilion of purple silk.

Inside, General Beladai, a tall, grey-haired veteran of many campaigns, is there to meet you. His face is fixed into an expression of determined efficiency, like a granite slab. Around him are the other leaders. Lek, Wing-warrior Chief of the Mannekyn People is a small, purple-furred, bat-winged humanoid. The trau warlord, Marack Mander, squats in a shadowy corner, wreathed in shadows. Olog Khan, a wiry, hawknosed nomad, is leader of the troops of the Horde of the Thousand Winds.

They explain that the citadel is all but invulnerable to their army, as they have no means of breaching the walls.

'You are our only hope,' growls General Beladai. 'A single spy could infiltrate the citadel and open the Great Gate from the inside.'

If you want to take up the mission, turn to **241**. If not, you are shown out.

'Come back if you change your mind,' grunts Beladai.

Turn to **145**.

589

The villa of Avar Hordeth, which you robbed with Luroc Bans, the former nomad turned thief looks as quiet and peaceful as before – except, that is, for the mercenary guards patrolling the grounds in sizeable numbers. It seems Avar Hordeth is taking no chances this time. You can count at least forty guards on patrol.

There is nothing you can do here, so you leave.

Turn to **280**.

590

The creature wanders off mournfully. If you have some **uncanny salts**, turn to **303**. If not, you cannot find a way through the panel, so you return to the surface. Turn to **320**.

591

No sooner have you left the square than you are set upon by a typical local – a huge, hulking bear of a man, his breath sour with ale. He wields a large cudgel, and is intent on robbing you. You must fight.

Mugger, COMBAT 5, Defence 6, Stamina 10

If you win, turn to **322**. If you lose, turn to **169**.

592

You remember the request made of you by the spectre of Tayang Khan, one fearful night at sea on the Violet Ocean. You shout to the four winds that Tayang Khan was foully slain at sea.

An eerie silence falls for a brief moment, and you fancy to hear faint laughter on the wind.

Erase the codeword *Cull* and turn to **683**.

593

You manage to find your way to the cavern from which the trau teleport tunnels lead to different parts of Harkuna. The plaques above the tunnels are carved with trau runes, but they are protected by sorcery, making them hard to read. You try to decipher them once more.

Make a MAGIC roll at Difficulty 13.

Successful MAGIC roll	turn to **495**
Failed MAGIC roll	turn to **233**

594

There is a sudden ominous grating sound, as the keel of your ship scrapes against some rocks. Then you are thrown violently forward as the ship comes to a dead stop.

'We've run aground, cap'n,' says the mate, 'We'll have to wait for high tide to float us off.'

The ship has caught itself on a sandbar.

Disembark, and explore the sandbar	turn to **166**
Wait for high tide and sail on	turn to **471**

595

What little game there is to be had in the area is quickly snared by the nomads. You will need all your skill if you are to avoid going hungry tonight. Make a SCOUTING roll at a Difficulty of 16. Success means that you catch a few voles and can make a stew. Failure means you are left with nothing to eat and must lose 1 Stamina point owing to hunger and cold.

If you survive the night, turn to **65**.

596

The guards turn you away. A continuous stream of carts, pack animals and the like, however, goes in and out of the citadel, carrying supplies. You could approach a trader and try to bribe him into letting you hide amid his wares.

Try bribery	turn to **611**
Leave	turn to **400**

597

Desperately, you grab on to the branch. It takes all your strength to haul yourself out of the marsh and on to dry land, where you lie, exhausted and gasping for breath. When you look back, the light has gone, and in the drawing darkness, you cannot even see the rock from which it glowed. Turn to **92**.

598

The tunnel is circular. Permafrost makes the earthern walls harder than stone. About halfway along the tunnel there is a side-passage with stones heaped across it.

Unblock the side passage	turn to **347**
Press on down the main tunnel	turn to **487**

599

You manage to keep a close tab on the rivers, and navigate your way across the plain.

Head west to Tigre Bay	turn to **669**
Head north east to the pyramid	turn to **472**
Go south to the Rimewater	turn to **320**
Head east into the plains	turn to **281**
Go south east into the plains	turn to **29**

600

You can bank money with the merchants' guild simply by writing the sum you wish to leave in the box here. (Remember to cross it off your Adventure Sheet.) It can be useful to have money banked – if you are ever robbed, your money in the bank won't be touched and you may have to use your banked money to pay off a ransom, if you ever get captured. If you have banked any money with the guild in another book in the Fabled Lands series, add it now to this box and erase it from the other book.

MONEY BANKED

To withdraw money from your account, simply transfer it from the box to your Adventure Sheet. The guild charges 10% on any withdrawals. (So if you withdrew 50 Shards, for example, the guild would deduct 5 Shards as its cut. Round fractions in the guild's favour.)

Return to city centre	turn to **10**
Paying a ransom	turn to **501**

601

Luroc is not happy with your decision. 'You lily-livered coward – I don't need the likes of you anyway!' he hisses before turning tail and disappearing into the shadows of the night.

You hurry off to the villa. Avar Hordeth is most interested to hear your story, and his guards catch Luroc and Floril red-handed in his vault. They are hauled off in chains, but not before Luroc curses you as a 'treacherous rattlesnake' and swears revenge.

Hordeth, a thick-set, sly-eyed man, is all smiles. He rewards you with 250 Shards, and offers you a room in the villa.

'You can stay here whenever you like, for free!' he says.

Gain the codeword *Drop*. If you ever return to the villa, you will find a place to store your equipment and to rest.

For now, you leave. Turn to **280**.

602

You are able to get your bearings. You sail the ship westward until you spot land. It is the coastline of the Great Steppes, and the harbour city of Yarimura. Turn to **580**.

603

The redcaps lie dead at your feet. You find that one was carrying a small sack. Inside you find a **Shadar scroll** and some **faery mead**. The scroll is mundane, but may have some value to a collector of Shadar antiquities. Note them on your Adventure Sheet.

The rest of the night passes peacefully. Turn to **144**.

604

The running footsteps are those of a rabid wolf. It leaps at you, frothing at the mouth, intent on ripping out your throat.

Rabid Wolf, COMBAT 7, Defence 5, Stamina 6

If you win, you get a wolf pelt. If you lose, turn to **7**. When you are finished, turn to **666**.

605 ☐

If there is a tick in the box, turn to **335** immediately. If not, put a tick there now, and read on.

The crew nervously turns the ship about. You head straight for the ghost ship. As you draw nearer, it seems to fade away, dissolving around you as you cut through its position. It was just an illusion, presumably set here to scare people away from the Isle of Mystery. Your men give sighs of relief. They eye you with new respect – your courage has inspired them.

If the crew quality is currently poor, you can upgrade it to average; an average quality crew can be upgraded to good; and a good quality crew can be upgraded to excellent. Note the change on your Ship's Manifest, if applicable. If the crew is already of excellent quality, there is no further improvement.

When you are ready, turn to **296**.

606

Gain the codeword *Deliver*.

Beladai's men are fighting their way into the courtyard, but resistance is stiff, as the garrison reinforces the gate rapidly. A dozen soldiers rush up the stairs of the winch-house to try to close the gates. You hold them off long enough for Beladai's army to get into the citadel. It is not long before the garrison is overwhelmed completely, and forced to surrender. The citadel is taken.

Turn to **61**.

607

You wake up to find yourself lying on a road, near the city of Yarimura. Two trau have just heaved you up out of a hole in the ground.

'Bored of that human now,' says one of them, as they disappear back below the earth, filling the hole as they go.

A farmer, and his family are standing there, looking at you in stunned disbelief. You learn from them that several months have passed since you were kidnapped by the trau.

Cross off all your possessions and money on your Adventure Sheet but restore any lost Stamina points. Any blessings you had are also lost. Instead, you are carrying a **wolf pelt**, a few gems worth 75 Shards (note the cash), **leather armour (Defence +1)**, some **selenium ore**, and a **verdigris key**. Although you have lost one point of SANCTITY, permanently, you have gained one point of MAGIC.

When you are ready, turn to **280**.

608

Your ship, crew and cargo are lost to the deep, dark sea. Cross them off your Ship's Manifest.

Your only thought now is to save yourself. Roll two dice. If the score is greater than your Rank, you are drowned – turn to **7**. If the score is less than or equal to your Rank, you manage to find some driftwood, and make it back to shore. Lose Stamina points equal to the score of one die roll and, if you can survive that, turn to **549**.

609

Despite their vast size the doors are so closely fitted that you could not get a hair between them. It goes without saying that they are too heavy to shift, and your strongest blow resounds leadenly without leaving a dent.

Climb the cliffs	turn to **221**
Go on your way	turn to **15**

610

You find the remains of the snake demon that you slew here. Its rotting flesh adds to the stench of decay that permeates the tomb.

At the far end of the hall, you find a large plaque which is inscribed: 'Here lies Xinoc the Priest-King, exalted under heaven.' There is a small hole in the plaque.

If you have an **obsidian key**, turn to **434**. If not, there is nothing you can do but leave.

Visit the Cave of Bells	turn to **657**
Visit the Vault of the Shadar	turn to **107**
Leave the City of Ruins	turn to **266**

611

You approach a fat fellow on a cart laden with barrels, at the far end of the queue waiting to enter the citadel. He wants 75 Shards to hide you in a barrel. If you haven't the cash, or don't want to pay that much, you'd better leave – turn to **400**.

If you have, the merchant becomes very agitated when he realizes you will actually go through with it. He eyes the guards nervously. You will have to convince him.

Make a CHARISMA roll at Difficulty 14.

Successful CHARISMA roll	turn to **36**
Failed CHARISMA roll	turn to **112**

612

'The Fane of the Four Winds – that is to be found in the domain of the Horde of the Thundering Skies. But it is a sacred to Tambu, Khan of the Endless Blue, and you must not offend the guardian spirits of the fane. Those initiates who wish to win Tambu's favour make sacrifice there.'

With that he falls silent, indicating that the audience is at an end.

If you have the codeword *Cull*, turn to **463**. If not, turn to **33**.

613

You spin through a yawning blackness, speckled with stars, and then find yourself falling through the air. You hit the ground with a crash. Lose 1-6 Stamina points (the roll of one die).

If you still live, you get up and look around. It appears to be the western coast of the steppes. Turn to **669**.

614

The temple of Nai is a sturdy, low blockhouse. Nai is the god of earthquakes and of ferocity in battle.

Inside there is a huge idol of Nai, as a mighty warrior, shooting his Arrow of Earthquakes from his bow, the Shatterer of Worlds. The idol is hollow bronze, and the priests of Nai climb inside during important festivals. Using huge metal hammers they create a thunderous booming in honour of their god. As the bringer of earthquakes, Nai is to be placated rather than worshipped, but many warriors pray to him for aid in hand-to-hand combat.

Become an initiate of Nai	turn to **267**
Renounce his worship	turn to **427**
Seek a blessing	turn to **554**
Leave the temple	turn to **58**

615

In the chaos, you manage to make it out of the camp alive. Turn to **218**.

616

The man in the black mask introduces himself as Lochos Veshtu of Aku, Master Knave of the Brotherhood in Yarimura. To join the brotherhood you have to pass a test.

'If you can sneak into the private bedchamber at the palace of Lord Kumonosu, the Daimyo of Yarimura, you will have proved your worthiness to join us,' he says.

`And what do I have to steal?' you ask.

`Oh, nothing. That would be rather — unwise. Just prove that you are capable of getting in there unseen — that will suffice.'

`But how will you know whether I've done it or not?'

`We'll know, believe me, we'll know,' he replies enigmatically. `Return when you have done as I ask.'

You are shown out. Record the codeword *Dare*.

Turn to **633**.

617

You manage to evade the worst of their assault, but several jagged stone teeth gash your arm. Lose 1-6 Stamina points (the roll of one die). If you still live, turn to **172**.

618

If you have the codeword *Discover*, turn to **537**. If not, but you have the codeword *Double*, turn to **105**. If you have neither codeword, read on.

The high priestess is covered from head to toe in bright white silks — all you can see are her eyes, like twin orbs of amber. She tells you that the mirror of the Sun Goddess, a holy relic of the temple, has been stolen. She believes it has fallen into the hands of a steppe nomad, one of the Horde of the Thundering Skies, and asks that you retrieve it for them. In return, the temple will reward you.

`Only a priest is worthy enough to handle the mirror,' she adds.

If you want to take up the mission, record the codeword *Double*.

You leave her. Turn to **89**.

619

You are in between the Gemstone Hills and the Citadel of Velis Corin. Once a huge army was encamped here, the army of the Northern Alliance, but now it has gone.

Go south to the citadel	turn to **308**
North to the Gemstone Hills	turn to **426**
West into the plains	turn to **668**
North west into the plains	turn to **234**

620

You tie the rope to a tree-trunk, and climb down. The rope gets you to a part of the mountain you can traverse, but you have to leave it behind.

Cross the **rope** off your Adventure Sheet. You think you are in the mountains of the Spine of Harkun. Turn to **100**.

621

To renounce the worship of Molhern, you must pay 40 Shards to the priesthood by way of compensation.

The sorcerer-priest shrugs his shoulders. 'As you wish — turn your back on knowledge, it's only the road to power, after all,' he comments.

Do you want to change your mind? If you are determined to renounce your faith, pay the 40 Shards and delete Molhern from the God box on your Adventure Sheet.

When you have finished here, turn to **274**.

622

The wreck is the tattered remnants of an Uttakin trader. Washed up nearby is some of its cargo. If you have a ship docked in Tigre Bay, you can fetch some of your crew, and take whatever cargo you can fit on board your own ship. If you haven't got a ship here, you can't carry the cargo — turn to **669**.

☐ Metals   ☐ Minerals   ☐ Timber

Each time you take a unit of cargo, tick the relevant box. If a box is already ticked, then you took that cargo the last time you were here. Note any cargo on the Ship's Manifest.

Head inland	turn to **669**
Board your ship	turn to **336**

623

As you step up to the arch of the tunnel, you notice that the air in the entrance shimmers with a bluish light. As you pass through it, you feel a momentary sense of dislocation. You travel upwards for hours, until you emerge through a hole in snow-covered ground. Turn to **472**.

624

You have come to the platform above a celestial harbour, the entrance to the underworld. A silver barge is moored here.

If you want to board the silver barge, it will take you to the celestial harbour below. Turn to *Into the Underworld* **199**.

Your only other way of getting out of here is a means of teleportation. Otherwise, you will die – turn to **7**.

625

Record the codeword *Drink*.

You are about to finish the creature off when it changes shape into a small, furry fellow with webbed hands and feet, and a thick, heavy tail. It drops to its knees, begging for mercy.

'Wait!' it cries. 'Spare me and I will give you my treasure.'

'Where is it?' you demand.

'In a sunken grotto beneath the river. I will go and fetch it, if it pleases you, my lord,' it says, grovellingly.

Agree	turn to **162**
Kill it	turn to **701**

626

Luroc leads you to the back of the villa. After one of the patrols has gone past, he throws his grappling hook, muffled with cloth, up on to the rooftop. He clambers up the rope like a monkey, and sits on the gable, waiting for you to follow.

Make a THIEVERY roll at Difficulty 12.

Successful THIEVERY roll	turn to **66**
Failed THIEVERY roll	turn to **104**

627

As you draw nearer to the hill, dozens more rise up from behind the crest of a low mound. At the sight of you they give a roar of blood-lust and charge! There are so many of them, that you have no choice but to flee for your life.

Roll one die and add one. If the result is less than or equal to your Rank, turn to **460**.

If it is higher, turn to **180**.

You struggle through the sleet and rain, pursuing the voice. Suddenly, something explodes at your feet, showering you with hot particles of molten ore. Lose 1 Stamina point.

You look up to see a man-shaped creature of greenish, flickering light, flying through the air on a storm cloud. Its eyes are burning orbs of blue fire, and it is hurling lumps of molten metal at you. It laughs wildly, a sound like pealing thunder.

Make a SANCTITY roll at Difficulty 14.

Successful SANCTITY roll   turn to **700**

Failed SANCTITY roll   turn to **536**

<h1 style="text-align:center">629</h1>

You realize you are marooned on the Isle of Mystery. The chances of being picked up by a passing ship are remote, considering the fog bank that surrounds the isle. You have only one option — building a raft. There are plenty of materials at hand, and after a few days of hard work, you have built a serviceable raft. You push out into the waters.

Roll one die.

Score 1 or 2	turn to **422**
Score 3 or 4	turn to **506**
Score 5 or 6	turn to **576**

<h1 style="text-align:center">630</h1>

This far north, the days are short, and the nights long. Everywhere, the snow stretches away like a bright white blanket. To the north, the snow rises up, clinging to the flanks of the Peaks at the Edge of the World. Roll two dice.

Score 2-5	A tunnel in the snow	turn to **278**
Score 6-7	No event	turn to **226**
Score 8-12	A tower in the air	turn to **385**

<h1 style="text-align:center">631</h1>

You find a poor shipwrecked sailor, clinging to a piece of driftwood. Unfortunately, he has expired — still holding on even in death. It seems he was once a captain. You find his log, the last entry of which reads: 'We set sail today with a good wind behind us. I am worried, however, that we couldn't afford to buy a blessing from the temple of Alvir and Valmir.'

You sail on. Turn to **236**.

632

You try to blow the right note. Make a CHARISMA roll at Difficulty 13. Add one to the roll if you are a Troubadour.

Successful CHARISMA roll	turn to **329**
Failed CHARISMA roll	turn to **464**

633

The streets are a maze of smoky alleys and dark passages built around a central square. The square contains a hulking mansion of dilapidated stone. A large door, with several dodgy-looking cut-throats loitering around outside, has a banner hanging over it that reads: Brotherhood of the Night.

Around the square, Thieves' Kitchen is divided into three areas: rough, very rough, and extremely rough!

Visit the brotherhood	turn to **560**
Head for the rough area	turn to **591**
Enter the very rough area	turn to **494**
Go to the extremely rough area	turn to **448**
Leave	turn to **182**

634

The fishman puts his spear down, and all three of them squat down around you, and lay out various wares in front of you. It is obvious they wish to trade! They speak with bubbly squeaks and clicks that you cannot understand but sign language is enough for both parties.

They are offering two **ink sacs**, one **mariner's ruttier**, and one **magic trident (COMBAT +2)**. They will accept in exchange **bags of pearls, silver nuggets** and **smoulder fish**, one for each. Simply delete one of the items from your sheet and add the one you want. When you're finished, or if you don't have any of the items they are interested in, the creatures leave, diving into the waters. You return to your ship and crew. High tide comes, refloating your ship, and you sail on. Turn to **471**.

635

Cross off 10 Shards. The old woman tosses some dirty old bones into a wooden bowl. She scrutinizes them and then fixes you with a beady stare. 'Go to the High King's Seat. You will find your answer there!' she rasps. You leave the wood. Turn to **280**.

636

You are traversing the barren windswept peaks at the very rim of the world. To the south is the bleak vista of the steppes; north will take you to a realm only spoken of in myths.

Go north	turn to **362**
Go south	turn to **164**

637

Molhern is the god of knowledge. Here on the island, the mages worship an aspect of the god called Molhern Magister, whose domain is the magical arts.

Most of the mages of Sokara and Golnir reject the gods. Here, a peculiar sect of mages has embraced the worship of Molhern. The temple is a single spire reaching skyward, with a great eye painted on its topmost pinnacle. A sorcerer-priest welcomes you to the temple.

Become an initiate of Molhern	turn to **517**
Renounce his worship	turn to **621**
Seek a blessing	turn to **384**
Leave the temple	turn to **274**

638

You are crawling in the grass near the general's tent when you trigger a magical trap. A circle of black dust has been spread around the tent – as soon as your skin comes into contact with the dust, it begins to glow with a bright yellow light. You are instantly spotted by the guards and captured.

The punishment for spies and assassins is swift and immediate: death by hanging. or 'kicking Nagil's jig' as the expression goes. Turn to **7**.

639

He embraces you and offers you a strip of jerky. You realize that, although these nomads do not speak any language you've ever heard, they recognize the word fineitri as indicative of friendship. Turn to **246**.

640

The tall hill where the manbeasts had their lair is deserted now. Since you killed Chizoka of the Black Pagoda, their evil master, they have dwindled away because of their lack of leadership. There is nothing else here.

Climb down to the shoreline	turn to **688**
Go west to Fort Mereth	*The War-Torn Kingdom* **299**
Go west to Fort Estgard	*The War-Torn Kingdom* **472**
Go west to Fort Brilon	*The War-Torn Kingdom* **259**

641

Your offering is rejected. Tambu is displeased! Lose a blessing (your choice), if you have one. You can keep the +1 item.

Make another offering	turn to **456**
Leave	turn to **118**

642

A darkening of the heavens heralds the gathering of the storm. Rain is swept in sheets over your ship, and the waves rise and fall inexorably, lifting you up and then dashing you down. Strangely, the fog that surrounds the Isle of Mystery is not dispelled by the high winds.

If you have a blessing of Safety from Storms, you can ignore the storm. Cross off your blessing and turn **580**. Otherwise the storm hits with full fury. Roll one die if your ship is a barque, two dice if it is a brigantine, or three dice if a galleon. Add 1 to the roll if you have a good crew; add 2 if you have an excellent crew.

Score 1-3	Ship sinks	turn to **608**
Score 4-5	The mast splits	turn to **489**
Score 6-20	You weather the storm	turn to **580**

643

Grasslands – an infinite sea of flat plains. You begin to dream of rolling hills, and cities awash with people. Here there is only desolation. Roll two dice.

Score 2-5	A beguiling flute	turn to **680**
Score 6-7	No event	turn to **224**
Score 8-12	A ring of stones	turn to **84**

644

You tell Orin Telana about the tunnels you have mapped that lead through the Spine of Harkun, thus outflanking the Pass of Eagles. He is amazed at the news. He decides to send troops through the tunnels, to ambush Beladai's army in the flank.

'As soon as we hear that you have killed Beladai, we will attack. Not only will we catch them by surprise, and leaderless, but our assault will give you a chance to escape.'

Erase the codeword *Deep* and gain the codeword *Dim* instead. Now turn to **152**.

645

A darkening of the heavens heralds the gathering storm. A ferocious wind sweeps the rain in sheets over your ship, and the waves rise and fall inexorably, lifting you up, and then dashing you down.

If you have the blessing of Alvir and Valmir, which confers Safety from Storms, you can ignore the storm. Cross off your blessing and turn to **533**.

Otherwise the storm hits with full fury. Roll one die if your ship

is a barque, two dice if it is a brigantine, or three dice if it is a
galleon. Add 1 to the roll if you have a good crew; add 2 if you
have an excellent crew.

Score 1-3	Dashed against rocks	turn to **288**
Score 4-5	The mast splits	turn to **358**
Score 6-20	You weather the storm	turn to **533**

646

You have come to the long hall, painted with murals of the life of
Xinoc the Priest-King. At the far end, the archway is completely
sealed with a solid block of stone. Beyond it is the chamber in
which you had to leave your equipment when you were magically
shrunken. From this side, you notice a small triangular hole in the
block. If you have a **pyramid key**, turn to **528**. If not, you leave.
Turn to **472**.

647

Throughout a short day the sun has hovered in the west like a
guttering candle, throwing long deep gullies of shadow across the

bleak landscape. Now it dips lower, grazing the horizon, and frost starts to speckle the ground.

In the gathering twilight you see a band of nomads about four hundred strong. They ride on beasts that at a distance resemble bulls, but as they get closer you see their muzzles are like broad hairy parodies of human faces.

The outriders dismount, glaring at you. You see the nomads' distrust of strangers in their eyes. They plant themselves between you and their wagons. Then, jabbing the ground with their spears, they start to chant a shrill song.

'We are making the koa-kaon — the ceremony of marking the borders of our camp site,' growls one of them. 'Begone, outlander!'

To convince them to let you remain with them during the night you must make a CHARISMA roll at Difficulty 15 (or Difficulty 13 if you are a Wayfarer).

Successful CHARISMA roll	turn to **474**
Failed CHARISMA roll (or don't try)	turn to **595**

648

If you have the codeword *Double*, turn to **189** immediately. If not, read on.

The dead nomad has red blotches all over his face and his eyes have been pecked clean by the birds.

Search him   turn to **332**

Leave him   turn to **698**

649

'Once it was a great gathering place for the Golden Ones, the people called the Shadar. Our people never go there now, for it is cursed, the abode of ghosts and spectres. Even Tambu himself shuns it.'

With that he falls silent, indicating that the audience is at an end. Turn to **33**.

650

You explain that you have an urgent message for Lochos Veshtu, the head of the brotherhood here in Yarimura from The Master of Shadows, the head of the brotherhood in Aku.

You are shown in to see Lochos, who stares at you enigmatically from behind the shiny black mask he wears. You recite the message you memorized though you don't know its meaning. Lochos understands though and he seems agitated. He thanks you, however, and rewards you with 500 Shards.

Erase the codeword *East*.

You leave the brotherhood. Turn to **633**.

651

You have tackled difficult climbs before. Now you know the meaning of impossibility. The rock here is as smooth as polished steel.

Make a SCOUTING roll at a Difficulty of 21; you can add 1 to the roll if you possess either a **rope** or **climbing gear**.

Successful SCOUTING roll   turn to **70**

Failed SCOUTING roll   turn to **399**

652

Musing on the victim's unknowable crime and the reasons for such harsh punishment, you compose a ballad which you later sing to a family of nomads. They are so moved that they give you shelter, food and drink for as long as you like. Restore your Stamina to its normal unwounded score if you were injured, then turn to **52**.

653

You have incurred the displeasure of Tambu, for it is his decree that only the dead shall pass through the arch. Erase the title Blessed of Tambu from the Titles box.

You descend stairs of shining black marble that lead down to a platform below.

Behind you, the stairs retract into the sheer surface of the Peaks at the Edge of the World as you descend, cutting off your route back.

Turn to **195**.

654

The hut heaves itself out of the mire with a horrible sucking sound, and a voice, cracked and gnarled with ancient evil, shrills at you from inside, 'I'll teach you to disturb my rest, impudent one!'

Spiked thorns spring forth from the jointed legs of the hut as it begins to lumber towards you.

If you have some **rope**, turn to **545**. Otherwise, turn to **578**.

655

Gain the codeword *Deliver*.

Beladai's men are fighting their way into the courtyard, but resistance is stiff, as the garrison reinforces the gate rapidly. But then, many of the soldiers have to be sent to the other side of the citadel. Beladai's men have moved through the tunnels you discovered, and are attacking the citadel from the rear. It is not long before the garrison is overwhelmed completely, and forced to surrender. The citadel is taken.

Turn to **61**.

656

As you step up to the arch of the tunnel, you notice that the air in the entrance shimmers with a bluish light. As you pass through it, you feel a momentary sense of dislocation. You continue on for hours, until you come to a ladder leading upward to a manhole cover.

Turn to *Over the Blood-Dark Sea* **716**. If you haven't got that book yet, turn to **495** and choose again.

657

The Cave of Bells is, in fact, a cathedral of great size. Inside its cavernous interior hang dozens of huge bronze bells. All the bells are etched with Shadar Runes; they have names such as The Thunderer, Knell of Doom, Ringer-in-Darkness and so on.

If you have the codeword *Egret*, turn to **704**. Otherwise choose from the following options:

Ring a bell at random	turn to **68**
Visit the Vault of the Shadar	turn to **107**
Visit the Crypt of Kings	turn to **298**
Leave the City of Ruins	turn to **266**

658

Your opponent falls to your superior combat skills. You join the fray, and soon it becomes clear that the wreckers are losing, caught out by the ferocity and excellence of your attack. They fight to the last man, knowing that capture means execution – the law shows no mercy to criminals.

'Worse than pirates, these scum!' yells your first mate, as he hammers a wrecker with a belaying pin.

Afterwards you take stock. Your ship and its cargo are lost for ever – cross them off your Adventure Sheet.

Moored on the other side of the island, however, is the wrecker's ship. It is only a barque but it will do. Note it on your Adventure Sheet, and rename if it you want: it is currently called Scavenger. It has a capacity of 1 Cargo Unit but no cargo is loaded. You find some other things of worth on board, however: a chest which contains 100 Shards and a **sextant (SCOUTING +3)**.

Also, the battle has improved the morale and experience of your crew. You can upgrade Crew Quality one level. A poor quality crew becomes average, an average quality crew becomes good, and a good quality crew becomes excellent. There is no change for an excellent quality crew. Note the crew with the barque on the Ship's Manifest.

Afterwards, you prepare to set sail. You have a new ship, but you still have the problem of navigating Disaster Bay. Where do you go from here?

Turn to **533**.

659

You will have to fight them. Treat them as one opponent.

Undead Warriors, COMBAT 8, Defence 7, Stamina 16

If you win, turn to **78**. If you lose, turn to **7**.

660

The camp is huge. Nomad warriors, winged Mannekyn People, soldiers of the king of Sokara and, at night only, many trau, rub shoulders here.

It is an easy matter to get into the camp – you are one among many attracted to the economic opportunity an army represents.

At the centre of the camp is a wooden stockade, where General Beladai and the other leaders of the army have their tents. This is well guarded.

There are plenty of armourers and weaponsmiths here, buying and selling for the army.

Armour	*To buy*	*To sell*
Leather (Defence +1)	50 Shards	45 Shards
Ring mail (Defence +2)	100 Shards	90 Shards
Chain mail (Defence +3)	200 Shards	180 Shards
Splint armour(Defence +4)	400 Shards	360 Shards
Plate armour (Defence +5)	800 Shards	720 Shards
Heavy plate (Defence +6)	–	1440 Shards

Weapons (sword, axe, etc)	*To buy*	*To sell*

Without COMBAT bonus	50 Shards	40 Shards
COMBAT bonus +1	250 Shards	200 Shards
COMBAT bonus +2	500 Shards	400 Shards
COMBAT bonus +3	—	800 Shards

After making any purchases or sales, if you have the codeword *Dread*, turn to **544**. If not, but you have the codeword *Assault*, turn to **588**. Otherwise, there is nothing else to do but leave the camp. Turn to **145**.

661

They torture you until you confess everything. They learn that you are the King's Champion and the assassin of Marloes Marlock, Governor of Yellowport. Retribution is swift, and you are executed. Turn to **7**.

662

You raise your arms, and call upon the power of the gods to dispel this travesty of life, this evil ship of ghosts. Unfortunately, your efforts have no effect whatsoever. In fact, the spectral sailors seem more determined than ever to plunder your ship.

A wave of fear seems to emanate from the ghost ship, terrifying you and your crew. Without waiting for your orders, your men take the ship about and flee. Turn to **492**.

663

You step into the darkness. It is much colder here, a marrow-freezing, bitter, biting cold that reaches into your chest with talons of frosty iron and squeezes your heart.

You must have a **lantern** or **candle** to proceed, otherwise it is too dark and you must turn back — turn to **22**.

If you have a light source available, you press on into a maze of tunnels.

Make a SCOUTING roll at Difficulty 13.

Successful SCOUTING roll	turn to **273**
Failed SCOUTING roll	turn to **140**

664

The nomads hastily string their bows and have a little sport. There is little or no cover on the barren plain, and you are punctured by several arrows before you are out of range. Roll four dice and subtract your armour's Defence bonus (if you have any armour); the total is the number of Stamina points you lose.

If you are still alive, turn to **52**.

665

If you have the title Hatamoto, turn to **256**. If not, read on.

You are turned away from the palace gates. Only members of the White Spear Clan are allowed within. Turn to **10**.

666

The sun is sucked below the horizon, casting its wan rays across the flat and desolate steppes. You camp for the night. If you have a **wolf pelt**, the fur helps to keep you warm. If you do not, lose 1 Stamina from the cold.

You need to hunt for food. Make a SCOUTING roll at Difficulty 11. If you succeed, you find a wild hare to eat. If you fail, you go hungry and must lose 1 Stamina point.

Go north	turn to **472**
West to the rivers	turn to **91**
Go south	turn to **29**
Go east	turn to **383**

667

Luroc is not happy with your decision. 'You lily-livered coward. I don't need the likes of you anyway!' he hisses before turning tail and disappearing into the shadows of the night.

You return to the city. Turn to **10**.

668

You are travelling across the plains. To the south lie the mountains of the Spine of Harkun, with white-peaked Sky Mountain towering above the rest.

Night falls, and you make camp.

The plains are flat and desolate, and you need to hunt for food. Make a SCOUTING roll at Difficulty 11. If you succeed, you find a grouse to eat. If you fail, you go hungry and must lose 1 Stamina point.

If you still live, the new day dawns. Sky Mountain casts its morning shadow over you.

Go west	turn to **266**
Go east	turn to **145**
Go north	turn to **44**
Climb up Sky Mountain	turn to **175**

669

You are on the rocky, windswept coast of Tigre Bay. Ice floes litter the bay, and the sky is grey and as cold as iron. You spot the wrecked timbers of a ship, washed up on the cruel rocks.

If you have a ship docked in Tigre Bay, and want to put out to sea, turn to **336**. Otherwise, you can:

Investigate the wreck	turn to **181**
Head east into the river plain	turn to **91**
Head south east to the Rimewater	turn to **320**

670

You have a mission from General Beladai of the Northern Alliance. Your job is to open the gates of the citadel. If you want to try now, turn to **498**. If not, turn to **152**.

671

'At night, it is cold enough to freeze your blood. Always take good furs,' he mutters. 'Be prepared for hard hunting. Do not make an enemy of the nomads – any nomad! But most of all, do not offend Great Tambu.'

With that he falls silent, indicating that the audience is at an end. Turn to **33**.

672

Vodhya is thriving under the benign rule of Duchess Nastasya, whom you freed from the evil clutches of Kaschuf. The villagers welcome you as their saviour. You can stay here and restore any lost Stamina points.

Duchess Nastasya will also see to it that you are cured of any poison or disease you may be suffering from, such as the Blight of Nagil.

You can also get a blessing from the local priestess at no cost. Mark SCOUTING in the Blessings box on your Adventure Sheet. The blessing works by allowing you to try again when you fail a SCOUTING roll. It is good for only one reroll. When you use the blessing, cross it off your Adventure Sheet. You can have only one SCOUTING blessing at any one time.

When you ready to leave, turn to **398**.

673

You drop anchor and take a small party of men ashore in the row-boat. Climbing a beach of flinty shingle, you see a number of caves set into the cliff face.

Enter a cave	turn to **6**
Press on inland	turn to **41**

674

You sneak through the shadows of the night, to make it to the courtyard at the gates. On either side of the massive steel doors, stairways spiral upward to the heavy stone towers that flank the gates. The winch-house is inside the tower on the right.

You crawl up the stairs, unseen, until you reach the winch-house. Inside, there are huge cogs, ropes and levers for operating the doors. Two guards are on duty; you will have to get rid of them silently.

Make a COMBAT roll at Difficulty 15.

Successful COMBAT roll	turn to **119**
Failed COMBAT roll	turn to **530**

675

The snapping jaws bite off your head with clinical precision. Your headless corpse flops to the ground. Turn to **7**.

676

You camp for the night. If you have a **wolf pelt**, the fur helps to keep you warm. If you do not, lose 1 Stamina point because of the cold.

You need to hunt for food. Make a SCOUTING roll at Difficulty 11. If you succeed, you find a snow-hare to eat. If you fail, you go hungry and must lose 1 Stamina point.

If you still live, the next day a thick mist has sprung up over the River of Destiny to your west.

West into the mist	turn to **91**
Head north	turn to **281**
Head east	turn to **118**
Head south	turn to **643**

677

You try to wrest it off your head, but the cursed thing has attached itself to you somehow. Tendrils of something horrible extrude themselves from the inside of the helmet and bore through your skull into your brain.

Everything goes dark. Turn to **7**.

678

The rukh is defeated at last. Inside the nest, you see the remains of a previous victim. In a satchel, you find a **silver flute (CHARISMA +2)**, and 100 Shards. There are also several rukh eggs, but they are too large to carry.

You now have the problem of getting back to earth from this remote peak. If you have some **rope**, turn to **620**. If not, you realize you are trapped, for the nest is set at the top of a pinnacle of rock. You will starve to death here – turn to **7**.

679

You run for the doors, but you are struck by several large chunks. Lose 3-18 Stamina points (the roll of three dice). Your armour helps – subtract its Defence rating from the total.

If you are dead, turn to **7**. If you still live, you stagger towards the exit, hoping not to be hit again. Turn to **441**.

680

You meet a troupe of people, marching through the steppes. There are nomads, townsfolk, even sailors by the look of them. Their clothes are in tatters, but they dance along tirelessly, a crazed, uncontrolled look in all their eyes.

At their head, a white centaur with a long white beard leads them a merry dance. Half horse, half man, he plays a haunting melody on a silver flute. The music is so beguiling that it fills your heart with a terrible, yearning desire to follow him, wherever he may go.

Make a MAGIC roll at Difficulty 18.

Successful MAGIC roll	turn to **522**
Failed MAGIC roll	turn to **408**

681

You scour the land for miles around, but you are unable to find a single trace of a tree. The crewmen lose confidence in you and return to the wreck where they tear off more of the hull for firewood.

'Just leave us alone,' says the mate, 'We don't need no false messiahs here, raising our hopes.'

'Yeah!' yells another. 'Go and jump in a river!'

Shrugging your shoulders, you leave. Turn to **669**.

682

You manage to reach a ledge half-way up the mountain where you pause to rest. Suddenly, you are struck by a shower of pebbles. A dozen winged creatures are hovering in the air above you, pelting you with small rocks. They are like little purple-furred monkeys, with leathery bat-like wings — Mannekyn People. They wear simple strips of leather, and wield small javelins.

'Get away, you big ox!' shrills one of them. If you have the codeword *Altruist*, turn to **368**. Otherwise, turn to **445**.

683

You come to a man-made hollow in the ground. In the middle is a shrine, bedecked with offerings from nomad worshippers, and covered in symbols of the god Tambu, Great Spirit of the Steppes. The wind howls all around, buffeting you from all directions. You have found the Fane of the Four Winds.

If you have the codeword *Cull*, turn to **592**. If not, but you are an initiate of Tambu, turn to **456**. Otherwise, read on.

You notice some of the offerings are quite valuable.

Leave	turn to **118**
Loot the shrine	turn to **389**

684

You are high up in the peaks, struggling on through swirling eddies of snow and ice. Lose 2-12 Stamina (the roll of two dice) because of the harsh conditions. If you have the codeword *Calcium*, however, lose only 1-6 Stamina, as you can breathe the thin air normally.

Go on up	turn to **575**
Go back down	turn to **271**

685

You trigger the rod. You disappear in a flash of brilliant blue light, to reappear in Yarimura. Reduce the rod's charges by one. If it is down to zero charges, it is used up, and shatters – cross it off your Adventure Sheet.

Turn to **10**.

686

You find the house of Etla. Inside, you come across a grisly scene. Etla lies dead across a table – his throat has been cut. He is clutching a note in one hand.

You take it and read, 'To the bearer of Etla's map. Meet me in Kunrir, Uttaku, and we'll divide the treasure. You will find me at the House of Sweet Repose.' It is signed Nyelm Starhand.

Erase the codeword *Dirk* and gain the codeword *Dregs*.

You leave the bloody scene. Turn to **77**.

687

Since the High King's awakening, the Rimewater has thawed almost completely, and the land around it is green and verdant. The ice has retreated, and spring has come after an absence of five hundred years. Geese and ducks swim on the water. They will have to change the name of the lake! The wooden buildings of the mine complex are still there, though.

Visit the ice mine — turn to **440**

Go north to the river plain — turn to **91**

Head into the mountains — *The Court of Hidden Faces* **35**

688

A passing merchantman spots you on the shore. They think you have been marooned, and send a small boat to pick you up. The captain offers to take you to Yarimura in the north.

Hitch a lift — turn to **10**

Climb up the cliff — turn to **32**

689

You remember something you read in old log book about the pyramid, during your sea-faring days on the Violet Ocean: 'It is only possible to gain entrance when the gods are not looking.'

Taking no chances, you heave the idols round so they are looking away from the gate. Then you step inside. Turn to **172**.

690

You have instructions from Lord Shiryoku, the Shogun's spy-master, to gather any information you can. While you are in the palace, you use the time to pick up the latest rumours, finding out the general state of the Clan of the White Spear.

Erase the codeword *Fog*, and acquire the codeword *Dog*.

Afterwards, you leave. Turn to **10**.

691

You pass the **witch's hand** and the **parrot fungus** across the table to Bakhan. Cross them off your Adventure Sheet. Bakhan hisses in delight, and shuffles out of the room. Some hours later, a woman with ice-blue eyes, and long black hair, serene and beautiful, walks in.

'I am Bakhan,' she says in a voice like honey. 'I cannot thank you enough. Bring me some selenium ore, and I will fashion you a gift as a token of my gratitude.'

Acquire the codeword *Drake*.

If you have some **selenium ore**, turn to **259**. If not, you leave. Turn to **10**.

692

You beat them off, killing a few in the process. You find 15 Shards and a set of **lockpicks (THIEVERY +1)** on the bodies. When you are finished looting them, turn to **182**.

693

You crawl up the side of the tower. Below you, the city is spread out like a carpet, fiery pin-pricks of light a mirror to the stars.

You complete your dizzying ascent, and come to a window ledge, near the top of the tower. The shutters are open to the warm night air, and you steal like a shade into the daimyo's bedchamber.

He lies asleep on a massive bed, a concubine at his side, snoring loudly. A casket lies open on a table nearby. Inside, is a necklace of fabulous jewels, within easy reach of your hand.

Take the necklace	turn to **177**
Leave the way you came	turn to **38**

694

The black stallion leads his herd straight at you. Make a COMBAT roll at Difficulty 15.

Successful COMBAT roll	turn to **207**
Failed COMBAT roll	turn to **16**

695

It seems to recognize the banner.

'Pass, friend,' it booms, and then fades away.

You enter the ruined city along a road lined with gigantic stone heads. Each granite face sheds carved tears of stone. You trek past mounds of rubble and wild, overgrown gardens. The wind whistles a doleful dirge through the deserted streets and shattered houses.

You come to a large central square in the middle of which has been laid a wide, circular mosaic that depicts a map of the city. Most of the places marked on the map are no more, but a few have stood the test of time.

Visit the Cave of Bells	turn to **657**
Visit the Vault of the Shadar	turn to **107**
Visit the Crypt of Kings	turn to **298**

Leave the City of Ruins   turn to **266**

696

Make a SANCTITY roll at Difficulty 13.
    Successful SANCTITY roll   turn to **324**
    Failed SANCTITY roll   turn to **286**

697

You get lost, and wander aimlessly amid the freezing fog. Roll one die to see where you emerge.

Score 1	Still on the river plain	turn to **91**
Score 2	The coast	turn to **669**
Score 3	A pyramid	turn to **472**
Score 4	A lake	turn to **320**
Score 5	The plains	turn to **281**
Score 6	The plains	turn to **29**

698

You camp for the night. If you have a **wolf pelt**, the fur helps to keep you warm. If you do not, lose 1 Stamina from the cold.

You need to hunt for food. Make a SCOUTING roll at Difficulty 11. If you succeed, you find a snow-hare to eat. If you fail, you go hungry and must lose 1 Stamina point.

If you still live, the sun rises, its wan rays barely warming the morning air.

Go north	turn to **630**
Go west	turn to **281**
Go south	turn to **118**
Go east	turn to **17**

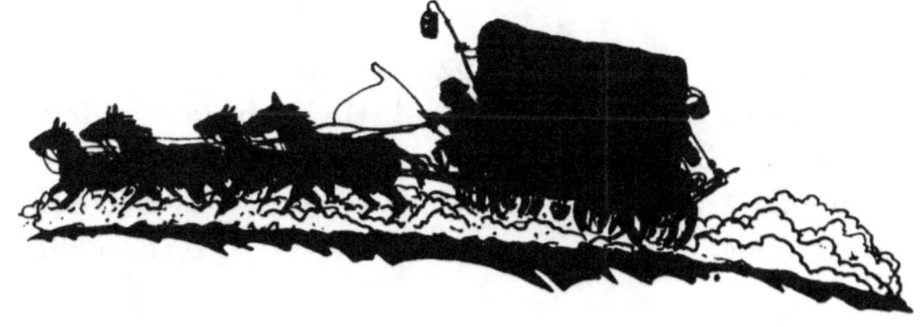

699

You are taken to see Akradai, prince of the Azure Sky tribe. He is
an old friend, and his shamans will cure you of any disease or
poison you may be suffering from (but they cannot lift a curse).
After a fine dinner at the table of a prince of the steppes, you retire
to bed, warm with Kvass, the intoxicating liquor of the nomads.
The next day, you continue on your way.

Go north	turn to **15**
Go east toward Yarimura	turn to **280**
Go south	turn to **234**
Head west deeper into the steppes	turn to **17**

700

You are quite aware of the nature of this flickering creature of the
clouds. It is a storm demon, one of the riders of thunderclouds that
delight in causing havoc among mortals. Elnir, god of the skies,
frowns on them, for they cause thunder and lightning without his
permission.

You try to invoke Elnir's power by calling upon him with a
prayer. Make a SANCTITY roll at Difficulty 16. If you are an initiate
of Elnir, add 2 to the roll.

Successful SANCTITY roll	turn to **43**
Failed SANCTITY roll	turn to **511**

701

You lift your arm to finish the creature, when it throws some coins,
and a jug on to the ground. You hesitate for a moment, just enough
time for it to turn and flee, diving into the river with a splash. You
find 50 Shards and a jug of **faery mead** on the riverbank.

Turn to **676**.

702

You come across the body of a nomad. He has been dead for quite
a while, judging by the smell.

Examine the corpse	turn to **648**
Leave it alone	turn to **698**

703

You dodge aside, grab the lance, and heave. The birdrider is yanked out of the saddle and crashes headfirst into the ground. He doesn't get up. The other riders rein in their beaked steeds, and look you up and down. Your courage and skill have impressed them.

Make a CHARISMA roll at Difficulty 13.

Successful CHARISMA roll	turn to **449**
Failed CHARISMA roll	turn to **504**

704 ☐

If there is a tick in the box, turn to **147** immediately. If not, put a tick there now, and read on.

You remember an old Shadar codex you discovered in the Icicle Woods. It told of the Cave of Bells, and the ancient rituals of the Shadar priest-kings. They always rang a bell called The Whisperer first, so you go over to it, and rattle its clapper.

There is no sound at first, but then the other bells begin pealing, weaving a harmonious tapestry of sound.

A wooden panel slides open at the other end of the cathedral. You walk through into a large, granite chamber where you find 2000 Shards, some **plate armour (Defence +5)**, an **enchanted sword (COMBAT +4)**, a **gold holy symbol (SANCTITY +3)** and the **sceptre of kings**. The sceptre is made of a hard, bluish metal, its tip fashioned into the head of a hawk.

Visit the Crypt of Kings	turn to **298**
Leave the City of Ruins	turn to **266**

705

A brightly painted caravan, pulled by horses, rumbles into view. It pulls up, and the caravaneers open up the back to display their wares. They are travelling pedlars.

Armour	To buy	To sell
Leather (Defence +1)	50 Shards	45 Shards
Ring mail (Defence +2)	100 Shards	90 Shards
Chain mail (Defence +3)	200 Shards	180 Shards

Weapons (sword, axe, etc)	*To buy*	*To sell*
Without COMBAT bonus	50 Shards	40 Shards
COMBAT bonus +1	250 Shards	200 Shards
COMBAT bonus +2	500 Shards	400 Shards

Other items	*To buy*	*To sell*
Flute (CHARISMA +1)	200 Shards	180 Shards
Compass (SCOUTING +1)	500 Shards	450 Shards
Rope	50 Shards	45 Shards
Lantern	100 Shards	90 Shards
Wolf pelt	100 Shards	90 Shards
Parrot fungus	100 Shards	90 Shards
Uncanny salts	100 Shards	90 Shards
Shadar scroll	100 Shards	90 Shards

When you have finished, they ride on. Turn to **676**.

706

You arrive at a high bronze double door set in sheer cliffs. If you have the codeword *Duress*, turn to **343**. If not, turn to **609**.

707

If you have the codeword *Dispel*, turn to **237** immediately. If not, read on.

Dusk is sweeping its twilight robes across the steppes when you notice a glowing, nacreous light flickering from what looks like a half-sunken rock in the centre of the marsh.

Investigate	turn to **431**
Ignore	turn to **92**

708

You don't get very far. One of the beetles manages to seize your leg, and then another latches on. You fall, and the insects swarm all over you. You are devoured in minutes. Turn to **7**.

709

You tell General Beladai about the tunnels you have mapped that lead through the Spine of Harkun, thus bypassing the Pass of Eagles. He is amazed at the news. He decides to send a small force through the tunnels, to attack the citadel from the southern side.

'As soon as you have opened the gates, some of the Mannekyn People will fly over the citadel to give the word to our troops there. We will crush them like an acorn in a nutcracker!'

Lose the codeword *Deep* and gain the codeword *Dim* instead. Now turn to **145**.

710

The high priestess is overjoyed when you hand over the mirror. Cross it off your Adventure Sheet. Also erase the codeword *Double* and gain the codeword *Discover* instead.

She rewards you with 150 Shards, and the blessings of the Goddess of the Sun, Nisoderu. Gain 1 Rank. This means you gain 1-6 Stamina points permanently: increase your normal (unwounded) Stamina score by the roll of one die. Remember that going up a Rank also increases your Defence.

Afterwards, you leave. Turn to **10**.

Adventure Sheet

NAME

PROFESSION

GOD

RANK

DEFENCE

ABILITY   SCORE

CHARISMA

COMBAT

MAGIC

SANCTITY

SCOUNTING

THIEVERY

POSSESSIONS (maximum of 12)

STAMINA

When unwounded

Current:

RESURRECTION ARRANGEMENTS

MONEY

TITLES and HONOURS

BLESSINGS

Codewords

- ☐ Dangle
- ☐ Dare
- ☐ Dark
- ☐ Dawn
- ☐ Dead
- ☐ Deathless
- ☐ Deep
- ☐ Defend
- ☐ Deliver
- ☐ Diamond
- ☐ Dim
- ☐ Dirk
- ☐ Dirty
- ☐ Discover
- ☐ Dismal
- ☐ Dispel
- ☐ Divest
- ☐ Dog
- ☐ Dotage
- ☐ Double
- ☐ Dove
- ☐ Dragon
- ☐ Drake
- ☐ Drape
- ☐ Draw
- ☐ Dread
- ☐ Dregs
- ☐ Drifter
- ☐ Drink
- ☐ Drizzle
- ☐ Drop
- ☐ Duress
- ☐ Dwarf

Ship's Manifest

SHIP TYPE	NAME	CREW QUALITY	CARGO CAPACITY	CURRENT CARGO	WHERE DOCKED

THE PEAKS AT THE EDGE OF THE WORLD
MOUTH OF HARKUN
PYRAMID OF XINOC
THE RUBY CITADEL
KASCHUF'S KEEP
N
HORDE OF THE THUNDERING SKIES
HORDE OF THE THOUSAND WINDS
YARIMURA
ISLE OF MYSTERY
TIGRE BAY
OLD AGE RIVER
RIVER OF LIFE
RIVER OF DESTINY
THE GREAT STEPPES
GEMSTONE HILLS
SKY MOUNTAIN
BELADAI'S CAMP
DISASTER BAY
THE RIMEWATER
CITY OF RUINS
NERECH LAND OF THE MANBEASTS
ICE MINE
PASS OF EAGLES
CRAGDRIFT SEA
ICICLE WOODS
THE SPINE OF HARKUN
CITADEL OF VELIS CORIN
FORTS OF THE EASTERN MARCHES

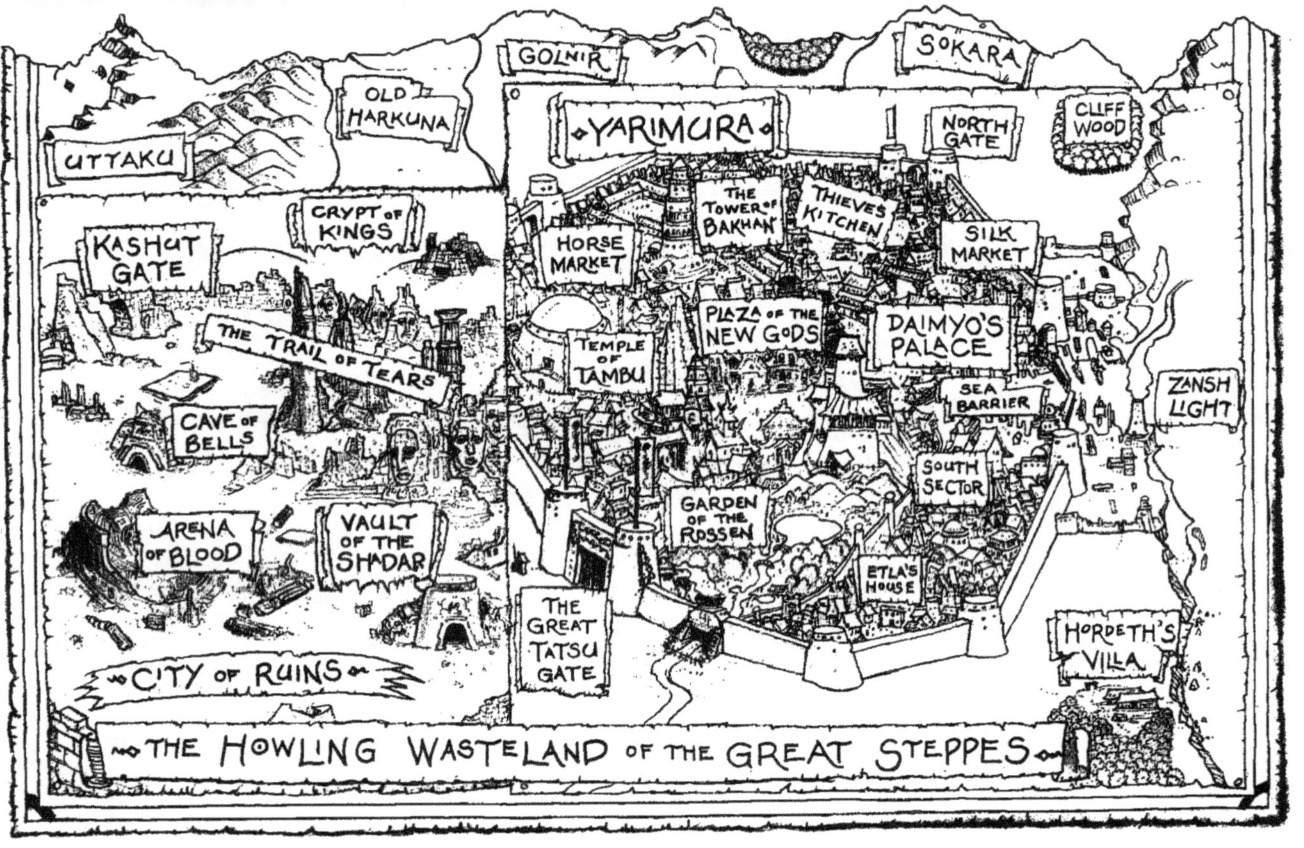

GOLNIR
SOKARA
OLD HARKUNA
UTTAKU
YARIMURA
NORTH GATE
CLIFF WOOD
CRYPT of KINGS
THE TOWER of BAKHAN
THIEVES KITCHEN
SILK MARKET
KASHUT GATE
HORSE MARKET
PLAZA of THE NEW GODS
DAIMYO'S PALACE
ZANSH LIGHT
THE TRAIL of TEARS
TEMPLE of TAMBU
SEA BARRIER
CAVE of BELLS
GARDEN of THE ROSSEN
SOUTH SECTOR
ARENA of BLOOD
VAULT of THE SHADAR
ETLA'S HOUSE
THE GREAT TATSU GATE
HORPETH'S VILLA
CITY of RUINS
THE HOWLING WASTELAND of the GREAT STEPPES

9 780956 737236